Merciless Lies

An Asha Kade Private Detective Mystery Thriller

Tikiri Herath

REBEL DIVA ACADEMY

The use of any part of this publication, reproduced, transmitted in any form or by any means electronic, mechanical, photocopying, recording, or otherwise or stored in a retrieval system without prior written consent of the publisher—or in the case of photocopying or other reprographic copying, a license from the Canadian Copyright Licensing Agency—is an infringement of the copyright law. ***

All rights reserved.

This is a work of fiction. Names, characters, businesses, places, events and incidents are either the products of the author's imagination or used in a fictitious manner. Any resemblance to actual persons, living or dead, or actual events, situations, and customs is purely coincidental.

Merciless Lies

Asha Kade Private Detective Mystery Thriller Series

www.TikiriHerath.com

Copyright ©2021 Tikiri Herath

Edition: 2021

Library & Archives Canada Cataloging in Publication

E-book ISBN: 978-1-989232-55-2

Paperback ISBN: 978-1-990234-11-8

Hardback ISBN: 978-1-990234-12-5

Audiobook ISBN: 978-1-989232-98-9

Large Print book ISBN: 978-1-989232-38-5

Author: Tikiri Herath

Publisher: Rebel Diva Academy Press

Copy Editor: Stephanie Parent

Back Cover Headshot: Aura McKay

Tikiri

A Gift For You

Thank you for picking up my latest novel. There's a gift for you for picking up this book!

HER DEADLY END is a 250-page twisty serial killer thriller about an unusual murder-suicide case that Tanya (Tetyana), Asha, and Katy accidentally stumble upon while vacationing in Paradise Cove.

It's a pulse-pounding, nerve-shredding mystery of a devious serial predator stalking a small seaside town in Washington State.

You'll learn about the characters in the Merciless murder mystery series which features private detectives, Asha Kade & Katy McCafferty, and those in the new Tanya Stone FBI K9 series which features Special Agent Tanya (Tetyana) & Max, her K9 German Shepherd.

Join the VIP Red Heeled Rebels Club and receive your exclusive gift. Click the link below to join.

HER DEADLY END: A gripping thriller with a twisty end
https://books.tikiriherath.com/ts-b0-mmm-herdeadlyend

There is no explicit sex, heavy cursing, or graphic violence in these books. There is, however, a closed circle of suspects, many twists and turns, fast-paced action, and nail-biting suspense.

NO DOG IS HARMED IN THESE BOOKS. EVER. But the villains always are.

The Red Heeled Rebels Universe

The Red Heeled Rebels universe of mystery thrillers, featuring your favorite kick-ass female characters:

Tanya Stone FBI K9 Mystery Thrillers
www.TikiriHerath.com/Thrillers
NEW FBI thriller series starring Tetyana from the Red Heeled Rebels as Special Agent Tanya Stone, and Max, as her loyal German Shepherd. These are serial killer thrillers set in Black Rock, a small upscale resort town on the coast of Washington state.
Her Deadly End
Her Cold Blood
Her Last Lie
Her Secret Crime
Her Dead Girl
Her Perfect Murder

Her Grisly Grave
Coming soon!

———◦∞◦———

Asha Kade Private Detective Murder Mysteries
www.TikiriHerath.com/Mysteries
Each book is a standalone murder mystery thriller, featuring the Red Heeled Rebels, Asha Kade and Katy McCafferty. Asha and Katy receive one million dollars for their favorite children's charity from a secret benefactor's estate every time they solve a cold case.
Merciless Legacy
Merciless Games
Merciless Crimes
Merciless Lies
Merciless Past
Merciless Deaths
One more to come.

———◦∞◦———

Red Heeled Rebels International Mystery & Crime - The Origin Story
www.TikiriHerath.com/RedHeeledRebels
The award-winning origin story of the Red Heeled Rebels characters. Learn how a rag-tag group of trafficked orphans from different places united to fight for their freedom and their lives, and became a found family.
The Girl Who Crossed the Line
The Girl Who Ran Away
The Girl Who Made Them Pay
The Girl Who Fought to Kill

The Girl Who Broke Free
The Girl Who Knew Their Names
The Girl Who Never Forgot
This series is now complete.

The Accidental Traveler

www.TikiriHerath.com

An anthology of personal short stories based on the author's sojourns around the world.

The Rebel Diva Nonfiction Series

www.TikiriHerath.com/Nonfiction

Your Rebel Dreams: 6 simple steps to take back control of your life in uncertain times.

Your Rebel Plans: 4 simple steps to getting unstuck and making progress today.

Your Rebel Life: Easy habit hacks to enhance happiness in the 10 key areas of your life.

Bust Your Fears: 3 simple tools to crush your anxieties and squash your stress.

Collaborations

The Boss Chick's Bodacious Destiny Nonfiction Bundle
Dark Shadows 2: Voodoo and Black Magic of New Orleans

Tikiri's novels are available around the world, on all Amazon stores everywhere. The nonfiction books are available on Apple, Kobo, Barnes & Noble, Indigo Chapters, and all good bookstores around the world.

All these books are also available in libraries everywhere. Just ask your friendly local librarian or your local bookstore to order a copy via Ingram Spark.

MERCILESS LIES

A MERCILESS MURDER MYSTERY THRILLER

The Corpse

I t would take him four hours to dig the grave and pull up the coffin.

Four hours of silent, focused work.

He cracked open the icy ground with his shovel, ignoring the stinging spasms on his back and the sweat streaming through his black mask.

It was three A.M.

A time when the night sky was the darkest that even snow owls didn't dare to fly. The man's eyes darted back and forth, constantly on alert to anyone spotting the peculiar activity at the graveyard that night. But he carried on, knowing his efforts would soon be rewarded.

Four more hours.

He kept digging.

Chapter One

The train lurched to a screeching stop.

Passengers slammed back in their seats.

Theodore Henry, Alaska's most notorious gold baron and owner of the railroad, dropped his cup of coffee on his lap. He jerked up from his wheelchair, cursing, as the hot liquid seared his thighs.

Connor McNamara let out a roar as his head slammed against the antique lamp on the oak paneled wall behind him.

My best friends and business partners, Tetyana and Katy, sprang up and grabbed the crystal wine glasses just as they were about to slide off the buffet table.

Outside, the ear-splitting shrill of steel against steel reverberated in the arctic air.

The train lurched again.

Violently, this time.

A mechanical shudder rumbled through the train carriages, like a mini earthquake had erupted underneath us.

Emergency brakes.

Someone pulled the emergency brakes.

"What in heaven's name is going on?" shouted Connor, swiveling his head around, his gray hair standing straight, looking like a mad version of Einstein.

Neil Wilson, Theodore Henry's personal physician, who sat across the dining table from his patient, stared at the wall mutely, as if unsure how to react. I wondered if he even knew where he was, given the copious amounts of premium wine he'd been imbibing since we left Black Eagle Town.

The fifty-year-old Château Talbot I'd poured for him only moments ago had rolled over the edge of their table and crashed to the floor. Its precious contents were now spilling onto the Persian runner in the middle of the dining car. An ominous blood-red stain spread on the carpet.

But I didn't have time to pick it up. I had more urgent matters on my hands.

A female voice shouted in panic up front, near the engine cab.

The train conductor.

"Everyone stay where you are," I said, and turned to Katy. "You're with them."

"Roger that," she said.

"Let's go!" I hollered to Tetyana, but she was already dashing through the car toward the engine room. I raced after her.

Why did we stop so suddenly in the middle of nowhere?

We were two hours into our journey, scheduled to arrive in Anchorage, Alaska, late that evening.

We were traveling on a private luxury train through America's northern frontier, a region few people got to see. We had just entered a rugged mountain pass on an elevated terrain, a place so remote and so isolated I'd wondered if even grizzly bears found it lonely here.

Robin and Dwayne, the train's two crew members, came rushing out of the engine room as Tetyana and I reached the front. Their faces were pale, like they had spotted a phantom.

Did we hit something?

"What's going on?" I asked.

Giving me a wild look but without answering, Robin thrust the door open, jumped down the steps and ran along the tracks, her heavy boots crunching on the snow.

Dwayne ran after her, panting loudly. That was when I noticed the man had a limp.

"I'm with them, Asha!" shouted Tetyana, as she leaped down the steps to run after the duo, who'd been operating the train smoothly on its maiden voyage.

Until now.

I raced after the three of them, trying to keep up with their long strides.

There was something up ahead. About five hundred yards in the distance. Something strange on the snow-dusted tracks.

My heart raced.

Is it an animal?

Is it dead?

I wished I'd put on my jacket before running out of the warm compartment. The frosty air seeped through my shirt, nipping at my skin. Whispery clouds burst through my lips, like I was breathing white smoke.

Suddenly, out of nowhere, an unearthly howl rang through the air. I halted, my heart pounding, a primal fear swirling up my spine.

That came from the woods.

A wolf.

Tetyana turned around and gestured at me to hurry.

She was well ahead of me, but I could see her forehead was scrunched and her eyes were narrowed.

There were few things in the world that ruffled my ex-paramilitary friend who'd fought off Russian militia groups before she even hit eighteen.

This isn't good.

I resumed running.

When I caught up to the small group congregated around the tracks at the far end, they had all been stunned into silence. They were staring at the thing I'd seen on the train tracks, stark horror etched on their faces.

I stopped, shocked.

It was a dead body.

A dead body with a brown paper bag over their head.

Chapter Two

M inutes before we had stopped, Katy and I had been serving drinks in the dining car.

Tetyana had stayed behind the buffet table, pretending to be the bartender, when she was really on guard, armed and ready, her eyes watchful, alert to anything out of the ordinary.

"I said vodka on ice. Not water!"

Connor had been shouting, slurring his words, angry spittle shooting from his mouth.

Gritting my teeth, I'd taken his glass to add another two ounces of hard liquor. Connor was my client's—Theodore Henry—right-hand man. As much as I'd yearned to, I couldn't truthfully tell him what I thought about his pal.

If you keep this up, Connor, I swear I'm going to strangle you myself before nightfall.

I couldn't wait for this contract to be over.

I was thankful we were heading back to civilization, back to where we could catch the first flight to New York. Back home.

Katy and I had been excited when I got called for this job two weeks ago. Tetyana had sniffed at the idea of a boring train ride at first, but had eventually joined us. How could anyone say no to a luxury ride on a private steam train through the mountains of Alaska?

All we had to do was make drinks and serve meals for a paranoid mining baron who was sure someone was poisoning him. That would be easy money.

I just hadn't expected to be stuck with a group of the most eccentric individuals on earth.

Despite our clients' morose personalities, it had been pleasant to listen to the clickety clack of the train and feel its gentle sway as we trundled through this majestic landscape filled with snowcapped mountains.

Though it was early spring, it felt like we were in the heart of a winter wonderland Christmas card.

The days were getting longer, and the air was getting warmer in this northern region, but the coniferous trees along the tracks were still laden with pristine snow and the ground was an undulating terrain of pure ice.

It would have been a magical ride, except for our petulant passengers.

"How much longer do we have?" Katy had whispered in my ear, as she'd mixed another drink.

"Ten hours," I'd whispered back.

She'd made a face.

I couldn't blame her. We were all counting the hours down to our destination.

"Please don't take another contract from mean old rich men again," Katy had muttered as she picked up the ice tongs and dropped a cube into a crystal glass.

Unlike Tetyana, who looked like Furiosa from *Mad Max* on a good day, Katy cut an elegant figure with her modelesque frame. Katy and I couldn't be more different. I was five-foot and petite with long black hair, while she was tall and curvaceous with fiery red hair.

It was Katy who'd fought by my side in our youth, but ever since she had become a mother, her Irish fighting genes had cooled. They only showed up when someone pushed her to the limit.

Like right now.

This had been a peculiar job from the start. It wasn't every day I got a call from a billionaire for my private investigation services.

Theodore Henry, sole owner of the Black Eagle Mining company, had required our presence as he traveled from Black Eagle Town to Anchorage via train, on his way to Seattle for his first thoracic cancer treatment.

He already had a personal bodyguard. So, I was perplexed when he asked me and my team to join him, and to come disguised as caterers so no one would know there was a group of private detectives on board.

But I'd shrugged it off as the idiosyncrasies of a wealthy man, one who had more money than he knew what to do with.

He was paying me well.

And I was curious.

Theodore Henry was a controversial figure in the business community, one who had notoriously extorted his way to the top of the food chain. He was both reviled and respected in the mining world for good reason.

But it was his pal and business partner, Connor McNamara, who had got on our nerves the most.

"Happy to pistol whip the bastard. Just say when," I'd heard a low voice say next to me.

I'd looked up to see Tetyana had sidled up to us, one hand on her holster, an annoyed look on her face.

"Just hang on a few more hours, girls," I'd said to my two friends.

It was my job to keep everyone in line, plus I couldn't afford to lose the hefty payment coming our way.

"We'll be done here soon. We'll pick up our check and head back home before you know it. Promise."

"We get to Anchorage in *ten* hours," Tetyana had growled.

"It's going to be pure hell," Katy had hissed. "If McNamara carries on like this, I swear I'll mix strychnine into his vodka."

With an indignant flip of her hair, she had spun around and stomped over to the head table with the drink tray in hand. With a resigned sigh, I had followed her, carrying a plate of olives, blue cheese, and figs.

Four guests had been waiting for us at the main table.

They were the only passengers on this private train. The rest were staff.

Theodore's personal bodyguard was snoring in the back, near the kitchenette. Despite his baby face, it was clear why the man was named Tank. But even with his imposing size and build, he came across like a blundering buffoon.

Why the gold baron had hired such an incompetent bodyguard, I couldn't fathom. But Tank hadn't shown any resentment for our presence, so we let him be, just like he was doing for us.

A father and daughter duo from Black Eagle Town operated this restored steam train. Dwayne, the father, was the engineer while Robin, the conductor, was a multitasker who managed everything else, from maintaining the fire, to watching the water levels, and making sure the boiler ran smoothly.

Moments before the train had come to an unexpected halt, Theodore Henry had been in his wheelchair, a woolen blanket over his knees, staring out the window, his mind seemingly elsewhere. In front of him, next to his glass of wine, had been an array of pill bottles.

I wondered if anyone had explained to him about the dangers of mixing medication with alcohol, but it wasn't my place to say. Besides, his physician was on board, and he didn't seem to mind.

Doctor Neil Wilson sat across from the oligarch, a heavily overweight man in his late sixties. He was the type of medical doctor who never took his own advice.

He'd been in that chair ever since we started the journey, wheezing hard, and drinking, and drinking some more, like his life depended on it. Katy had already opened a second bottle of wine just for him.

Next to the doctor sat Stella Green, the only female passenger on the train.

With her medium-length, dirty-blonde hair tied back into a neat ponytail, she looked like the fit, outdoorsy type you'd expect to find in these parts. But from my research, I knew she had a graduate degree in mining engineering and a post-doctorate in geology. In her mid-thirties, she had already proven her worth at Black Eagle Mines and had risen up the ranks quickly to join the executive suite and was now the vice president of research and development.

But she had looked uncomfortable that day. She'd sat, leaning against the expansive window, not eating or drinking, but staring at the bleak and snowy landscape outside.

Something had been troubling her.

I wondered if I'd be despondent too, if I'd been forced to spend twelve hours in the close vicinity of a bunch of cantankerous, drunk men—all old enough to be my father.

Until I did my research, I'd expected the infamous mining baron from Alaska to be a big, brawny man, the kind who spent most of his days outdoors, hunting and fishing and snowmobiling in the wilderness. Someone who'd look like he could fight off a black bear with his bare hands.

To my surprise, Theodore was a small and wiry man with a high-pitched, almost child-like voice. He looked even more innocuous with his shaven head, ready for his cancer treatment.

Innocuous, that is, until you looked into his steely black eyes.

That was when you knew you were dealing with one of the most cunning businessmen in this region, one who'd stop at nothing to get his way. Even at seventy-six years old.

Connor McNamara had sat to the right of Theodore. Connor, I'd read, was Theodore's childhood friend, a surly man who didn't think twice of yelling obscenities at anyone who crossed him.

There was something about these two septuagenarian friends.

It was the way they joked and sparred with each other. Blood is supposed to run thicker than water, but in this case, these two men seemed closer than blood brothers.

The second Katy had sat the drink tray at the edge of the table was when we had come to the sudden stop.

The train had lurched fiercely, making Katy lose her grip. The tray had fallen on Connor, splashing the liquor all over him. He'd sprung from the table, cursing and yelling, but there was little anyone could do after that.

That was the beginning of the end of our train ride.

We were stuck in this snowed-in valley in the middle of nowhere, surrounded by the shadows of the mountains.

And I had no clue what was to come.

Chapter Three

I stepped closer to take a look at the corpse lying on the tracks.

Though the face was concealed by the paper bag, it looked to be a male—a tall, suited man. The hands were frozen, but the wrinkles on the skin told me he'd been in his sixties or seventies at least.

Dwayne, the engineer, crossed himself and muttered something incomprehensible. Robin, the conductor, looked like she was about to throw up, one hand over her mouth.

"If I wasn't going so slow and if Robin didn't have that drone scouting for moose along the tracks..." Dwayne trailed off with a shudder at the thought of his train plowing through the cadaver.

"He'd have become minced meat," said Tetyana, who had no qualms stating things exactly as they were.

She kneeled next to the dead man to examine him.

"If I had to guess," she mumbled, as her eyes swept the body, looking for signs of what might have killed him. "He's been dead for a while. A few days, maybe more."

I covered my nose and leaned over.

I braced myself for a putrid odor, that of rotting flesh, but instead a strong chemical smell hit my nostrils.

He was wearing an ill-fitting black suit and a white shirt. His skin was deathly pale, almost white. He had his arms by his side, looking like someone you'd see inside a coffin at a funeral home.

Except for that paper bag that covered his head.

I stared at the corpse.

"He couldn't have just stumbled here," I said.

My eyes searched for telltale tread marks on the snow that would show me where the man had been dragged from.

"Fresh snow," said Tetyana, as she saw me look around. "I see our footsteps, but no one else's."

"Either that, or they covered their tracks really well," I said.

"If they used a vehicle or a snowmobile to transport him here," said my friend, her hands on her hips, "it would take a lot of work to cover those tracks. An almost impossible task."

"Let's take a look," I said.

Tetyana jumped up, her gun at the ready.

For the next ten minutes, we stalked the area around the tracks and close to the tree line, scouring for clues. Footprints, drag marks, disturbed snowbanks, anything that would tell us where this corpse had come from.

But we found nothing.

When we returned to the cadaver, Dwayne and Robin were still standing by it, shivering and clutching each other, looking too petrified to move.

Tetyana and I exchanged a glance over the dead body.

I knew she was itching to yank that bag away from his face. I was too, though neither of us would have recognized him even if we saw his face. But we didn't have protection. No gloves. No access to a CSI-type lab kit. Not out here.

"Been riding these trains all my life. Never seen anything like this," said Dwayne, shaking his head. "Who on earth would do something so nasty?"

That was when I noticed his daughter was clutching a large black electronic device. She saw me look and extended her hand.

"The drone," she said, making a face. "Lost control and hit a tree. It's busted now."

I shook my head and turned back to the body.

"This looks like a mafia job," I said. "The work of a local gang."

Tetyana frowned.

"I'd expect this in Chicago, or Sicily. But here? In the middle of Alaska?" She reached over to the bag. "Let's see who this is, shall we?"

"No!" With a panic-stricken gasp, Dwayne stepped back, faltering on the ice. Robin sprang toward her father and grabbed him by the arm before he slipped.

"You go wait in the train, Dad," she said. "Me and these ladies will take care of this."

He stared at his daughter, his face almost as pale as the dead man's skin.

"Don't touch...," spluttered Dwayne, a confused look on his face. "What are you going to do, anyway?"

Robin nudged her father away from the body. "We'll figure out something, Dad. Go to the train."

I looked at him in mild surprise. I'd want to see who this was, especially if I were from here.

That was when I saw something move from the corner of my eyes.

"What the hell?" said Tetyana, jumping up.

I scampered away in a hurry, almost falling back.

Dwayne crossed himself again. Robin stared at the body in horror.

The dead man's right hand was twitching.

Had the body come alive?

"My goodness," cried Robin. She pulled her father by the arm and staggered farther back.

"Wait," I said, putting a hand up. "Everyone shush. I heard something."

"Me too," said Tetyana, frowning.

Unless I was going insane, it was a high-pitched cat's mew.

I stepped closer.

The mew.

Again.

I was sure now. An animal was trapped underneath the corpse or had taken shelter under it.

I reached toward the body.

"Don't touch it!" cried Dwayne from behind me, his voice tinged with fear.

I didn't have to.

A small gray fur-ball stumbled out from under the man's immobile hand and gazed at me with its big blue eyes.

I stared back at the kitten, half-wondering if the glacial arctic air had gone to my head, and I'd gone mad.

"My goodness," gasped Robin. "That poor thing was stuck under him?"

I extended my hand toward the kitten, who took a few unsteady steps toward me, and sniffed my fingers.

"It's feral," I heard Robin say, a warning in her voice. "It could have rabies, and who knows what germs."

But it was too late.

The kitten was crawling onto my outstretched palm, probably attracted by my body heat after hiding under that cold corpse.

"Poor thing," I said, stepping away and straightening up, the kitten curling into a ball in my hand now. "It's shivering."

I glanced around me.

We were in a snowy ravine, surrounded by dark pine woods that ran along the tracks. Beyond the trees, on both sides, rose the incomparable Alaskan mountains, their white peaks glistening in the distance.

I felt their eyes on us, as if they were silently watching us.

"Wonder where the kitten came from?" I said, turning around slowly. But there was no other sign of life except for us.

There was a deathly quiet in this dark valley. A quietness you didn't want to disturb.

Behind us, the black hulk of the train looked like an ominous steel monster, ready to mow us down.

I wondered what everyone was doing inside. Were Theodore, Connor, and the doctor still drinking away, oblivious to our macabre discovery? Was Stella still staring out the window, that unhappy look in her eyes?

Poor Katy, I thought. She was stuck dealing with them all by herself.

"Maybe that's not a cat," said Tetyana, who had been watching me warily, keeping her distance ever since Robin mentioned rabies. "Maybe it's a kind of wild lynx or something. Put it back, Asha."

I looked down at the animal, who was purring now.

"Looks like a regular house kitty to me," I said, scratching behind its ear. "I'm not leaving it out here."

"But what are we going to do with *him*?" said Dwayne, pointing a trembling finger at the corpse. "We can't leave him lying here either."

A movement near the train caught my eye.

I snapped my head around.

Tetyana frowned.

We had told everyone to stay put on the train, but someone had disembarked and was walking our way.

Chapter Four

We watched as the man, who, unlike us, had bulked up in hat, coat, scarf, and gloves, ambled alongside the train.

"Connor?" I said, a bitter taste coming to my mouth.

The last thing I needed was to manage an obnoxious drunkard while we figured out what to do with this dead man.

"Tank," said Tetyana, with a scornful look. "He finally woke up."

"What do you have over there?" called out the bodyguard as he got within shouting distance.

"Come, see for yourself," hollered Tetyana. "I think you're going to like this."

When Tank got closer, Tetyana and I stepped aside so he could see what we'd discovered.

He stopped in his tracks. His eyes bulged, and a look of horror slowly crossed his face.

"Did we hit him?" he spluttered.

I raised my eyebrows. Tetyana was right. Tank wasn't the sharpest knife.

"We were traveling in this direction," I said, speaking slowly. "So, no, we didn't hit him."

"Jeez," said Tank. "Who is it?"

Tetyana turned her attention back to the corpse.

"Whoever it is, this sure was no accident," she said. "Someone brought him up here and deliberately placed him here. What I want to know is, did they kill him or did they dig him up?"

"D... dig him up?" stammered Tank.

"Who would do this? And why?" I said, frowning. "We're miles from anywhere."

"This is a message," said Tetyana, thoughtfully. "Possibly, a warning."

A message to whom?

To Theodore Henry and his team?

Maybe Theodore wasn't being as paranoid as I'd suspected.

Tetyana instinctively touched her waist, where she carried her sidearm. With her hand on her holster, she scanned the surroundings, a grim look on her face.

I wished I had my weapon on me, too.

My own Glock was safely locked up in my cabin. Alaska recognized our New York firearms licenses, but I hadn't wanted to advertise our true vocation to everyone on the train. I just hadn't been prepared to come across a scene like this.

I glanced around, wondering if the culprit was behind those tall pine trees, watching us. Waiting.

For what?

I turned to Robin and Dwayne, who were standing several feet away from us, clutching each other, fearful expressions on their faces.

"Are there any villages or settlements nearby?"

Silence.

It was like the father and daughter had both gone mute in shock.

Next to me, Tank shrugged. "No idea. I'm from Seattle."

I looked at Robin.

"Robin? Do you know this area well?"

She shook her head, like she was too stunned to speak. "Settlements out here? Why would there be any?" she said.

I frowned. A simple yes or no would have sufficed.

"Are you sure?" I said, feeling like I was missing something.

Dwayne merely stared unblinkingly, like he hadn't understood my question.

"Nothing for miles around here," said Robin.

"Is this railway used frequently?" I asked.

"Just by the freight train."

"Freight train?" I said, straightening up.

"It brings supplies to the mine from Anchorage," replied Dwayne, finally finding his voice. "Comes once a week."

"When did it come this way last?"

"Five days or so ago."

"When is it due next?"

"Hard to say," said Dwayne with a shrug. "Gets delayed at the port, sometimes for weeks. If the shipments are late, the train's behind too."

"My hubby drives that train," said Robin. "I never know when he can make it home. It's always different depending on the weather and all that."

"Hey," came my friend's voice from behind me.

I swiveled around.

"Look at this," said Tetyana.

Holding the kitten close to my chest so it wouldn't fall, I bent down to see what she was pointing at. There were mud marks on the man's suit intermingled with the light snowflakes.

"Dirt," I said. "From getting dragged here?" I paused. "But there's no mud anywhere and the snowbanks are several feet high."

"He was probably underground," said Tetyana. "If you ask me, someone dug him out of his grave and placed him neatly across the tracks."

"Jeez," said Tank. "That's crazy stuff right there."

"How does someone dig up a grave this time of year? The ground's still frozen," I said, trying to think this through. "You'll need equipment and that won't go unnoticed, unless he was buried recently, and the ground was still loose."

I stared at the man, his face still covered with the brown paper bag.

"Is there a way to take that thing off without disturbing the remains?" I asked, turning to my friend.

Tetyana had been waiting for me to ask that. Her hand hovered over the bag as she searched for the best place to yank it off.

"Don't touch it," cried Dwayne.

I looked at him, bewildered. "Don't you want to see who it is?"

Without waiting for an answer, Tetyana wiggled the paper bag gently to loosen it, moving the head back and forth on the tracks.

My stomach churned.

Dead bodies weren't new to me. I had seen them before. I had even killed before. More than once.

They were all deserving kills. Some had been the most vile men on earth who had subjected many innocents to horrific acts. But it always agitated me to see a lifeless body, especially one in such a beautiful but hostile environment as this.

Dwayne and Robin were stepping backward, moving toward the train as if they couldn't bear to see what was to come next.

Using my free hand, I pulled my phone out of my pocket, ready to snap a few pictures.

Tetyana kept coaxing the paper bag, while Tank and I watched, breathlessly.

Then, with a final tug, she yanked the bag free. The dead man's head dropped back on the tracks with a sickening thud from the momentum.

Robin let out a horrified gasp.

"Frigging hell," said Tetyana, dropping the bag and jumping to her feet.

Tank made a retching noise from behind me.

Oh, man.

I wanted to look away, but my eyes were stuck to that face like a magnet. I struggled to keep my breakfast down.

For good reason.

The dead man's face was unrecognizable.

Someone had taken a knife to it and carved every inch up. His nose and eyes were sunken deep into that deathly skin. His lips had been shredded and white bone stuck out where his cheeks had been cut up.

His face was so disfigured that, for a moment, he looked like a freak from a grotesque, surrealistic painting.

But this man wasn't a painting. He had been alive.

It was a sight I was never going to unsee.

Chapter Five

"**K**ick the body off the tracks and start moving!"

Theodore glared at me, then turned his furious eyes on the kitten in my arms.

"And keep that thing away from me. I'm allergic to cats, for goodness' sake."

Katy plucked the cat from my arms and deposited it gently behind the liquor cabinet, out of Theodore's line of sight.

Theodore's face had turned a dark maroon and his hands were clenched into fists. If he could walk, I was sure he'd be stomping up and down the dining car.

Now I understood why Dwayne and Robin had looked so relieved when I told them I would share the news with their boss.

I knew his wrath would fall on his crew and I hated it when good, honest people trying to do their job got into trouble. I was a contractor and had more leeway. At least, I hoped.

Tetyana and Katy flanked me in the dining car, as I tried to talk some sense into the mining baron.

We had left Tank behind to keep an eye on the dead body. He'd only agreed to the job when we told him he could stand several yards away so he wouldn't have to see the disfigurement. For a trained bodyguard, he was the biggest wimp of them all.

Tetyana was sure the body was a "Mafia kill."

I had to agree.

The dead man could have been a thug, a member of a local gang, or someone who had the misfortune to cross them. Either way, I wasn't going to allow Theodore to treat a human corpse like roadkill. Billionaire or not, there was some basic decency I expected from my clients.

"It's a crime scene, Mr. Henry," I said, trying to keep my voice level. "If we're going to move the body, we have to do it with care."

Theodore's nostrils flared at my words. This was a man not used to disagreement, let alone anyone refusing to obey his commands.

He didn't know I'd faced much more formidable adversaries. I was well aware my five-foot petite frame made me look years younger and weaker than I truly was.

I always got the opposite reaction my friends got when we met strangers.

Katy's height gave her an advantage. Given her buff, athletic built and her military crew cut, Tetyana intimidated most people. While she could be deadly and was trained to kill, they didn't realize it was me they'd have to watch out for, if they ever crossed me, my friends, or my family.

"We have to call the authorities first, Mr. Henry," I said, keeping my voice firm and my gaze steady. "Before we move the body, we'll have to take pictures, document as much as we can, and make sure we don't mess with the evidence."

"What evidence?" shouted Connor, who'd been fuming on his side of the table. "What the heck are you going on about?"

I turned to him.

"This wasn't an accident, Mr. McNamara. This wasn't some lost hiker who'd stumbled onto the tracks and frozen to death. We're miles from anywhere. That man was dressed in a suit and that body was embalmed. That tells us there's more involved here than meets the eye."

"What are you now? The FBI?" snarled Connor. "Why don't you shut up and get me another drink, wench."

I glared at the man. Tetyana took a step closer to him, her eyes so fiery, they'd have burned him to cinder if she could. With an irate hiss, Connor looked away.

I knew his type.

He was a bully until you stood up to him. Then, he turned into a coward.

"Katy's already calling the authorities," I said. "As soon as we get their permission, we can start moving."

"If you think I'm going to stay stuck here while the stupid pigs from the nearest county figure out how to get here, you're wrong," said Theodore, jabbing a finger in the air, inches from my nose.

"We need to be patient," I said, not flinching.

"I didn't pay you to play cop, dammit!"

"That no longer concerns me," I said, suppressing the urge to slap this man down. "There's a dead body on the tracks with a face mutilated beyond recognition. We can't just toss him off and go on our merry way."

"I'll be happy to kick him out myself," mumbled Theodore while turning back to his drink, as if he'd given up the debate.

A part of me felt bad.

He was traveling to Seattle for cancer treatments, after all. He was stuck in a wheelchair with a potentially incurable disease, having to wait for everyone around him to help him out. That was probably weighing him down.

But another part of me was sure he was being his usual egocentric and pompous self. I wasn't about to take rushed action I'd regret later, however much he had promised to pay us.

My eyes swept over his companions.

Stella was sitting immobile in her chair, like she was glued to it. Her face remained expressionless. She hadn't even blinked an eye when we came over to tell them about our discovery.

Something was wrong with that woman. I wondered if she was also sick. Whatever it was, she was hiding it well.

Doctor Wilson merely gazed at us with dull eyes. He was so infused in alcohol, I could almost see fumes emanating from the top of his head.

He was an old friend of Theodore, but I still couldn't help but wonder why the gold baron, who could afford any physician in the world, had hired a drunk for such an important treatment.

Footsteps from the back kitchen made us all turn.

It was Katy.

"Asha," she said as she appeared on the threshold, her mobile phone in her trembling hand. Her voice had notched up several octaves, like she was at the verge of panic.

"All okay, Katy?" I asked.

"There's no cell phone reception," she said, sounding out of breath. "Been walking up and down. Went all the way to the back and even tried the bathroom. Nothing."

She stared at me with wide eyes.

Tetyana and I pulled our phones from our pockets while Connor and Theodore fumbled in their pockets for their mobiles as well. Stella sat still, like a statue, watching us.

I looked at my phone in dismay. All the bars were red.

No amount of clicking or swiping or even restarting the phone was going to do anything.

"You're right," said Tetyana with a disgusted sniff. "Did you try outside?"

"No," said Katy. "I came to tell you first—"

Tetyana whirled around. "Lemme try."

She stomped out of the train carriage and pretty soon we saw her pacing along the tracks, holding her phone in the air.

As we watched, a flash of light came from near Tetyana's hand. She'd turned on the flashlight app.

It was getting dark outside. I'd forgotten how quickly day turns to night in this region in spring.

I stepped up to the window and waved. Tetyana shook her head.

My stomach sank as I heard her shout through the window.

"Negative reception!"

"We'll try the radio in the engine car," I shouted back.

She nodded. "I'll go check on Tank," she said, pointing in the direction of the cadaver on the tracks.

In the distance, I could make the silhouette of Tank huddled in his overcoat as he stood under a pine tree, several yards away from the body.

"Roger that," I called out. "We'll keep fort."

With a quick salute, Tetyana marched toward Tank.

The sound of heavy footsteps from the front of the car made me turn. Someone was dragging their feet.

It was Dwayne.

He stopped and stared at his boss, like he was reassessing what he'd come to share.

"Sir..." He swallowed hard.

"Stop gawking like an idiot and get this thing moving!" shouted Theodore. "Do your damn job."

"But sir..."

"What is it, Dwayne?" I asked.

From his expression, there was something other than a dead body on the tracks that was bothering him. Dwayne's eyes darted from Theodore to Connor, then to me and back.

"What the hell's wrong with you?" said Theodore. "Speak, man."

"Sir," said Dwayne, withering under his boss's glare. "The radio's dead."

Chapter Six

Theodore slammed the table with his fist, making everyone jump.

"What the hell do you mean it's dead?" he shouted, his flinty eyes protruding. "I paid good money for this operation. Make it work!"

"Sir," said Dwayne, swallowing. "We're in a dip, in the middle of a valley and it's getting dark."

"What does that have to do with anything?"

"SATCOM doesn't work in these conditions and latitude, especially at this time of day."

"What about your backup radio?" I asked.

Dwayne nodded, a somber expression on his face. "I need a clear line of sight for VHF to operate, and we're nowhere near a tower or station."

"Why the heck didn't you prepare for this, man?" shouted Theodore, his face turning red. "What do I pay you for?"

The engineer gulped and looked like he wished he could melt into the floor.

"It's just that we don't normally stop in the middle of nowhere like this, sir. This is highly irregular."

"Contingency planning," yelled his boss, who appeared ready to explode. "Why didn't you make one before we left? You should have known better than that!"

I looked down at my phone. Those red bars on the top right-hand corner of my screen looked even more ominous.

"What about the cellular networks?" I said. "There must be a tower in the vicinity?"

Dwayne shook his head sadly. "We're thirty miles from the nearest cell towers in both directions."

"What the hell? I need a drink," said Connor, grabbing the vodka bottle from the doctor's hands, who'd just opened it to pour himself a glass.

"So," said Katy, her eyes widening, "does this mean we're stuck in this valley with no way to reach anyone?"

Dwayne was silent for a moment as if afraid to answer her question.

"Problem is we're in the middle of a mountain range," he said. "If this happened fifteen miles either way, we'd have been able to pick a signal. But even then, there wouldn't have been any guarantee..." He trailed off.

Nobody spoke for a while.

I wondered if Theodore's idea was actually a good one. Maybe we needed to move the body and get to the nearest station before anything else.

I turned to Dwayne, trying to come to terms with where we were at.

"With no cell towers or radio working, this is the perfect spot to drop a dead body, isn't it?" I said. "Someone wanted to hold us up."

Dwayne looked away, like he didn't even want to consider the thought.

Connor swore. Theodore looked like he was about to throw something at someone. Dwayne wiped the droplets of sweat that had gathered on his forehead.

"If I wasn't stuck in this wheelchair—" growled Theodore.

He didn't get to finish.

The sound of a gunshot echoed through the woods outside.

Tetyana!

Pushing Katy aside, I dashed through the doorway into the sleeping carriage behind us.

I slammed my cabin door open and dove into my suitcase, which lay open on the luggage rack. I'd just plucked my sidearm from its secure case, when the door banged and Katy came in, her hair standing up, like a lion's red mane.

"What was that—"

"Get your gun," I said, checking my weapon.

Not waiting for her to reply, I ran past her to the exit nearest to our cabin.

I yanked the handle down, expecting the door to open, but it didn't budge. That wasn't a surprise as until a half hour ago, the train had been rolling. Dwayne must have secured all exits.

"It's locked?"

I spun around to see Katy, her Glock in her hand now.

"This way," I said, pulling her away from the door.

We rushed back to the dining car.

Given the circumstances, I had expected chaos, but Doctor Wilson and Stella were still seated, immobilized in fear. Dwayne had disappeared from the dining car.

Theodore had half risen from his wheelchair, and was holding shakily to the table, staring out the window. His eyes were darting back and forth, as he muttered darkly to himself.

Connor was hiding behind the liquor cabinet, looking pale and flustered. His eyes widened as he saw our Glocks.

"What the hell are you doing with those?" he asked.

I didn't have time to answer.

"Come on, Katy," I said, as we stepped up to the exit which Tetyana had jumped out of, just moments ago.

But the door was shut and Robin and Dwayne were bolting it with a steel rod.

"Hey, open up!" I yelled.

They spun around. Dwayne's eyes widened when they fell on our weapons. He shot us an alarmed look.

"I said, open the door."

"You... you can't go out," he stammered. "I don't know what's going on, but the train is on lockdown."

"But Tetyana's out there," said Katy.

"There was a shooting," said Robin in a stern voice. "Didn't you hear?"

"There are two people outside right now," I snapped, pushing her away from the door. "Get out of the way, for heaven's sake."

Someone stepped through the door toward the gangway connection. It was Connor marching toward us, his finger pointing accusingly.

"Why are these damn catering girls running around with guns, telling us what to do?" he shouted. "Who the hell do you think you are?"

I'd have gladly pistol whipped him. But Tetyana was outside and could be in trouble.

"Get away from the door," I said, ignoring Connor and pushing Dwayne away. I pulled the steel rod from the door.

"Are you trying to get us killed?" shouted Connor.

"Let the girls out," came Theodore's voice from behind us.

We all turned to see him wheeling in through the connecting door and onto the gangway.

"They're not caterers," he said, turning to his friend. "They're my private investigation team."

Connor's eyes bulged. Dwayne and Robin gave us shocked looks.

"You're *PIs*?" said Robin in a breathless voice.

"And didn't you tell me?" spluttered Connor, his cockiness evaporated, looking dejected for a change.

"I brought them over from New York," said Theodore, his voice wavering. "I had an inkling something bad would happen on this trip. Something told me in my bones."

He turned to his crew members.

"Let them do what they're here to do."

Without a word, Robin and Dwayne stepped away from the door.

I pulled out the steel rod and yanked the handle. The door flew open, and a swirl of cold air blasted inside.

With my gun aimed forward, I popped my head out and swiveled around.

Where's Tetyana?

It was getting darker and harder to see. The only light came from the train carriage windows, but they didn't go far.

I peered into the distance to spot the silhouettes of Tetyana and Tank, but twilight had already enveloped the side of the tracks where the corpse lay.

Strange.

I'd expected to see the flashlights from their phones at least.

If anyone had been waiting to take a shot at me, I'd have made a perfect target, standing by the train's doorway.

We had to move. And move fast.

With my heart in my mouth, I jumped down the steps and jogged along the tracks toward the dead body, with Katy right next to me.

Who fired that shot? Please let Tetyana be okay.

We were halfway there when she grabbed my arm and pulled me back.

"Did you hear that?" she whispered.

I stopped and strained to listen.

"Someone's in there," she said, pointing her gun at the shadow of a large tree, fifty yards from us.

"What did you hear?" I whispered back.

That was when an anguished yell came from the woods.

Chapter Seven

"Tank?" said Katy.

"Keep it down," I whispered.

"Sounded like he's in trouble," she whispered, looking around nervously. "Is Tetyana in danger too?"

I didn't know what the woods held. But I wasn't about to leave our friend alone with whatever was going on, despite her training.

Katy and I crept across the icy ground toward the thicket of trees.

We were doing our best to stay in stealth mode, but to my ears, the sound of our boots crunching on the snow was as loud as a herd of bison thundering across the plains.

It was getting darker, and the temperature was dipping. I shivered, thankful I'd pulled on my jacket and my gloves this time.

As soon as we crossed the threshold into the snow-covered woodlands, I slipped behind the nearest tree trunk. Keeping my hand steady on my gun, I craned my neck to spot anyone through the trees. Katy's anxious breaths fell on my neck as she peered over my shoulder, inches behind me.

"To the left," she whispered. "Something's going on down there."

She was right.

Suddenly the sound of thrashing came from deep within the woods, like the herd of bison had wandered in there now.

What's going on?

Katy and I stepped carefully from tree to tree, our backs to each other, scanning our surroundings to make sure we weren't being followed.

Or watched.

Another yell came from the direction we were heading.

It was Tank.

A loud and angry curse followed the shout.

"Tetyana," said Katy, relief in her voice. "She's alive, and she sounds mad."

It seemed like there was a scuffle up ahead in the middle of the woods.

We quickened our pace, trying not to make any noise. But my heart was pounding so hard, I was sure the entire world could hear it.

Did they find the person who dumped the body? Are they fighting an attacker?

Tetyana could and would single-handedly take on the entire Alaska Army National Guard, if she put her mind to it. But for her sake, I hoped she was being prudent. And I wasn't about to make any stupid assumptions and get us in trouble too.

I stepped up to the next tree.

"Frigging hell!" came an angry voice.

That was definitely Tetyana.

That's when I saw them.

Two figures were brawling underneath a massive Douglas fir, about five yards ahead of us. Tank was trying to get away, but was doing a lousy job at it, and Tetyana, was trying to grab him and hold him back.

"I said, calm down!" she shouted.

Tank looked like he spent all his spare time at the gym. Or in a prison. He was putting up a good fight, but Tetyana had a strong hold on him.

"Lemme go!" he roared and lifted his hands to push her away or punch her.

I jumped out from behind the trees.

"Freeze!" I shouted, pointing my weapon at him.

Tank stopped moving, hands in mid-air, and stared at us, his mouth open.

"I got him," said Tetyana, grabbing him by the shoulder and forcing him to turn around.

"Stand right where you are," said Katy, pulling her phone out of her pocket. She turned the flashlight on and shone it at his face.

Tank looked away to shield his eyes.

"What were you running away from?" said Tetyana, shaking him by the shoulders.

He didn't answer, just stared at us like he was seeing ghosts.

Tetyana turned to us.

"One minute, we were guarding the body. The next, this meathead runs off, screaming bloody murder."

"Who fired the gun?" I asked, keeping my eyes on Tank, my weapon still aimed at him.

"Sorry, that was me," said Tetyana. "It was a warning shot. I was trying to get a cell signal when I caught him bolting off to the woods."

"I... I saw her," stammered Tank, now limp in Tetyana's grip. He was breathing heavily and sweat was streaming down his face, though he'd stopped struggling. "She was gonna get me. She's gonna get us all."

Tetyana shook her head.

"He's been babbling about this all along. I dunno what the heck he's talking about."

"Who is it, Tank?" I said. "Did you see something?"

He turned to me, blinking rapidly as Katy's flashlight cut across his eyes.

"She's here, I tell you."

He stared past my shoulder, like he was searching for something. I turned around, but there was no one. Just stillness. Not one branch moved, or a pinecone dropped.

"Who is this *she*?"

"The… the elders in the village told us. They knew about her. She did this to that man. It was her. We're all gonna end up like him."

"You mean like the dead man on the tracks?" I said.

He took another sharp breath in, which sounded like a sob.

If it hadn't been for Tetyana's firm hold on his shoulder, Tank would have bolted like a jittery jackrabbit.

"What did you see, Tank?" I said, lowering my weapon and my voice.

"It's the woman they told us about. In the white dress and a feather in her hair." He stumbled over his words, like he was scared to speak but wanted to get it out in a rush. "If she doesn't like you, she'll get you. I'm telling you."

His eyes darted back and forth, like he expected this strange woman to jump on him at any moment. He was a blubbering basket case.

"I saw her coming on the other side of the tracks." He shot a fearful look at Tetyana, who was still holding him tightly. "I saw her, I tell you. I wasn't going to hang around waiting for her to get me too. That's why I ran like that."

Tetyana rolled her eyes.

"You should have warned me, dude," she said. "The way you ran, you looked pretty suspicious. I didn't shoot to hit you."

Tank stared at her.

"I'd take a bullet to my head any day, rather than get torn to shreds by that woman."

"Do you expect us to believe in these ghost stories?" I said. "Really, Tank?"

When researching for this trip, I'd come across the many urban legends of Alaska. The state seemed rife with haunted tales, especially about monsters lying in wait for their prey in remote lakes or Big Foot roaming the snow-covered landscape, its inhuman roars terrifying local inhabitants.

But that's what they all were. Made-up stories. Tales to be told around a campfire or an ice-fishing hole.

"Do you think what happened to that poor man on the tracks was the work of some crazy poltergeist?" said Katy in a soft voice, like she felt sorry for the man.

I decided to wait before I made any judgments, myself. Though he looked and sounded genuinely shaken, I wasn't sure if this was all a first-class act.

Tank's shoulders dropped. He shook his head and looked down at his feet.

"I don't know, man. I don't know what the hell is going on here. Whatever it is, it isn't good. I'd take a bullet for Mr. Henry. That's my job. But I don't do ghosts. That's not in my job description."

"Come on," said Tetyana, pulling him by the arm, impatience laced in her voice. "We have a job to do. Until the authorities come over, we have to guard that dead man."

She pulled him toward us. Tank lurched but followed her.

"Hey, Tetyana," I said, lowering my voice. "Bad news. Radio is down. Both SATCOM and VHF."

She whirled around.

"Are you kidding me?"

"Didn't have time to double-check. Had to take Dwayne's word for it, but we'll try it when we get back."

"I tell you it's her," mumbled Tank. "Why don't you people believe me?"

"How the heck does that happen?" asked Tetyana, ignoring him.

"Cell towers are too far away and SATCOM doesn't work that well up in the mountains," said Katy. "That's what Dwayne said."

"Maybe Theodore is right," I said. "The best solution might be to move the body carefully, get to the nearest cell tower station and call the authorities."

Tetyana gave a shrug.

"Roger that."

She turned and scowled at Tank.

"As long as no one tries any more funny moves."

He gave her a miserable look.

Pulling him forward, she marched toward the tracks, dodging the tree trunks. Katy and I kept close behind them, our weapons out, our eyes and ears alert.

Perhaps he'd seen a nocturnal animal hiding among the trees, but had conjured up that old tale to justify what he'd seen. If Tetyana had been busy trying to get a cell signal, that would explain why she'd missed it at the edge of the woods, despite her eagle eyes.

But something about Tank's ghost-woman-in-a-white-dress story had disturbed me.

We stepped out of the tree line and walked toward the tracks.

It was comforting to see the train parked behind us, the bright yellow lights emanating from its windows. It signaled warmth and safety, in contrast to our sinister surroundings.

"Frigging hell!" said Tetyana, pulling Tank back.

"What?" I said, snapping my head away from the train and toward them.

"I told you," said Tank, in a hoarse whisper. "I told you. Why didn't you listen to me?"

I walked around them to see what had stopped them.

"The body," whispered Katy, as she stepped next to me. "It's gone."

Chapter Eight

"Do you recognize this man?"

Connor and Theodore leaned across the table and peered into my phone.

I had expected to share the photo with the authorities to show them how we'd found the dead man. But now, with contacting them a remote possibility and the body having disappeared into thin air, I was glad I had something to prove what we had seen on the tracks.

Theodore adjusted his eyeglasses and scrunched his forehead. Connor peered at the image. They both looked sincerely curious.

Stella Green sat straight in her chair, her lips contorted into a grimace. She had given my phone one glance and had quickly turned away, as if it had been too distasteful to even contemplate.

I didn't blame her. It was a gruesome image.

The physician had left the table by the time we had returned to the train. According to Robin, he'd walked off to his cabin saying he needed a nap, just as we had jumped out to inspect the gunshot.

Tank had positioned himself behind Theodore's chair now, like he was seeking protection from us. I wondered who was guarding whom in this relationship.

He stood with his hands clasped, looking like a bodyguard on duty, but Tank's eyes told a different story. The man was frightened. I wasn't certain if it was the mystery of the disappearing cadaver or the phantom-in-a-white-dress he'd dreamed up that had unnerved him the most.

"Very interesting," said Connor, leaning in, considerably calmed down compared to our last encounter.

I wondered if Theodore had told him to settle down or if it had been our guns that had quietened him. I didn't know or care. I was just glad he was co-operating.

I pulled my phone out from under his nose.

"Let me zoom it," I said, using my fingers to enlarge the photo. I placed the mobile back on the table.

"How interesting," muttered Connor, picking up my phone, his nose five inches from the screen.

"What do you see, Connor?" asked Theodore, narrowing his eyes. "It's not a pretty picture."

"That it ain't, my friend," said Connor, not looking up, his brow furrowed.

Tetyana was standing by the doorway, her eyes alternately scanning the outside and sweeping the room, watching everyone's movements. The black gun in her hand gleamed under the dining car's light.

For the tenth time that day, I was grateful she had come with us on this trip. She'd scoffed at the train ride at first. It was David, my fiancé, who'd encouraged her to take a break from teaching classes at his martial arts dojo and join us. I knew he had an ulterior motive, always worrying about my safety whenever I took these private cases.

Sitting at an empty table in the back of the dining car were the father and daughter. Robin and Dwayne sat side-by-side, leaning against each other, their faces drawn and lined with worry, and their shoulders stooped.

They looked exhausted.

I'd read about how railway deaths and suicides traumatized train crew. We hadn't run over those human remains on the tracks, but this incident had shaken them to the core.

"Connor, do you know the man?" said Theo. "Talk to me."

There was a hint of anxiety in his eyes, like he'd recognized the dead man, but was looking for confirmation.

Or denial.

I was on full guard.

We had been so focused on reining in Tank in the woods, we didn't know if someone from the train had somehow walked over and removed the body in our absence.

Theodore couldn't walk, or at least he wanted us to think that. Could he and Connor have moved the body together? Or was it Dwayne and Robin?

Stella Green looked too fearful and Doctor Wilson too drunk to do anything of significance.

It was strange how the physician had disappeared from the dining car, the minute we'd stepped out of the train. But he'd been too inebriated to walk straight, let alone drag the body of an adult and cover up the tracks on the snow.

Besides, when Katy and I went to check, we heard the distinct sound of snores from his cabin in the sleeper car.

One thing was for sure.

Tetyana didn't trust Tank.

She didn't like the way he dashed into the woods, shrieking like a scared kid. It wasn't what anyone would expect from a well-trained bodyguard. Either he was pretending to be the security detail or what we had seen in the woods had been an act.

Why would he do that?

A ruse to get us all away from the body?

Katy was sure there were people hiding in the woods, watching, lingering. For what, we didn't know. Yet.

If she was right, whoever left the body on the tracks had wanted to stop the train for an unknown reason we still had to figure out.

Robin and Dwayne had been adamant. We were stranded in the middle of one of the most remote regions of Alaska. There were no settlements, villages, or roads for hundreds of miles.

I hadn't made up my mind on any of this yet.

But the question remained.

Who moved the body?

Connor was zooming in and out of the image, his eyes intently focused.

"Tell me," said Theodore, a sense of urgency in his tone. "What do you see, my man?"

"There's only one person who had a scar on his neck like this," his friend replied, speaking thoughtfully, as if he was still thinking it through.

"See this?"

I leaned across the table to see what he was pointing at. There was a small scar in the crude shape of an inverted cross on the man's neck.

I had hardly noticed it when I saw the man on the tracks. The lighting had been bad and the shock of seeing his face had been a distraction.

"Speak up, Connor," shouted Theodore, startling us all. "If you know who it is, tell us."

There was a nervous twitch on Theodore's hand. He was blinking rapidly and his chest was heaving, like he was about to hyperventilate.

I smelled fear.

Why did the mention of the scar alarm him?

The research I'd done on this man prior to our arrival in Alaska had been limited but revealing.

Despite his unpleasant personality, he had done well for himself. He had a knack for discovering precious ore in the most unlikely of places and for convincing the right experts to do all the hard work for him.

His competition, almost every other mining company executive and owner in this part of the world, despised him. If I'd read between the lines correctly, there were many people who'd do anything to see him fail.

That kind of history laid you wide open to revenge.

Now, with cancer eating into him and mortality staring him in the face, I had no doubt his fears had only grown larger. And his paranoia heightened.

Theodore was a man waiting for his dark past to catch up to him.

"Jim Johnson," said Connor, placing my phone on the table and leaning back in his chair.

Theodore's eyebrows shot up.

"Jim?" he whispered. "How is that possible?"

"Who's Jim Johnson?" I asked.

Nobody answered.

Theodore's hands were shaking, and he had a strange expression on his face. Stella was staring at the wall in front of her, withdrawn and aloof, like she didn't want to have anything to do with any of this. Connor sat back in his chair, rubbing his eyes.

"Could any of you tell us who Jim Johnson is, please?" I asked the group.

Someone cleared their throat behind me.

I turned to see Dwayne shift in his chair.

"Who is he?" I asked. "Do you know?"

"Used to be head foreman at the mine," replied Dwayne, speaking slowly, like it pained him to talk about the man. "I used to work for him ages ago."

"How come you didn't recognize him when we saw him on the tracks?" asked Katy.

"You asked me who Jim Johnson was," said Dwayne, suddenly on the defensive. "I didn't know it was him. Didn't see any scars or anything, and his face was all smashed..." He trailed off, and dropped his head.

Next to him, Robin was absentmindedly playing with the corner of a napkin. I could see her mind was elsewhere.

They both had pained expressions on their faces. They were both avoiding eye contact.

They knew more than they were telling us.

Chapter Nine

"I was at his funeral four days ago."

We all turned to Connor who was gazing at the ceiling, his chair tipped back, his hands behind the back of his head. Unusually reflective for a man who loved to bluster.

"So, he was dead then?" said Katy.

"Pretty much," said Connor, not looking at her. "It was an open casket, and he was in that suit. I remember it because I told his wife I would have paid for a better one if she had only asked me. He looked exactly like this... except for the face."

He put his hands on the table and brought his chair back down.

"I saw them bury him," he said, locking eyes with Theodore, who was leaning in, listening intently. "Six feet underground. Even saw his grandkids throw flower petals or some stuff on the coffin after it was lowered."

"Where was he buried?" I said.

"City burial lot, behind the church," said Connor, his eyes still on Theodore. "Where everyone gets buried in Black Eagle town."

"Why would anyone dig a dead man up?" I asked.

Connor and Theodore continued to stare at each other. I couldn't gauge what they were thinking from their expressions. Just that they were worried. Nervous.

"You didn't go," said Connor to his friend.

"Urgent meetings," replied Theodore in a quiet voice. "I sent flowers and a gift basket to his family."

"Was he one of your employees?" I asked.

No answer.

The two men were still looking at each other, faces drawn. It was like they were speaking a silent language that only they understood.

Dwayne and Robin sat huddled in their corner, their faces turned down, while Tank stood behind his boss, head bowed, like he was at a funeral.

What's going on here?

They were all hiding something. I racked my brain, struggling to figure out how to get them to open up.

"Why disfigure him?"

Everyone jerked their heads up. Even me.

We all turned to Stella. She had hardly spoken a word throughout the journey, so it was strange to hear her voice.

"It doesn't make any sense," she said, looking with distaste at my phone. "Why would anyone dig him up, smash his face, and put him on the tracks?"

"That's exactly my question," I said.

But no one answered.

"What do you all know about Jim Johnson?" I said, scanning the room. "Was he involved with gangs or mafia types?"

Theodore's lips curled into a snarl. He turned his head slowly, his dark eyes falling on me.

"That man worked at my mine since the day I dug the ground. None of my employees have anything to do with drugs or gangs. If they did, I'd fire their asses."

"Darn right," said Connor, turning to me with a scowl. "He was the best foreman we had. Don't sully a good man's reputation."

"But someone did that to him," I pointed out. "I'm trying to figure out why anyone would dig up and cut up a good man and throw him on the tracks in the middle of a valley with no roads to get to."

"If I ever find out who did this to Jim, I'd smash their faces in," growled Connor.

I turned to Theodore.

"When was the last time you spoke with Jim Johnson?"

"Haven't talked to the man in years. He retired ten years ago, I think."

"Nine," said Connor.

"What did he do after retirement?" I asked.

"Started a garden and kept chickens. Got on the town's volunteer firefighter list after his wife nagged him to get out of the house," said Connor, looking genuinely sad.

Theodore shook his head. "I got more gold out of this mine under his watch. That man was efficient, a hard worker. He knew how to get everyone to pull their weight."

"Aye," nodded Connor. "It was difficult to find his replacement. They don't make men like him anymore."

A rustle came from behind me, like someone was shuffling their feet.

"He was a tough man," said Dwayne.

I was about to ask him what he meant by that, when Theodore slammed his hand on the table. He glared at his crew in the corner.

"Whatever happened to Jim, let the authorities deal with it," he growled. "Now the tracks are clear, let's get moving."

Neither Dwayne nor Robin looked up.

"Get this beast rolling and let's get outta here, Dwayne. Now."

The engineer didn't budge. He looked like he was struggling to control his emotions.

"We just found a dead body on our path, sir," stammered Dwayne. "I can't in good faith drive across the tracks right now."

"Why the hell not?" asked Connor.

"Protocol says—"

"Damn the protocol," shouted Theodore.

Dwayne's face scrunched up.

"How do I know there's not another body on the tracks, sir, or god forbid, someone moved Jim further down? I can't risk it, sir. It's dark outside now."

"You have headlights, don't you?" said Connor. "Use them. If you see something, you can stop just like you did this time."

Dwayne rubbed his face.

"Only reason I stopped on time was because Robin's drone caught sight of Jim from the air a mile away. This isn't a sports car, this is a steam engi—"

"Don't you tell me what this is," said Connor. "Get the drone back up. Do I have to think of everything around here?"

"At night?" said Robin, looking up and frowning at Connor. "First of all, my drone's busted. Second of all, this ain't military-grade equipment with night vision. I got it from Walmart to catch animals crossing the tracks."

"Are you suggesting we spend the night in this god forsaken valley with some crazy grave digger out there trying to frighten everyone?" Theodore raised his voice. "I don't care if we run over a hundred dead men. If they're dead, they're dead. Let's get rolling!"

Dwayne swallowed hard and looked down. I could see he was summoning all his strength to speak up.

"Since when did you stop taking instructions?" said Connor, frowning at the engineer.

"This goes against everything I've been trained to do," replied Dwayne, his voice feeble. "We have to wait till morning and see what's left on the tracks at least, before we can start moving."

Connor rose from his chair and leaned across the table, his knuckles digging into the tablecloth.

"When Theo or me tell you to move the damn train, you move the damn train."

"I'm really sorry, sir," said Dwayne, not looking at the two men directly anymore. Sweat droplets streamed from his face. "A dead body on the tracks is—"

He didn't get to finish.

Connor grabbed the half-empty vodka bottle from the table and hurled it at the engineer.

"Watch out," shouted Tetyana.

I ducked, pulling Katy away.

Robin moved just in time.

But Dwayne wasn't so lucky.

The bottle slammed against his head, spouting vodka everywhere.

"Dad!" screamed Robin.

Dwayne crumpled, face first, onto the table.

"Oh no," gasped Katy, running toward him.

Blood trickled out of the cut on the right side of his forehead, but he remained motionless. Robin reached over and touched the wound, then stared at the blood on her fingers in horror.

"What the hell did you do to my father?" she shouted at Connor, her face turning purple with rage.

Snatching up the vodka bottle from the floor, she stomped toward Connor.

Chapter Ten

Tetyana leaped over a chair and pulled Robin back.

Robin wiggled furiously, but Tetyana held on to her tightly. "Enough!" I shouted.

Connor stared at the conductor like she was mad.

Theodore shot Tetyana a frustrated look.

"Get that woman away from us," he growled. "I hired you people to protect me."

Tetyana glowered at him, but she had a job to do. She pulled Robin away from the men. But if no one had been around, I was sure she'd have happily pistol-whipped Connor.

"How dare you?" shouted Robin, looking like she was ready to slug Connor, if she could only reach him. "You could have killed him!"

Tetyana snatched the bottle from her hand and slammed it down on the nearest table.

"Stop this," I said, stepping in between Robin and the head table.

"Throwing things at your crew isn't helping," I said, using all my energy to not lash out at the two men.

Theodore stirred in his wheelchair, as if suddenly realizing what had happened.

"That was a stupid thing to do, Connor," he said, in the tone one would use to scold a naughty child. "You shouldn't have hit him, for Pete's sake."

Connor slouched in his chair, eyes down, turning his vodka glass around and around, seemingly oblivious to the havoc he'd created.

If I had despised this man before, I positively hated him now. He was a boor, a bully who seemed to get away with a lot.

"I was only trying to get us moving," he mumbled into his drink.

Katy was at the table in the back, leaning over Dwayne. She had pulled the first-aid kit from the wall and had it opened in front of her.

Tetyana let Robin go. She walked over and took her father's hand, talking to him in a soft voice.

Dwayne's fingers twitched.

He's alive.

Thank goodness.

"Oh, Dad," said Robin, reaching over with a napkin to dab the blood from his face.

"I can stop the bleeding," said Katy, pulling a roll of bandage from the kit. "It's going to hurt, but he'll be okay. He'll need rest before anything."

She looked at Connor, her face sour.

"If he had become unconscious, we'd be stuck here for good."

"With no comms to the outside world," I said.

"At least we have a doctor on board," said Theodore with a shrug.

A drunk one. Practically useless.

"Worse comes to worst, we wake Neil up," he continued.

I wondered if this man had any empathy at all.

He turned to me and to my surprise, lowered his voice.

"Clean up quickly and start the train. Best we get out of here or I swear we'll kill each other."

But Robin heard him.

"Dad's all cut up and you want to put him to work?"

Theodore looked away. Though he may not have cared, he knew the repercussions of his friend's actions.

"Dwayne's the only one who can operate the train," said Stella, speaking up unexpectedly. Her accusing eyes landed on Connor first, then Theodore.

"We're in a real spot now, aren't we, gentlemen?" she said.

There was a note of smugness in her voice, the kind you'd feel when someone you hated got cornered. There was no love lost between her and her employers.

"Seems like you made the decision for us," I said to Connor. "We stay put till tomorrow morning."

He curled his mouth into a snarl but didn't reply.

Theodore turned to Robin.

"You know how to operate this thing?"

"Go to hell," she said, not even looking at him.

Theodore turned to me.

"What about your team?"

I shook my head. "Helicopters, small planes, and maybe a small boat, but no one in my team has operated a train before."

Dwayne lifted his head so Katy could bandage his wound, but his eyes were closed, and his face showed pain.

"Best to let Dwayne rest and recover tonight," I said, and turned to Tetyana. "We'll need to secure the compartments."

She straightened up.

"I'll be on guard all night," she said to the room. "I suggest you folk move into your cabins and stay inside until morning."

No one moved.

"It'll make my job easier, and you'll be safer."

Theodore opened his mouth to speak but closed it.

He and Connor were in their mid-seventies at least, and Theodore had serious health issues. I could see the recent incidents were wearing them out. If they'd been younger and sober, we'd have had a fight on our hands.

Tetyana raised her voice.

"Happy to hand you all a watch shift. Who's with me?"

That did it.

Stella jumped to her feet and clutched the edge of the table.

"I'll be in my room," she said in a low voice, before squeezing past Connor and heading toward the sleeping car behind us.

With a loud curse, Connor pushed his chair back and got up. Without another word, he stomped out, and we heard his door slam shut.

Theodore pushed his wheelchair back and rolled it around the table. "If I could walk, I'd move the damn train myself," he muttered, as he rolled to the back of the dining car.

Tetyana commanded Robin to take position in the engine car upfront and for Tank to take watch in the luggage compartment at the very back.

That left the dining car and the sleeping cabins in the middle, which Katy and I would patrol, while Tetyana did a full turn, from the front of the train to the back, and back again, every hour on the hour.

It was going to be a long night.

Chapter Eleven

D wayne gave Katy a glazed look.

"What happened?" he said, slurring his words.

"It's you who needs our protection, not your boss," I said, giving him a wistful smile. "How are you doing?"

"Not the first time that happened." Dwayne grimaced.

"Is it Connor?" I asked. "A nasty boss, is he?"

"All of them," he mumbled, wincing as Katy placed a bag of ice on the bump on his head.

"What do you mean?"

"A mining town's a rough place. Nothing like the good life you ladies are used to."

Katy and I exchanged a glance over his head.

He didn't know of the terror we had experienced in our youths. Escaping human traffickers, fighting slavery gangs, and running from country to country, making sure everyone we cared about was safe, wasn't what I'd call a *good life*.

I shook off the haunting memories of my dark past. I had work to do and I couldn't lose my composure now.

"Fights?" I said. "Bar brawls and that sort of thing?"

"I'll take a bar brawl any day," said Dwayne in a somber voice. "It's when your bosses treat you badly that it gets.... complicated."

"How complicated?"

"That foreman, Jim, had a nasty temper, and he made sure everyone knew it."

"What did he do?"

Dwayne didn't answer.

"How bad was it?" I tried again.

Without speaking, Dwayne stretched his left leg out from under the table and pulled his pant leg up.

Katy gasped.

This was why Dwayne limped. He had a prosthetic steel rod in place of a flesh and bone leg.

"How did that happen?" I asked.

"Jim was a hard boss. He worked us to the bone. Never gave a second thought to safety."

"You worked at the mine too?" said Katy.

"Everyone in town started at the mine. I was lucky my family ran the trains. Better than getting stuck underground all day and night for your whole life." Dwayne shivered. "I had an escape to look forward to."

"How did you lose your leg?" I said, softening my voice. "Something Jim Johnson did?"

"Jim wasn't the most popular man in town. He put a lot of men in hospital more than once. Doctor Wilson just patched us up and sent us back down the shaft."

Dwayne paused. He had a pained and faraway look in his eye, like he was recollecting memories that had been buried a long time ago.

We waited quietly. He was going to tell his story in his own time.

"The shafts and passages were never built for us to work. They were built for efficiency. The elevator was real bad. People got stuck in the mines for several shifts some days." He sucked in his breath. "I happened to put my foot in the wrong place at the wrong time and I fell down the space between the elevator and the floor. Fell one hundred feet. That's what they told me afterward, anyway."

Dwayne looked down at his hands. They were shaking.

"I was a kid, fourteen. I try not to—"

"Fourteen?" cried Katy.

A red-hot flash of anger went through me.

I had my own dark memories about child labor. It was all my parents talked about when they used to inspect mining operations for Environ Africa, a long time ago. The tales of horror they told would have chilled the blood of anyone. They had died trying to get their stories out to the world.

"Do they use child labor here in Alaska?" I said, pushing those thoughts back. My own history was done and dealt with. I had to focus on this moment.

Dwayne shrugged.

"It's not like in the Congo where they send eight-year-olds down the shafts," he said. "I was a strapping young teen. Plus, the wages were good. Every boy in town wanted a job there. They don't do that anymore, but it was a different time back then."

I sighed.

It didn't help when those who were exploited excused horrific practices. It happened in Africa. It happened in South America and in Asia. That, I knew. What was shocking to hear was it had happened here too.

"Do you think Jim's exhumed body was a message to the mining company?"

"Message?"

"To remind Theodore and Connor of what Jim did to their employees?"

"Nah..." Dwayne shook his head. "All mines operate like this. It's worse in other places. Miners are a hardy bunch. Nobody talks about it. That's all."

Because they don't live to talk about it?

"What about the city council?" I said. "The mayor? The sheriff? Surely, they can't hide these practices from the local authorities for too long."

He shrugged. "It's a small town. Mr. Henry has good connections. He knows everyone, and they know him. Guess who funds their re-election campaigns?"

He raised a brow as if to say *you know what I mean?*

So, they were all in Theodore's pockets.

Dwayne was sharing a lot more than I'd bargained to hear.

"You aren't from here," he said with a sigh. "You don't understand what it's like. This is our life. To tell the truth, I've forgotten half the things that happened in the mines. Best to forget and move on."

"Memories run deep," I said. "They pop up when you least expect it. Maybe someone is holding a grudge and wanted to strike back."

He shook his head.

"You're reading too much into this."

He turned his tired eyes on me.

"This was the act of a nutcase, if you ask me. When you get six months of night like we do up here, it can do funny things to you. Some go a little loony after a while."

I raised an eyebrow.

"You seriously think there's a lunatic on the loose?"

"Who else would dig out a dead body and throw it on the tracks?"

"Jim Johnson wasn't a coincidence."

"His grave was fresh," replied Dwayne in a grim voice. "That's all there is to it."

"What are you saying?" said Katy.

"It was easy to dig him up. They probably didn't even know who the body belonged to."

Chapter Twelve

"**I** swear there are eyes in the woods," said Katy, giving a visible shudder. "They're watching us."

"Eyes have bodies, and bodies are things I can deal with," said Tetyana, gripping her gun and peering out of our cabin room window. "I just wish I brought my night goggles."

It was pitch black outside.

The only light was coming from a string of small spotlights Tetyana and Robin had rustled up from the engine room and had hung outside the train compartments while Katy and I talked to Dwayne.

All the inside lights had been turned off except for a few security lights. All the doors had been secured, and the windows shuttered.

Except one.

The window in our cabin, which was where we had stationed ourselves momentarily while we took stock of our situation.

Tetyana had drawn up a roster for Katy and me to take turns keeping watch. That way, we'd get some rest in case we needed to be up and running the next morning, but neither of us could sleep.

Not now.

My gut told me our problems were just beginning.

"We should have expected this," I said, as I absentmindedly petted the kitten that had made Katy's pillow her bed.

A warm bowl of milk and a good clean up with a face towel were all it had taken to transform the cat from a shivering, matted-down creature to an ordinary house cat.

After playing with Katy for a while, she had curled up into a ball and fallen asleep, her chest moving up and down in rhythm and her white paws twitching every once in a while, like she was dreaming of chasing little white mice.

"If this cat belonged to Jim Johnson, the gravedigger's a psycho," I said, turning to my friends. "They left her inside a dead man's sleeve. On a train track."

Tetyana shook her head. "Not a fan of cats, but that was a sick thing to do."

Katy turned to me, an accusing look on her face. "We never learn, do we?"

I raised an eyebrow. "About what?"

"Why did you take this job?"

"It was a call from Madame Bouchard's estate," I said.

"She's dead," grumbled Katy. "Why do we let her pull our strings like this? Look what she's got us into now? Stuck in the middle of nowhere with a screwball gravedigger running around outside."

"Hard to say no to the money," I said, giving my friend a wistful look.

"She's playing with us again, from beyond the grave," said Katy, letting out a resigned sigh.

"Don't forget Theodore promised us a hefty check for escorting him to Anchorage." I paused as I realized what would happen now. "We might have to say goodbye to any payment now thought. He's not going to want to pay up after I stood up to him like that."

"Why do you always do that?" asked Katy, shaking her head.

"I didn't like the way he was treating Dwayne. You didn't either. Admit it."

Katy nodded glumly.

"I don't care about the check anymore," I said. "As long as Madame Bouchard's estate donates to our nonprofit for taking these calls, I'd do this every day."

"It's just that I was expecting a quiet luxury train ride through Alaska's wilderness," said Katy, rubbing the kitten's ear gently.

"I'm cool," said Tetyana with a shrug, not taking her eyes off the window. "This is what I've been trained for. If I had to stay in New York, teaching martial arts to flabby corporate execs day in and out, I'd shoot myself in the head."

"I made a promise," I said, more to myself than my friends. "I promised Madame Bouchard I'd take every call that came in."

I'd given her my word at her deathbed. With her dying breath Madame Bouchard had promised a million-dollar donation from her estate to our anti-trafficking nonprofit every time I took a call for help from her friends or colleagues.

It had been impossible to say no.

But what I didn't tell anyone was, like Tetyana, I craved adventure. After racing across four continents, fighting trafficking gangs in my youth, it was hard to settle down. There was a fire burning in my belly, one I couldn't ignore.

Very few of my clients at my New York bakery, or those who signed up for martial arts classes at my fiancé David's dojo, knew of my moonlighting work. Work I did when no one was looking.

Like this one.

"I miss Chantelle," said Katy. "I always call her to see if she's done her homework for the day, but now…"

I gave my friend a friendly nudge.

"We'll get everyone out of here first thing in the morning and figure out that dead body later. Promise. Don't you worry."

"You're optimistic."

"Dwayne said a freight train heads this way every week. It's supposed to come in one or two or three days. Worst-case scenario, we flag it down and get help."

"Three days?" spluttered Katy. "What if it doesn't show up or is delayed even longer?"

"We have enough food, water, and supplies for more than a few days," I said. "The toilets are working. We have heat. Comfy rooms to sleep. Three days is more than enough for us to figure out what to do next."

"I wish we were stuck with nicer people," said Katy. "Robin and Dwayne seem normal, but I can't stand Connor and Theodore. They have evil in their eyes."

"The man I don't trust is Tank," said Tetyana, her back to us, her face glued to the glass. "Weird how he got scared of a ghost. Have a funny feeling about him."

"Stella is a head-scratcher too," said Katy. "It's strange why a really intelligent woman like her would come here to work. She'd do so well in New York or Chicago."

"She's a member of the executive suite. Probably gets paid well," I said.

"But after what Dwayne said, why would she work for a company with serious labor violations? Wouldn't she be worried about potential lawsuits?"

"Statute of limitations?" I said. "They wouldn't get away with hiring kids these days—"

"Hey, guys!"

Katy and I spun around to see what had startled Tetyana.

She was pointing her weapon at the sky.

Chapter Thirteen

Katy and I scrambled up to the window.

"Oh, my goodness," whispered Katy.

In stunned silence, the three of us watched the bursts of intense green and yellow colors ebb and flow high above us.

The sky was putting on a magical show over the snowy tundra landscape. The colors shifted across the starlit Arctic sky in undulating waves, like supernatural ribbons dancing in the wind.

"The Northern lights," I said in awe, my eyes turned upward.

"Aurora Borealis," said Tetyana. "Never expected to see it."

"People pay thousands for this," breathed Katy, creating a foggy shadow on the window. "And we're getting our own private show. There's no one else to see this but us."

A rustle behind us made me turn. The kitten had woken up from the commotion and jumped off Katy's bed. She gave me a curious look and blinked those adorable eyes.

I stared at the animal, Katy's words echoing through my mind.

There's no one else to see this but us.

"Hey," I said, nudging my friends. "How does a stray kitten turn up in the middle of a remote valley?"

Tetyana turned to me with a look that said, *huh?*

"She's not a feral cat," I said. "What if it wasn't the gravedigger who'd left her under the dead body?"

"What are you saying?" asked Tetyana, narrowing her eyes.

"What if there's a village or settlement nearby, one Dwayne, Robin or the others don't know about?"

"Behind the woods?" said Tetyana.

She opened the shutter to the second window in our cabin and leaned closer, her nose touching the glass pane, her eyes darting back and forth.

"Been thinking the same thing too," she said in a quiet voice.

"You guys can't be serious," said Katy. "Who would live here?"

"How else would a kitten show up like this?" I said.

"I told you," said Katy. "A kooky gravedigger brought her over and stuck her in the dead man's sleeve. They were cruel enough to dig up a corpse. Sticking a kitten in his sleeve is just one notch up on the scale of evil."

"This is an old track from the Klondike era," I said. "Communities settled along the train tracks all over the state during the Gold Rush. There are a dozen abandoned towns in Alaska from that time."

"That was a hundred years ago," said Katy, wrinkling her nose. "Who would be crazy enough to make a home so far from civilization today?"

"Hardy folk who prefer the outdoors? People who want to get away from the big city and live a simpler life?"

"Or serial killers," sniffed Katy. "This is the perfect spot for a serial killer to lie low while they plot their next murder."

"Hey!"

We both turned to Tetyana. She tapped the window with the barrel of her Glock.

"Do you see what I see?"

We jumped toward the second window and peered out, our heads turned up.

"Look down," said Tetyana. "Closer to the trees."

"Smoke," I said, as I watched the gray swirls rising from just beyond the woods.

"Part of the Northern Lights?" said Katy.

"No, that's smoke from fire," said Tetyana. "It's low to the ground. And it's white. I'd bet you anything that's coming from a chimney."

We stared at it for a minute, letting this sink in.

"But no one would live here. There aren't even roads up here," said Katy.

"Boats, float planes, ski planes, snowmobiles," I said. "None of those need a road."

"Shh...," said Tetyana suddenly, whipping around, her gun aimed at our open door.

Footsteps.

Someone was coming along the corridor.

Katy and I took position behind her.

Making a motion to stay quiet, Tetyana stepped out, holding her gun steady.

"Oh!" cried a female voice.

I jumped out after my friend, my weapon in my hand.

It was Stella, her hands in the air.

"Why aren't you in your room?" growled Tetyana.

"I... I couldn't sleep...," stammered Stella, her eyes still on Tetyana's Glock.

"Didn't I tell you to stay in your room till the morning?" said Tetyana.

"I'm sorry," Stella mumbled. "Just needed to get out for a moment. It's claustrophobic in there."

"Get back in your cabin," said Tetyana.

Stella stared at my friend, like she was too petrified to move.

I stepped around Tetyana.

"Stella," I said in a softer tone. "You can put your hands down. It would make our lives a lot easier if you followed instructions."

"What do you think is going to happen to us?" she asked in a low voice, almost a whisper. "What are we going to do?"

"We're going to keep an eye on the train all night, just to make sure no one gets close," I said. "As soon as day breaks, we'll examine the tracks and start moving."

"Start m... moving?" said Stella, looking confused. "Where to?"

What a strange question.

"To Anchorage or the next closest station," I said. "It's not like we can do a U-turn or turn around or get on the other track. Unless Dwayne knows how to push the engine backward to Black Eagle Town, we're heading south as planned."

"Sorry...," stammered Stella, and paused as if she was searching for the right words. "It's just what Tank said..."

"What did Tank say?" asked Tetyana.

"He saw the woman in a white dress. I've heard these stories before. When I was growing up here, my grandma said she haunted graves and bad places... I, er, feel like she's watching me through the window."

"Didn't I tell you to keep the shutters down?" said Tetyana.

"Y... yes...," said Stella. "But I can't help feeling like she can see right through them."

I stared at her.

Stella Green was a post-doctorate scientist who had published many articles on precious metals in prominent mining magazines. She had risen to the top of the hierarchy in one of the largest mines in this state. To hear her stutter about an apparition in a white dress was ludicrous.

"You don't really believe all that, do you?" I said, watching her carefully.

Stella shrugged unhappily and stepped away, like she didn't want to have this conversation any longer.

"I really should get back to bed," she whispered hoarsely.

After giving us another frightened look, she turned around and stumbled back toward her room. We watched as she groped her way through the darkened corridor.

"Poor woman," whispered Katy. "She may be a scientist but she's still human. She's probably spooked. Like we all are."

"Then she should have stayed in her cabin like I told her to," said Tetyana, turning to us. "That smoke worries me. That means someone lives near here and I'd bet you they put the body on the tracks. I'm gonna go check on Tank in the back."

I was about to tell her I'd join her when something furry pressed against my leg.

I looked down to see the kitten had ambled out and was exploring the corridor now.

Just as I bent down to pick her up, the cabin door across from us flew open with a loud bang.

I jerked my head up.

What now?

Chapter Fourteen

T heodore appeared in the shadows.

Tetyana cursed from under her breath.

Is everyone on the train up?

The old man was in his velvet dressing gown, shakily holding on to the open door with both hands.

Where's his wheelchair?

"What's all this noise?" he demanded.

"We're keeping watch," said Tetyana.

"Keep it down, would you?" snapped the old man. "I hired you to protect me, not make a ruckus and keep me up all night."

I stared at this small man, whose trembling hands and shaved head made him look so vulnerable. But even through the darkness, I could see the fire in his eyes.

"Mr. Henry," I said, speaking up before Tetyana made another retort. "We're doing our best to make sure everything remains secured. These are extraordinary circumstances."

He screwed his eyes as he swayed on his feet. That door was the only thing keeping him upright.

"Strange state of affairs, that's for sure," he said. "Who on earth would put a dead body on the tracks?"

"Why don't we let the authorities figure that out," I said. "They have the equipment and teams to investigate this sort of thing."

Theodore shook his head.

"That's what I'm afraid of. They'll make a big muck of it and next thing I know it'll all be in the papers. Like I need more attention right now." He shot us a fierce look and pointed at his shaved head. "I've enough to deal with, as it is."

I was about to answer when I spotted a gray ball of fur slip through his legs and enter his room.

The kitten.

Theodore didn't even notice it.

"There's probably an easy explanation for this," I said, taking a discreet step closer to him. "This could be just a sick prank."

"You call that a prank? It's madness, I tell you."

"A check on the graveyards near here should confirm the dead man's identity and maybe a clue to who did this."

I paused as my mind whirred, trying to figure out how to get that kitten out of the man's room, without arousing any more of his ire.

"The best we can do is to keep everyone safe and secure till the morning," I said, one eye on the cat and another on Theodore. "Dwayne should be feeling better by then and we should get rolling. You'll arrive at Anchorage and catch your flight to Seattle in no time."

I took another step closer, just as Theodore shuffled back to his room, muttering to himself. I peeked over his shoulder to see the kitten had jumped up to his bed and had curled up on the crumpled sheets.

Theodore's wheelchair was neatly folded against the bedframe. From where I was, I could see pill and syrup bottles of all sorts piled up on his bedside table.

I stepped up to the door quickly and held it open, bracing for the yell.

"What the heck is this?" Theodore's angry voice boomed through the carriage. "How did it get in here?"

I cringed, wondering how many people were up now.

"Here kitty," Katy called out from behind me. "Come back here."

"Who let this thing in here?" roared Theodore, picking up a hairbrush from the side cabinet. He raised it in the air, ready to smack the unsuspecting animal.

"Wait," I said, stepping inside.

"You can't come in here," said Theodore, turning around to give me a vexed look. "This is my private space."

I brushed past him and marched up to the bed and plucked the kitten from the pillow. I turned around to leave with the cat cradled in my arms when I spotted them.

I stopped in mid-stride, my mouth open.

Three large paintings leaned against the wall, across from the bed. They were oil paintings on canvas of the Aurora Borealis we just saw through the train's windows.

Even in the dark, they were vivid and stunning, as eye-popping as what I'd seen in real life.

"Wow," I said out loud, for a moment forgetting where I was. "These are gorgeous. So realistic."

I looked up to see my client's face had turned a shade darker. His jaw had tightened like he was gritting his teeth.

"Get the hell out of my room," he whispered hoarsely. "Get out. You lot are more trouble than I thought."

"Sorry," I said, stepping toward the door. I turned around at the threshold and gave him an apologetic smile. "I didn't mean to intrude."

Instead of acknowledging my apology, he leaned in and pinched my forearm. I pushed his hand off and stepped away. But he grabbed my arm.

His movements were so fast and his grip was so strong that for a split second, I wondered if he was playing at being sick.

"Hey!" Tetyana called from behind me. "Let her go."

Theodore leaned close, his fiery eyes boring into mine as he hissed in my ear.

I stared at him, wondering if I'd imagined his words.

"Excuse me?" I said. "*What* did you say?"

Theodore stepped back and slammed the door in my face. The bolt turned on the other side with a loud click, like it was giving me the finger.

I stood stunned for a moment.

I vacillated between surprise at how fast Theodore had moved without his wheelchair and disbelief at what he'd spat in my ear before pushing me out.

I turned to my friends who were watching me, confused expressions on their faces.

"What the hell is wrong with the old fart?" said Tetyana.

I gestured to my friends to follow me into our cabin.

"Did you see them?" I whispered, once inside.

"See what?" asked Katy.

"The paintings," I said. "They were beautiful. Surreal. Paintings of the Northern Lights."

"*Paintings?*" said Tetyana, her face falling, like she had hoped it had been another dead body or something.

"It's not the paintings, it's how Theodore reacted when he saw me see them," I said.

"What did he say before he pushed you out?" asked Katy.

"He told me if I told anyone what I saw, he'd hunt me down."

Tetyana's eyes narrowed.

"Are you sure it wasn't something else you saw?" asked Katy.

I shook my head.

"I was looking point-blank at them. I told him they were beautiful. He knew what I was talking about."

"It was dark in there. Maybe he thought you were looking at something else, next to the paintings maybe?"

"There was nothing else," I said.

"He owns the biggest private mining company in the state," said Katy. "Maybe he has a stash of diamonds in his room."

"There are no diamonds in Alaska, Katy. In the Canadian territories yes, but they haven't found any on this side of the border." I shook my head. "No. It was the paintings. He didn't like that I saw them. Weird."

Tetyana gave an impatient sniff.

"I don't have time to worry about an old man's art collection," she said, stomping to the door. "But he can't go around threatening us like that."

She stepped out of the cabin.

"You guys stay near Theodore Henry's room. Do everything to make him stay inside. And if he grabs you again, shove your Glock in his face."

"Watch your back," I said, a sense of foreboding coming over me.

Tetyana shot me a grim look and nodded.

"I'll be fine. But if there's one man I want to monitor right now, it's Tank."

Chapter Fifteen

Katy and I were making a quick breakfast the next morning when Dwayne limped into the kitchenette.

I knew the second I saw him that something was wrong.

We'd all had a slow and painful night.

The trail of gray smoke behind the woods had subsided soon after we saw it, but the Northern Lights had danced outside our window for hours.

I couldn't help but feel they were mocking us, partying it up in the night sky while we remained stuck and scared in the shadows of the valley below.

Katy and I hadn't got much sleep, though we had taken turns to keep watch with quick naps in between.

Tetyana had stayed up all night patrolling, standing in for Tank and Robin to give them some respite. She was up in the early hours, bright and bushy tailed, saying she'd been through worse.

Theodore, Connor, Stella, and Doctor Wilson had stayed inside their cabins. It was still early, and we hadn't heard a peep from any of them.

Dwayne had been up for an hour, tinkering in the engine room with Robin.

When he walked in, I was slicing bread and Katy was arranging a sandwich tray on the counter. Under the kitchen table was an empty milk saucer and a kitten with a full belly, purring next to it.

"Feeling better?" said Katy, looking up as Dwayne stepped inside.

"Surviving."

"Coffee pot's still hot."

He gave a somber nod, but stood by the door, his mouth turned down and his hands thrust in his pockets.

"There's a vial of painkillers in the first-aid kit," said Katy, always concerned for others' well-being.

He cleared his throat and shuffled his feet.

"What's going on, Dwayne?" I said.

"I don't know how to say this...." He trailed off unhappily.

I put my knife down and gave him my full attention. Next to me, Katy stopped bustling around.

"What is it, Dwayne?" I asked, feeling my stomach tighten.

"I don't want to be the one to break this news to Mr. Henry, but..."

"But what?"

"The boiler's gone."

"The boiler?" asked Katy, scrunching her forehead.

"The water tank that makes the steam for the train to run. Robin heard funny noises early this morning. Seems like a valve has broken off. Can't move till we fix it."

"How long will it take?" I said.

Dwayne scratched his head. "Couple of hours if we're lucky. It's a little risky...."

"Risky?" I said, my stomach tightening even more.

The last thing we needed after discovering a mutilated dead body on the tracks was to have a technical issue with the train's engine.

"Boilers are tricky," said Dwayne, looking depressed. "This is an old machine. It's refurbished, but it's the same equipment they used ages ago. They never fully replaced it."

"Between Robin and you, you can get it to work, right?" I asked.

"Sure, but this ain't no mini-mall train. It's going to take time. You tighten the wrong lever, and it could blow."

He shook his head and rubbed his eyes, looking like a man at the end of his tether.

"The thing is, it's going to get worse real soon."

I narrowed my eyes. "How much worse?"

"When I checked the forecast last time we had a cell signal, it said a hailstorm is on its way." He looked at me, his red eyes lined with worry. "A freak spring storm. Was planning to be near the next town when it hit these parts, but now…"

He shook his head miserably.

"Just don't want to be there when Mr. Henry hears about any of this."

"I'll take care of Theodore," I said, straightening up.

"Thanks, but he's going to burst a blood vessel…."

"Why don't you go and do your thing, and I'll bring breakfast to you and Robin," said Katy, giving him a sympathetic smile. "Take your time to do what you have to do, okay?"

I nodded. "Focus on the boiler, and I'll deal with your boss."

Theodore was going to explode no matter who gave him the news, but I would rather it be me than a valuable crew member without whom we'd never get out of this valley.

With a relieved sigh, Dwayne shot me a grateful nod and stumbled out of the kitchenette, almost bumping into Tank.

"Coffee?" Tank mumbled as he entered the kitchenette, rubbing his face.

"On the counter," said Katy. "Pour yourself a big cuppa."

Tank lumbered over to the coffee pot.

"So, when are we gonna start moving?" he asked, as he picked a mug from the cabinet.

I turned to him.

"There's been a delay. Engine trouble."

The mug Tank had just picked up fell to the ground and rolled under the table. The frightened kitten jumped in the air and scrambled behind Katy's legs, her fur standing up, like she'd been electrocuted.

"What?" said Tank, his eyes bulging.

"Boiler's out of order," I said.

"Are you kidding?"

I squared my shoulders and gave him a steely look.

"Patience. We just have to hang tight a few more hours."

He looked about him, apprehension etched on his face.

"You mean, we're stuck here all morning—"

"Tank," I said, speaking sharply. "We're all going to have to pull our weight. What you need to do now is to help Tetyana and guard your boss's room until we're done with breakfast."

A semblance of a scowl crossed Tank's face, but he caught himself just in time. He grabbed the mug from under the table, poured himself the coffee, and walked out without another word.

"Fishy," I whispered.

"What do you mean?" asked Katy.

"I asked him yesterday how long he'd been on the job."

"What did he say?"

"Awhile," I said.

"What does that mean? Weeks? Months?"

"He was hedging. Didn't even make eye contact."

"Maybe he doesn't like us nosing around, given we're technically interfering with his job?"

"He was pretty good at following Tetyana's orders last night."

"That's because Theodore told him to."

"Yes, but a normal bodyguard would be throwing his weight around, protesting to let him do his job," I said.

"That ghost scared the crap out of him. He must feel like an idiot after that. Maybe he's too embarrassed to complain."

I shook my head.

"I can't put a finger on it, but Tetyana's right. There's something funny about him."

"What do you mean?" asked Katy.

"I'm beginning to think he's an imposter."

Chapter Sixteen

I knocked on Theodore Henry's door.

No answer.

I knocked again. Louder.

Either he was fast asleep, or he was refusing to open the door.

Tank was standing in the corridor, in front of his boss's cabin, hands folded neatly in front of him, still in his wrinkled black suit. On the surface he looked like an obedient bodyguard on duty, but his face told me he resented being put to work.

"He didn't leave his room, right?" I asked him.

Tank shrugged and gave a slight nod, as if to say *sure, but leave me alone*. He was of no help.

I turned back to the door and tried the handle. To my surprise, it slid down, and the door opened ajar. I gently pushed it an inch and peeked in, half expecting a furious roar telling me to go to hell.

All I could hear from inside the stuffy cabin were the gentle snores of a man slumbering deeply.

Strange. I was sure I'd heard him turn the bolt after he slammed the door on me the night before.

Katy and I had patrolled the dining carriage and the sleeping car all night. We hadn't seen Theodore, or anyone else, get out of their rooms, walk about, or enter other cabins. That meant either Theodore hadn't locked the door properly, or had unlocked it later on for some reason.

Like everyone else, he had his own toilet and sink, so that couldn't have been it. The shower rooms were at the end of the car, near the kitchenette, but I was sure he hadn't got up in the middle of the night to take a shower.

I opened the door another inch, thankful to whoever had oiled the hinges during the refurbishment process. With a quick glance around to make sure the kitten wasn't making another attempt to invade Theodore's room, I pushed the door fully open.

Through the dim nightlight next to the bed, I could make out the man's reposing figure. He was lying on his side, his face to the antique oak-paneled wall, sound asleep.

I pushed the door gently against the wall until I heard the low magnetic click that told me it would stay open in place.

I tiptoed in.

Tank hadn't protested my creeping into his boss's room. I wondered if that was because he knew Theodore's wrath would fall squarely on me. I half imagined him smirking behind my back.

I wasn't looking forward to being the bearer of the bad news on the train's extended delay. But my client was in no conscious state for a chat.

I gingerly took another step farther in.

Suddenly, Theodore snorted and smacked his lips.

I froze.

He muttered something in his sleep. His chest heaved up and down for a few seconds, then, just as quickly, he fell back into sleep, snoring in gentle cycles again.

I crept up to his bed and bent down in front of the plethora of pill bottles at the bedside table. One bottle was opened, its screw cap and a half-empty glass of water next to it.

Taking care not to touch it, I scanned the label.

Ambien XR Extended Release.

If there was anyone who knew everything a layperson could know about sleeping tablets, it had to be me.

Sleeping pills were what had saved my life and kept the tormenting nightmares of my childhood at bay. Without them, I would never get any rest, instead succumbing to the demons that crept into my mind at night.

I knew this brand.

My own addiction was to the generic version of it. Same strength, different name. And much cheaper.

I looked at the man who was dead to the world now, wondering what nightmares he needed to smother to get his nightly rest.

My research had told me he had a privileged upbringing, born into a wealthy family with old money. After college, he had helped out with his family business until he'd gone out on his own and had literally struck gold.

I scanned the other medications. Their labels didn't tell me much, but I gathered they were related to the cancer treatments as prescribed by Doctor Wilson.

I straightened up and turned around, bumping into the folded wheelchair by his bed. The three paintings that had arrested me the evening before stared at me, stopping me once again.

They leaned against the blanket, their vivid colors dancing in front of my eyes like the Aurora Borealis had come alive on canvas in this darkened room.

I stepped up to examine them closely. Even not being a professional connoisseur of fine art, I could see the talent in these magnificent pieces. I couldn't take my eyes off of them.

But something nagged at the back of my mind. Something about these paintings bothered me.

Why do I feel like they're trying to send me a message?

A million and one questions swirled through my head. Why did Theodore threaten me if I talked about these pieces? Were they stolen?

Were they forgeries? Was Theodore involved in something more than just gold mining?

The frames were made of a cheap, light-colored material. They looked flimsy, almost plasticky. That was odd, especially for a man who had the means and the resources to take care of such striking art.

I had enough of an eye to know these pieces would have looked so much nicer mounted in sturdier and more ornate wood, worthy of what they would hold.

With a quick glance back to make sure the gold baron was still fast asleep, I stepped closer to scrutinize the signature on the bottom right-hand corner of each painting.

In place of a written signature was an inverted cross drawn in black ink. It was more an emblem than an artist's autograph.

With a chill, I realized what had been bothering me.

I took a sharp breath in as I remembered the scar of the upside-down cross on the dead man's neck. My heart ticked faster as I squinted in the dark, wondering if I was making connections where none existed.

Behind me, Theodore stirred and mumbled.

I straightened up and stepped toward the door walking backward, watching the man in case he woke up. I couldn't for the life of me think how I'd respond if he turned around and asked what I was doing in his room, but at least I'd be prepared.

Loud footsteps were coming along the corridor. I slipped out of the room and shut the door quietly behind me.

It was Tetyana.

"We don't have much time," she said urgently, marching up to me.

"What now?" I said.

"We have a narrow window to see where that smoke came from."

"How long is the boiler repair going to take?" I said.

She made a face. "They tell me they're still trying to diagnose the problem, but I was thinking more about the rest of the gang."

She pointed her chin at Theodore's closed door.

"Up yet?"

"Fast asleep," I said. "Sleeping tablets."

She raised an eyebrow.

"Everyone else is in their cabins," I said. "Still sleeping, I presume. Though in an hour or so, they'll be coming out one by one, demanding breakfast and asking when we're going to start moving."

Tetyana nodded.

"Hence the small window of time. I don't want to be out while this lot starts rumbling around."

She paused and turned to Tank who'd been standing in position, watching us with a curious expression on his face.

"I'm going to check out the woods. I need backup. You're with me."

That was a command, not a question. But for once, Tank resisted.

"No way," he said, taking a startled step back. "Mr. Henry hired me to stay close to him. It's you people he hired to take care of the extra stuff. I'm staying right here."

"Scared of seeing more ghosts?" Tetyana said, irritation in her voice.

"Let me do my job. I'm not moving."

From the corner of my eye, I caught Tetyana rolling her eyes.

"How long do you need?" I said.

"Twenty minutes tops," she said. "This is a recon exercise to get a lay of the land. I'll be going in and out fast."

"I don't like you being outside alone," I said, making a quick decision. "Katy's in the back and she has her Glock. It's still quiet, so she can hold fort for another twenty minutes. I'll come with you."

"Roger that," replied Tetyana.

"Let's see if we can find the kitten's rightful owner," I said. "I've a funny feeling they live behind those trees."

Chapter Seventeen

"**D**rag marks," said Tetyana, pointing at the snow near the tracks.

I peered at the ground, following her gloved finger.

I was glad I had my shades on. It had taken a second for my eyes to adjust to the morning sun reflecting against the bright white snow.

The drag marks were so faint, we'd missed them in the dusky light the day before. Whipping my phone out, I took a picture.

"What do you think happened here?" I said.

"Tank ran off that way," she said, pointing at the tree line. "While I was trying to rein him in, someone came here and dragged the body back into the woods. Looks like they went through the opening over there."

Her eyes were on two tall Douglas firs that stood at the threshold, looking like stern sentinels whose task was to guard this winter forest.

Something stirred in my jacket.

It was the kitten, its rose-colored snout peeking out, sniffing the cold air. I nudged her gently back in. It was still early, and the temperatures were well below zero. She was better off snuggled in my pocket, sheltered from the wind.

My plan had been to let her out once we got close to the tracks where we had found her. She wasn't a dog, but I'd hoped she'd show us the way to her home. But with these tracks on the ground, I couldn't risk having more prints muddying up the evidence even further.

Leaving the drag marks undisturbed, Tetyana and I carefully stepped up to the two Douglas firs.

"Check this out," said Tetyana in a low voice, pointing at the snowbank by the trees that had been disturbed. "They came this way."

I snapped another photo. That was when I saw it.

A boot print.

"Did you see this?" I said, breathlessly.

We kneeled next to it.

"Size twelve or thirteen," said Tetyana.

"A man, then."

"Or a large woman. I wear eleven."

We stood up.

Giving wide berth to the boot print, we stepped in between the fir trees and entered the woods. We stopped for a moment to take in the dramatic change of scene, our breath condensing into misty clouds in front of us.

The coniferous trees, their branches heavily laden with snow, grew close together as far as we could see, gently sloping upward.

We were at the base of a mountain.

In my mind's eye, I could see this arboreal forest covering most of the slope till it eventually gave way to thinner, shorter trees. These would, in turn, transform into the bare shrubs of the tundra until a point where only moss would grow on the mountain sides. Finally, all we'd find would be hard ice, jagged rocks, and deep snowbanks on top.

I shivered.

Compared to the brightness of the valley through which the train tracks ran, it was dark inside the woods. There was an eerie solitude around us, but I couldn't help but feel we weren't alone.

I was glad we'd suited up before we stepped off the train.

We were in our winter ops gear, as Tetyana liked to call it. We had on our thick tights, winter socks, and mountain boots. Fitted snugly on top of our layered long-sleeved shirts were our Kevlar vests, which acted as a holster for our Glocks.

We each carried an extra cartridge of bullets, a Tanto knife, and a flashlight tucked into our vest pockets. In addition to this, Tetyana always kept a pair of steel handcuffs in hers. I didn't recall a time when she pulled them out, and always wondered if she'd ever needed to use them.

Without speaking, we stepped among the massive trees, feeling like we were walking in the land of the giants. My eyes swept around, my ears alert.

We had taken fifty steps into the woods when I noticed the black piece of cloth flapping in the wind from behind a pine tree. It was like someone was standing on the other side, their jacket fluttering in the wind.

Other than the boot prints and the drag marks near the tracks, this was the best indication there was someone other than us in the woods. But whoever they were, they weren't doing a great job hiding from us.

Tetyana held out her arm, signaling me to stop.

We waited, quietly, our weapons aimed forward, barely breathing.

A long green vine curved across the tree trunk. A quick glance at the other trees told me none of them had this vine growing around them.

"Wait here," whispered Tetyana.

Aiming her Glock forward, she stepped stealthily toward the tree. I watched her, my heart in my mouth, my gun covering her back.

She stopped when she got within four feet of the tree and whipped around, shouting, "Freeze!"

To my surprise, Tetyana lowered her weapon and took a quick step back, with a look of disgust. She looked away, her face scrunching like she was about to vomit.

What is it?

My friend had a stomach of steel and I'd never seen her like this. But with her weapon down, I knew whatever she'd discovered wasn't hostile.

I made a fast beeline toward her. Tetyana waved me away.

"You don't want to see—"

But I'd already seen it.

The dead body had been propped against the tree, tied by a green rope which I'd mistaken for vine.

Though he was standing slouched, the man's disfigured face was even more graphic in the cold, stark morning light. His contorted eyes stared into the ground, like he was waiting to be swallowed up and return to where he belonged.

Underground.

"Someone's playing with us," I said, feeling sick to my stomach.

Tetyana turned around slowly, her weapon at the ready, scanning the surrounding woods.

"Stay here," she whispered, as she stepped away to stake out the area.

Something fluttered by the corpse. I turned back to it. That was when I noticed something white sticking out of the man's jacket pocket.

A piece of paper.

I didn't recall seeing it the night before. Then again, it had been dark.

While Tetyana stepped among the trees looking for more clues, I put a hand over my nose and reached over to ease the paper from the man's pocket, glad I had my gloves on.

I pulled out a piece of oblong paper, the size of a business card, folded in half. I flipped it open, wishing my hand wouldn't shake so much, and read the note.

Remember me?

A chill went down my back.

From what Dwayne had told us, Jim Johnson had been a modern-day Gestapo who'd ruled the underground shafts at Black Eagle Mines with an iron fist.

Was someone trying to get revenge for what he had done to the employees in the mine?

But he had retired a decade ago.

"Over here," came my friend's voice.

I looked up to see Tetyana gesturing me to join her.

She was standing beside a lone tree, staring up the mountain slope. I folded the note and slipped it into my pocket. In my other pocket, the kitten meowed loudly.

Hushing it, I stepped over to where Tetyana was.

I peered through the trees. Something glinted. The sunlight was reflecting off a smooth and shiny surface, and it wasn't snow.

"A settlement," I whispered.

"We found it," whispered Tetyana.

The kitty meowed again.

"Shh…" I said, patting her as she poked her head out of my pocket.

"How much do you want to bet that little one comes from here?" said Tetyana, looking down at the kitten, which was now struggling to get out.

I was just about to answer when Tetyana pulled me by the arm and flung me on the ground.

The arrow buzzed right by my ear and slammed into the tree trunk next to me.

It had missed me by five inches.

I stared at the weapon lodged firmly in the tree, my heart pounding madly against my chest.

"Come out or I shoot!" shouted Tetyana, springing to her feet.

I jumped up. We swiveled around, our backs to each other, our guns aimed forward.

But the forest had turned silent again.

"It's that dang cat," hissed Tetyana. "It gave us away."

I scanned the forest.

"They're camouflaged," I whispered. "We—"

I didn't get to finish.

A thunderous blast shook the ground underneath us, like a bomb had gone off.

That came from the railway tracks.

Chapter Eighteen

Tetyana and I hurtled through the woods.

The acrid smell of metal burning stung my nose as we reached the end of the tree line. Only one thought whirled through my mind like a hurricane-force wind.

Katy!

Why did we leave her behind?

We crashed out of the woods and halted, dumbfounded at the scene.

"Oh no," I cried.

An immense gray plume of smoke had engulfed the engine in front. Red and orange flames were shooting in the air, like the train was putting on its own ghoulish light show.

Tetyana got to Dwayne before I did.

He was lying on his stomach several yards from the locomotive, struggling to get up. His face was blackened with soot and his body shook.

But he was alive.

Leaving Tetyana with him, I whirled around.

"Katy!" I screamed.

I dashed toward the train carriages in the back which were still intact. The dining car door was open, and Robin was ushering everyone out of the back door.

Where's Katy?

I pushed past Stella, Tank, and Doctor Wilson, who were shakily making their way out, and leaped up the steps. My friend was at the back of the line, her hair as red as the blaze up in front.

I pulled her by the shoulders.

"You okay?"

Katy gave me a numbed look and a brief nod.

Holding her hand tightly, I pulled her out, just as another explosion shook the engine.

"Down!" I yelled, slamming to the ground, pulling Katy with me. Robin dove next to us.

Tetyana!

I whirled around to see her pulling Dwayne away from the engine. The others, who'd already had a head start, were scrambling toward the woods, not looking back.

"We need to get out of here!" I shouted to Katy and Robin.

The three of us army-crawled along the snow toward the group that had now congregated at the foot of a massive Douglas fir. They were sitting against a snowbank, watching the engine burn, terror in their faces.

Katy turned to me, her eyes wide. "Someone bombed the train."

Bombed?

Her voice was emotionless, like she hadn't yet come to terms with what had happened.

A few yards from us, Tetyana was half carrying, half dragging Dwayne. I dashed over to help her bring him toward the group and sat him next to Robin.

Robin pulled her father in close. They swayed back and forth, their heads touching, mute in shock.

The engineer was in bad shape. His forehead was still bandaged from the incident the night before when Connor threw the bottle at him.

That was when I realized two people were missing.

Another loud bang came from the engine, making us all dive for cover.

"Hey!" I shouted over the noise. "Where's Connor and Theodore?"

"Didn't see them," said Robin in a shaking voice. "I—"

I didn't wait for her to finish. I sprang up to run toward the train when someone grabbed me.

"Get back," said Tetyana, gripping my shoulder tightly. "Do you want to get hit by the debris?"

Dwayne turned a pale face to me.

"Connor... he..."

He was trying to speak, but his lips had swollen up like marshmallows on a campfire stick.

"What is it, Dwayne?" I asked.

He pointed a shaking finger at the engine car, then collapsed against the tree, clutching his heart.

"Dad!" cried Robin. "Dad, are you okay?"

Her father looked up and gave her a weak nod.

My stomach sank. Even if anyone survived those explosions, the fire would get them.

"We can't leave them inside," I said, turning to Tetyana.

Her face was bleak but stern.

"We wait till the blasts stop, so we live another day to save everyone."

She was right. I fought my instincts to run into the sleeper cabin where I was sure Theodore was, dazed with that heavy dose of sleeping tablets.

"The other cars... shouldn't burn," said Dwayne, drawling like it was too painful for him to speak.

"How can you be so sure?" I said.

"They put up a firewall when they refurbished it," said Robin. "Firewall?"

"Mr. Henry asked for it," she said. "A thick door to stop flames from the engine room spreading to the other cars."

I stared at the father and daughter duo, who stared back at me. "What happened here?"

"It was the boiler," said Robin. "It exploded. Dad knew it was going to give us trouble. It was an old system that had been refurbished more than once. A disaster waiting to happen."

"The fire should be contained, or help me god," muttered Dwayne, shaking his head.

I looked at the mangled engine. The flames were subsiding.

The billowy cloud engulfing the front had overpowered my senses. The blaze was actually smaller than what I'd first thought.

The smoke was now blowing away from the train. If Robin and Dwayne were right, the rest of the carriages should remain unscathed. But I couldn't ignore the calamity of our situation.

Our only transportation out of this valley of death had been destroyed.

Someone tapped on my shoulder.

I jumped and spun around, like a wound-up spring.

It was Stella, her face scrunched up like she was about to cry. She shook her head mutely, as if she was unable to speak, still reeling from what had happened.

"What is it?" I asked.

"He's gone," she said.

"Who?"

"Theodore."

"*What?*"

"Theodore disappeared before the explosion," said Katy, turning to me, her face ashen. "We were looking for him when everything blew up."

"What do you mean he's disappeared?" I asked, looking from Katy to Stella, and back to my friend again.

"I went to wake him up for breakfast," said Katy, "but he wasn't in his room. He wasn't anywhere on the train. We looked everywhere."

"How is that possible? That man can hardly walk."

I turned around, looking for Tank. He was squatting against a nearby tree, slightly away from the crowd, his head hung in between his knees, his arms lying limp on his legs.

"Tank?" I called out. "What happened to Theodore?"

He didn't look up.

"Tank!"

Nothing.

I wanted to walk over and shake him. He was supposed to guard his boss, ensure his safety.

What happened?

"Looks like the explosions have stopped," said Tetyana. She stepped away from the tree and turned to Robin. "Where's the hose?"

Robin got up and brushed the snow from her pants.

"On the other side, if it's not burned. The spare water tank is in the back car."

Tetyana and Robin walked over to the train, stepping carefully around the debris.

I looked at the raggedy group behind me, cowering by the trees.

"Katy, you stay with the others," I said. "Tank, you're with me. We need to find Theodore and Connor."

Katy nodded, but Tank sat like a hunched stone statue on the snow.

I didn't wait for him. I scrambled over to the dining car and jumped up the steps.

Someone yelled my name. It could have been Tetyana warning me not to enter, but I couldn't ignore my responsibility.

I had a contract to protect Theodore Henry, a man confined to a wheelchair and battling cancer. I didn't like the man much at all, but I wasn't going to abandon anyone in trouble.

Katy and Stella's earlier remarks echoed vaguely in my mind as I looked around the dining car. What did they mean *he was gone?*

That made no sense.

I whirled around.

The dining car was empty but in pristine condition. There wasn't even an overturned chair.

The only sign of a fire was the heavy metallic smoke that hung in the air. I grabbed a napkin and held it to my face, trying not to breathe in the smoke.

I weaved through the tables, heading to the kitchenette. I knew that little kitchen well, and there was no way for anyone to hide in there.

After a quick scan, I ran toward the sleeping car behind it.

I stepped up to Theodore's room, smashed the handle down and slammed the door open.

Chapter Nineteen

Theodore's wheelchair was propped against the bed, folded neatly. It was exactly where I saw it only an hour ago.

His medicine bottles sat crowded on the bedside table. The three paintings leaned against the wall, their backs protected by the blanket.

Everything looked the same as before.

Except one thing.

Theodore was missing. His sheets lay in a crumpled heap on his bed, but it was empty.

I sniffed the air.

Amid the smoky smell, I detected something else. The tang of sweet nail polish remover mixed with harsh disinfectant permeated the cabin, a smell I didn't recall when I had slipped in here earlier that morning.

My eyes swept the room. Theodore Henry was the most unlikely man to be a cross-dresser. I doubted that was nail polish remover. That smell had to be something else.

I leaned over the bedside table, but it was hard to say if any of the vials or jars had been disturbed. Theodore could have opened a bottle after he'd woken up, one that contained a pungent syrup or liquid medicine.

Where is he?

The sleeping cabins were luxurious but cramped. We were on a train after all. There was just enough space for a luggage rack, a bed, and a side cabinet. There was no place for an adult human to hide. Or even a child.

The mini toilet.

I yanked the bathroom door open.

But there was no one inside.

The commode lid was down, and the taps looked spotless. There was no indication the washroom had been used recently.

I stepped back into the room and turned around the space, trying to think.

How could he have taken off without his wheelchair? Did he walk out?

I remembered how fast he'd moved for a sick man the night before.

Or did someone take him?

I shuddered at the thought of the unseen gravedigger creeping in and pulling him away from his room.

Where had Tank been when he disappeared?

A quiet mew came from the bottom of my vest. I'd forgotten I was still carrying the kitten. A frightened eye peeked out from my pocket.

Should have left her with Katy.

It was too late now. Poor thing. It would have to finish the search with me.

I pulled open the shutters and checked the latches, but they were in locked position. Light drifts of snow had gathered along the windowpane on the outside, which told me no one had opened the windows for at least a day.

My mind whirred.

There was a reason Theodore had hired us. He'd been worried about someone trying to get him, but he had been nonchalant and vague about the threats, saying he already had a trusted personal bodyguard.

Just come as caterers and make my meals so no one can poison me, he'd said.

And now, he had vanished.

Was that what the fire was all about? A distraction while they—whoever they were—nabbed the richest gold baron in the state? Was this going to become a kidnapping investigation?

Or, was it murder?

I swiveled around in frustration, trying not to let the guilty panic bubbling inside of me take over my senses. I needed a clear head to think straight.

I continued the search, starting with the cabins, one by one. It didn't take long as they were all extremely confined spaces.

Outside, I could hear Tetyana holler for more water. I couldn't hang around in here for long. She needed help.

Even if Dwayne and Robin were right, and the firewall would protect these carriages, we needed to eliminate every bit of cinder that could ignite at any moment. We couldn't risk the entire train combusting.

I ran all the way to the last car where our luggage was stored. Everything looked exactly the way it had been, when we had placed this car on lockdown the night before.

The showers were next, but with one glance I knew neither Theodore nor Connor were here. With an exasperated sigh, I jumped out of the train through the dining car's door.

In the fifteen odd minutes I'd been rummaging inside, the flames had died down.

I ran over to where Dwayne was sitting, huddled by the fir tree with Doctor Wilson and Stella as they watched the rest of the group fight the fire. I handed the kitten to Dwayne, giving a side glance at Stella.

Why wasn't she helping out?

The doctor looked like he had barely slept off his alcoholic binge, and Dwayne was still recovering from getting blown off by the explosion. Stella looked healthier, fitter, and was much younger than the two men.

But she sat on the ground, immobile, her face drawn, and her lips set in a thin line. She was staring at the engine with such a faraway expression in her eyes, I wondered if she was actually present.

Leaving them be, I dashed back to the train.

Tetyana had the hose aimed at the engine, while behind her, Robin was unfurling the hose.

A few yards away, Katy was shoveling snow with her bare hands and throwing it onto the tracks.

While it melted almost immediately, every bit would help to keep the heat low and the oxygen away from the burning cinder underneath.

Tank was across from my friend, doing the same, but working at a much slower pace. While Katy's hands were a blur, he was picking a handful of snow and throwing it idly on the tracks, like a reluctant kid who'd been asked to put out a campfire after a weekend retreat.

At least he was cooperating. Sort-of.

I hurried over to Katy.

"Here, grab some," she said, not looking up. The two of us worked fast and furiously as a team, going from one end of the train to the other and back again.

It took me a few minutes to realize that Tank had stopped working and had retired under the Douglas fir, next to Dwayne and the others, as soon as I'd joined in to help.

"What happened to Theodore?" I asked Katy, as I threw a fistful of snow on the tracks. "His wheelchair's still in his room."

Katy stopped to wipe the sweat off her brow.

"One minute Stella and I were in the kitchen making sandwiches and the next minute, Tank runs in, in a huge panic, to say he lost Theodore."

"*Lost* him?"

"He supposedly took a ten-minute washroom break. When he returned, Theodore's door was open, and he wasn't inside." She shot an angry look Tank's way. "If he told me he had to go to the toilet, I'd have taken his place. The idiot."

"So, Theodore disappeared in all of ten minutes?"

"That's what he said. I didn't hear a thing." She let out a sigh. "Sorry, I know you wanted me to keep an eye on things while you were out."

"Hey, it's not your fault—"

"Asha!"

I spun around.

Tetyana was gesturing me to come over.

Katy and I jogged over to where she and Robin were standing by the mangled frame of the locomotive. Tetyana was still holding the hose, but the water was trickling out. I wondered if we'd run out of water or if Robin had turned off the tap.

"We found one of them," said Tetyana, her face grim.

I stepped closer and peered through the gap on the side of the train the explosion had created.

"Oh, no," gasped Katy.

The body was unmistakable.

It was Connor, his hair frazzled like a mad Einstein, just like it looked when he was alive, except he was now dead.

He lay facedown, behind the engineer's chair, hands curled in pain and his body scrunched up. His entire left side had been scorched.

His cloverleaf dressing gown had burned through and stuck to his skin, exposing dark welts inside. Red-hot bubbles simmered across Connor's raw open muscles.

Chapter Twenty

"What was Connor doing in the engine room?" I asked.

"He was looking for us," said Robin.

"And where were you?" I said.

"Dad and I were checking the gears outside. That was when we heard him."

"Connor?"

Robin nodded. She let out a sigh and rubbed her face.

"He was screaming at us."

"What about?"

"He wanted us to start the train. He was yelling, asking why we weren't rolling. Dad told me to check something in the back, but I think that was because he didn't want me to confront Connor."

She looked up at us, her face flushed.

"I'm not going to lie. I didn't like that man and he didn't like us. We did everything to avoid him."

"When did the boiler explode?" I asked, softening my voice.

"About two minutes after I went to the back," said Robin, shaking her head as if in disbelief. "Dad was near the front. I was in the back, but the engine room window was open. I heard Connor threatening to fire us if we didn't start the train and...."

"And?" said Tetyana.

Robin spread her hands wide.

"The whole thing blew up."

We stood quietly in a circle, digesting this information. I could feel Katy behind me, her hand on my shoulder, holding on for support.

"Theodore's disappeared from his cabin," I said, trying not to let the thread of guilt weaving through my spine take hold of me. "I checked everywhere. It's like he's vanished into thin air."

"How does a man who can't walk disappear just like that?" said Tetyana, frowning. "It's not like we were in the woods for more than fifteen minutes."

I turned to Katy.

"Did you see Connor when you were searching for Theodore?"

"He was in the engine room when we went to check for Theodore," said Katy. "He was stomping up and down, screaming like Robin said. He was throwing things too. We skedaddled out right away."

"And Tank? What was he doing at that time?"

"He was behind me, babbling about a curse from that woman in a white dress. Stella was with us too, but she just looked numb."

"Where was the doctor?" asked Tetyana.

"In his cabin, sleeping," said Katy. "I had to bang on his door for him to come and open it up."

"Did he look like he had been out?"

Katy shook her head.

"He came to the door in night shorts. No shirt. He looked so hungover, I don't think he even understood what I was asking. I did go in and check the bathroom and the window but there was nothing. He was alone, and to be frank, hardly able to speak."

"Was the front door of the dining car open at that time?" asked Tetyana.

"It was," said Katy. "I thought Robin and Dwayne had opened it to check something outside. I didn't think too much of it, with Connor rampaging around like a madman."

"It's how Connor was," said Robin, in a low voice. "He was worse when he was drunk."

I suppressed the urge to look at the man. He was no longer alive. There would be no more screaming, bullying, or threatening others.

I turned to my friends.

"You know what I think?" I said. "This was no accident. This fire was deliberate."

Tetyana nodded.

"My conclusions, exactly."

Katy's eyes widened, but she didn't say anything.

Robin merely stared at us, her face expressionless, like she was drained of her energy.

Robin, Katy, and the others still didn't know of our discoveries inside the woods.

The dead body tied to the tree.

The glint of a human-made structure among the trees.

The arrow that had missed me by five inches.

A shiver went through me as I wondered if whoever was causing this havoc was watching us from the woods.

Tetyana and I had been out in the open, vulnerable to an attack, especially as this was foreign territory to both of us. We had most probably been in their line of sight. Unless it had been a child or an inexperienced marksperson, that arrow shouldn't have missed me.

It had to be a warning.

A warning for what? To stay away? Why blow up our only means of transportation out of here, then?

I had to share these discoveries with the others, once the initial shock of the train fire and finding Connor's body sank in. There was only so much any of them could take in at one time.

"We have to find Theodore," I said. "He's central to this. Everything that's happening is related to his disappearance."

Katy furrowed her brow.

"Do you think this is a ransom kidnapping? If so, who did it?"

"Whoever it was," I said, "they knew Tetyana and I were out scouting. You were in the kitchen with Stella. The doctor was sleeping, and you, Robin, were fixing the engine with your dad. That means they had a fifteen to twenty-minute window to nab Theodore."

Tetyana raised an eyebrow and locked eyes with me.

I knew what she was thinking. Either the kidnapper got lucky when Tank went to the bathroom, or he was in on this.

The bodyguard was the most suspicious among us right now, but I didn't know if anyone else was involved. There were too many pieces to this puzzle and my gut told me not to trust anyone.

Not yet.

I turned to Robin.

"Good thing you and your dad were working outside. Otherwise, you'd have been in the engine room when it blew up."

Robin's face turned white. She swallowed hard and shook her head like she wanted to speak but couldn't.

Katy put an arm on her shoulder and gave me a hard look.

"Now's not the time to think of what would have happened," she said. "Now is the time to figure out what we're going to do next."

"One thing's for sure," said Tetyana, glancing at the blackened skeleton of the engine. "We ain't going anywhere now."

Footsteps crunching on the snow made us all turn.

It was Tank.

Chapter Twenty-one

Tank lumbered toward us in his wrinkled and ill-fitting suit, trailing his jacket along the snow with one hand.

He looked beat.

With an exaggerated sigh, he stopped a few feet from us and leaned against the charred front of the train.

"Don't!" shouted Robin.

But it was too late.

He jumped with a whelp and clutched his arm.

"Hot enough for you?" said Tetyana, shaking her head.

His face turned red. "Man," he winced. "Just when you thought things are getting better...."

"Speaking of," said Tetyana, pointing a thumb behind her. "You haven't seen Mr. McNamara yet."

Tank took a few steps forward and squinted through the gaping hole in the side of the train. His eyes widened and his face turned instantly white.

He dropped his jacket on the ground.

"Is... is that...?" he stammered, giving us a wild look.

"Connor McNamara is dead," said Tetyana matter-of-factly. "Burned to a crisp."

"And your boss is still missing," I said. "Any idea where he is?"

Tank turned to me, face ashen, speechless.

What a peculiar bodyguard, I thought. He acted like he had no training in crisis management or security, for that matter. And now, I wondered if he'd ever seen a dead body before this trip.

"Hey, Tank," I said. "Can you tell us what happened when Theodore disappeared?"

Without answering, he staggered back, gagging.

He put his hands on his thighs and doubled over. We watched as he vomited on the snow, his back convulsing so hard, I worried he might fall into his own puke.

That wasn't a show. Unless he was an excellent actor.

Suddenly, I realized I'd misjudged him.

Tank was a lot younger than I'd first thought.

When I'd met him the night before, his imposing hulk and height reminded me of the bouncers employed by seedy nightclubs to break up bar brawls and keep gangsters at bay.

But in the clear morning light, I could see this baby-faced man was barely out of his teens. A child in a man's body.

He may have been built like an NFL footballer, but he was just a kid.

Perhaps he was an innocent victim.

Like us.

"We found something in the woods," I said.

Stella looked up sharply. If I'd thought she couldn't look more frightened, she could.

"Something?" said Doctor Wilson, frowning.

"What is it?" said Dwayne, wincing as he tried to sit up using his bandaged hand. The kitten was now curled up inside his jacket, her gray ears poking out from under the flap.

Dwayne switched hands and leaned back against the tree. The man was in pain. Robin crouched by him, a concerned expression on her face.

We had all gathered at the root of the massive Douglas fir, fifteen yards from the wreck. Tank was standing silently on the outskirts of the group as usual.

The fire was now completely out, and the area around the train looked like a war zone that had been blitzed overnight.

Connor's body was still inside the burned shell of the engine room. We were waiting for the Arctic air to cool the steel down before we could look for more evidence inside.

Theodore Henry was still missing. And no one had seen him leave the train.

Or, someone in this group was lying.

"We found the missing body," I said, watching them carefully.

"Jim Johnson?" said the doctor, sitting up.

I turned to him. So, he had been paying attention after all. Maybe he was more sober than I thought.

"Where did you find him?" asked Stella.

"He was tied to a tree. Propped upright."

Stella's eyes widened. Robin shuddered visibly, and Dwayne looked away with a grimace, like he didn't even want to imagine it.

"There was a note in his pocket," I said.

Robin took a sharp breath in and Stella jerked her head back. Tank shuffled in place.

I pulled the note out of my vest pocket. Tetyana shot me an inquiring look as she hadn't heard about it either. We'd rushed back to the train the second I'd slipped it into my vest.

"What does it say?" asked Katy.

I read it out loud.

"Remember me?"

I looked around the group. "Does anyone know what this means?"

Robin shook her head. Stella put her head in her hands, like she wanted to curl into a ball and disappear. Except for my two friends, no one was making eye contact any more.

"You said you found a few things," said Katy. "Any sign of Theodore Henry?"

I shook my head.

"We definitely saw signs of someone watching us," said Tetyana. "Someone who didn't want us to be there."

"Impossible," whispered Robin to her boots. "We're in the middle of nowhere."

"Impossible?" I said, turning to her. "Someone put that dead body on the tracks, and someone shot at me."

Everyone jerked their heads up and stared.

"He shot at you?" said Robin.

I narrowed my eyes.

"I didn't say it was a *man*."

She shook her head, looking disoriented. "It's a figure of speech."

"How come we didn't hear the gunshot?" asked Katy, frowning.

"It was an arrow."

Katy gasped. "What in the world?"

"It flew past and missed me by five inches."

"It's quieter too," said Tetyana. "A gunshot could be heard for miles around and would have alerted everyone. That was a warning."

The doctor threw his hands in the air.

"The only message I'm getting right now is some crazy psycho is sneaking around the woods moving dead bodies, carrying bows and arrows, and we're stranded here with nowhere to go!"

I stared at him. That was the most he'd spoken since we'd met.

Dwayne shook his head.

"That's not fully true. There's a freight train coming this way. We just have to wait for it to take us home."

"If the psycho doesn't kill us first," said Stella in a doleful voice.

"Dad's right," said Robin. "The sleeping quarters and kitchen haven't been affected. We have supplies and a place to sleep. We'll just have to stay put in there, lock ourselves in, till Steve comes on the freight train and we can all head home."

"That might be days from now," said Katy.

"Do you have a better plan?" asked Robin.

"We need to find Theodore Henry," I said. "We don't know where he is, and given the circumstances, I'd say he's in grave danger."

"That's what the police are for," said Robin. "That's their job. The freight train can call for help."

Dwayne sighed loudly.

"I just want to see my wife right now, and I really don't like Robin being here in the middle of this... whatever is going on. Dead bodies, missing men, and someone shooting arrows. That's not our job. We were hired to drive the train."

"Well, it's *my* job," I said.

Stella sat up, suddenly interested. She narrowed her eyes. "Why are you *really* here?"

"Theodore Henry thought he was being poisoned," I said. "That's why he brought us in, but neither he nor we expected a hold up or a kidnapping."

"You think he was *kidnapped*?" said Stella.

"Why do you think that dead body was put on the tracks?" I said. "To stop the train and nab Theodore, one of the richest men in the state. Maybe they've already contacted his family or the company HQ for a ransom. I'd say that's a strong possibility."

No one spoke for a while. Everyone sat quietly, hunched over, heads bowed, defeatist expressions on their faces.

I exchanged a glance with Tetyana and Katy.

Tetyana nodded.

I knew my friends well enough to know they'd agree to my suggestion.

"I'm willing to bet anything Theodore is somewhere on this mountain," I said, turning back to the rest of the group. "We're going in to find out what or who is hiding behind these woods."

Everyone looked up, alarm on their faces.

"You're nuts," said Tank, shaking his head.

"Stay away from the woods," said Dwayne. "This is the time when the bears and wolves come out of hibernation looking for food."

"Are you asking to be Grizzly dinner?" said Robin.

"I'm not afraid of the animals," I said. "It's people I worry about."

Dwayne shook his head. "It's madness to walk in there. Even I wouldn't, and I'm from these parts. You'll never find your way out. You'll get lost and freeze to death."

"I've found my way around worse terrains in the middle of war," said Tetyana.

"But there's no one in there," said Stella. "There's no human habitat for hundreds of miles around here."

Something told me to stay quiet about the smoke we saw from beyond the woods the night before, or the glint from the metallic roof we spotted this morning.

"If no one is around here, how does a dead body end up on the tracks?" I asked. "And how does Theodore disappear into thin air?"

No one answered.

Chapter Twenty-two

We hiked in single file.

Tetyana was up in front. Katy was in the middle. I took the rear.

We stepped through the woods, navigating around the hulking trees, listening to any sounds that would tell us someone was nearby.

We were geared up and armed, except I knew our Kevlar vests wouldn't stop another arrow aimed at our faces. Or a bullet to our heads.

As a reconnaissance expert who'd navigated foreign territory during battle, Tetyana had mapped a preliminary route for us.

We were going to take the long way to the structure we'd spotted earlier. There was no guarantee we'd find that place, as we were going through this thicket blindly with only our friend's keen sense of direction to lead the way.

But it was the best way to circumvent the mysterious maniac playing these dastardly games.

Dwayne, Robin, Stella, and the doctor had crawled back inside the train, with strict instructions to stay in lockdown mode till we returned from our recon trip.

But we had needed a distraction. Someone to make a little noise, while the three of us circled the tracks and entered the forest.

That way, if anyone was watching us, they wouldn't notice us slip in. If there had been more than one person, we'd have to take the chance.

To my surprise it was Tank who had offered to be the decoy. Or bait, as he'd called it, saying he'd felt guilty for having "lost" his boss and had wanted to do something useful.

While Tetyana, Katy, and I had hid behind the far end of the train, Tank had gone for a walk along the tracks, in the direction where we had discovered the dead body.

Once in position, he'd fired three shots into a pine tree trunk using his sidearm. The harsh sound of the gunshots had reverberated through the valley, sending flocks of wild birds into the air, screeching their displeasure at being disturbed.

That was all we had needed.

We'd scrambled from behind the train and darted into the woods, crossing our fingers, hoping against hope no one had spotted us.

But Tank had one more job to do. That was to guard the train until we came back.

Though I wasn't sure if I could trust him or any of the others, I had no choice. And the others didn't object. All I hoped was he wouldn't get hit by an arrow as we scrambled out of sight.

The kitten mewed in Katy's pocket and popped its head out.

Tetyana snapped around.

"Keep that thing quiet," she said. "That's what got us into trouble last time."

Katy slipped a hand into her pocket and stroked the cat's head.

I glanced around.

It was too quiet for there to be a village or an encampment around here. I wondered if Katy was right, that this was the work of just a deranged individual. One madman who had known the wealthiest gold baron in the state would be riding this train through this valley.

But why dig up a dead body, lacerate the face, haul it all the way to this remote valley, and toss it on the tracks?

There were many ways to hold up a train. That wasn't the easiest one.

The only reason Dwayne hadn't plowed right through the corpse was because of Robin's drone. That had been a fluke.

Though he'd played it down, that grizzly finding had meant something to Theodore Henry. And Connor. Connor was now dead. I just hoped Theodore was still alive to tell us what was going on.

We had hiked for fifteen minutes, climbing slightly uphill, staying hidden among the trees, when Tetyana let out a low whistle.

"Stop."

We halted.

She was peering in between two tree trunks, swiveling her head. I craned my neck to see what she'd spotted.

"Wrong way," she whispered, turning around. "We've been circling the base of the mountain, but I think we went too high."

"Are we lost?" whispered Katy.

Tetyana shook her head.

"We're heading east. Shouldn't be too far off track, but we need to get back down a bit," she said. "I'm flying blind here, going with memory and instincts, which means I can't pinpoint anything, and that's not great."

"So, what do we do?" asked Katy.

Tetyana looked around thoughtfully. "I don't want us to stumble onto this place and get ambushed."

"Wait," I said. "Why don't we let the cat lead the way?"

My friends shot me a skeptical look.

"Sure, it's not a dog," I said, "but cats are known to find their way home too."

Katy put her hand in her pocket and gently pulled the animal out.

"Can you help us find your home, little one?" she asked the kitten, who mewed back.

"Put her by the tree and see which way she turns," I said, pointing at the base of a pine tree.

Katy set her down.

We waited.

The kitten stood for a while, trembling, now that she was out of Katy's warm pocket. Then, with a shiver, she sat down, curled into a ball and buried her nose in her tail.

"Jeez," said Tetyana. "We don't have all day."

I stepped up to the kitten, wishing I knew her name. Gently uncurling her and nudging her back up, I placed her a few feet away from the tree. After a few seconds, I placed her farther away, until she began to sniff around and move on her own.

It took a minute, but the kitten finally found her nose. Soon, she was ambling around the trees, stopping to sniff at twigs and pinecones, but heading in one direction.

East.

This was a long shot. The cat could be as lost as we were, but it was all we had to go by right now.

It was another ten minutes when Tetyana stopped us again.

"I recognize this place," I whispered, staring at the tree only six feet from where we stood. "We were here this morning."

"Our kitty is a puppy in disguise," said Katy. "She has a good nose."

"Stand by," said Tetyana, as she stepped away.

Her sidearm at the ready, she crept from tree to tree, following the cat. The kitten was several feet in front of her, confidently moving in the direction of the structure we saw earlier.

I nudged Katy and pointed at the tree.

"The dead body was tied to that trunk," I whispered. "And now it's gone."

Katy's eyes widened.

"The arrow's gone too," I said. "It hit this tree right here, but someone plucked it out."

"What do they—"

"Keep it down," said Tetyana in a low, warning voice and gestured for us to join her.

We tiptoed over and crouched behind the tree where she was hiding. Something metallic glinted through the branches.

My heart gave a leap.

We found the settlement.

"I see a roof," whispered Katy, craning her neck. "And a building."

"Let's get closer," I said.

We slunk through the woods toward the structure. Soon, the trees began to thin, exposing a clearing up front.

"Wow," said Katy, when we got to the edge of the clearing.

We gawked at the scene that lay beyond the tree line. A handful of snow-covered structures, in varying degrees of disrepair, sat silently along the slope of the snowy mountain.

"It's an abandoned mining town," said Tetyana in a hushed voice.

"It's like we're back in the Klondike Gold Rush days," said Katy in an awed whisper. "Except all the people are gone."

Chapter Twenty-three

The kitten strolled between our legs and entered the clearing. Soon, it was sniffing around a rundown cabin.

I braced myself, expecting to hear a yell from the owner, happy to find their pet again.

But the mountain was even more ominously quiet than usual. The cat ambled around the shed and then disappeared, like the ghost town had swallowed her whole.

The three of us stayed put, watching, waiting.

The encampment was on a steep slope which stooped upward toward the craggy crest. Below us was a valley which lay in the opposite direction of the train tracks.

A long, rusted pipe ran down to the valley from up above. I guessed the mine was somewhere near the peak.

Half a dozen buildings huddled along the pipeline, left to fend for themselves for almost a century. Their slanted roofs were covered in several feet of snow and their high windows had been shuttered up, with snowdrifts gathered against the panes.

It was a sad and lonesome place.

The trees had probably been clear cut a long time ago to build this bleak settlement deep in the mountains.

Katy nudged me. "Imagine the stories that could tell?"

I followed her finger.

A white-washed building with a tall, gabled roof stood in the middle of the clearing, silently watching over this desolate collection of crumbling structures. A rusted metal cross rose from the roof top, pointing to the skies above.

The town church.

I stared at the hypnotic scene, feeling the long-forgotten memories still lingering in this derelict village. At one time, I was sure, this place had been bustling with hope and dreams of gold.

I wondered who else knew of this abandoned place. Apart from the person we were tracking, that was.

"Wood smoke," said Tetyana, shaking me out of my trance. "Do you guys smell it too?"

I sniffed the air. She was right. I looked up, but couldn't see anything swirling in the frosty air above us.

"That must be the remnants of the fire from last night," I said.

"Smoke means fire, and fire means people," said Tetyana.

"How does anyone live here?" said Katy, glancing around. "There's no electricity. No water. You can build a fire to stay warm, but what about food?"

"You've never gone winter camping then?" asked Tetyana.

"No way. If Peace ever suggested it, I'd divorce him," said Katy with a shudder. "Have you?"

"It was what we had to do," said Tetyana in a quiet voice. "When we were trying to keep the Russian militia at bay. Away from our village."

We fell silent for a moment.

Tetyana had lost her entire family to the militia. She hadn't had the choice but to pick up a gun and fight for her life.

None of us had grown up in carefree, pretty suburban homes with happy families. The scars of our pasts ran deep, and sometimes the pain emerged when we least expected.

Like right now.

I put a hand on Tetyana's shoulder.

"Time to go in," I said, knowing the best remedy for our nightmares was action. "Let's stick close together."

"Follow me," said Tetyana, nodding.

The three of us crouched down and scampered to the nearest building.

We flattened ourselves against the old brick wall and scanned the area, our guns aimed forward, like a small SWAT team readying for attack.

"Where's the kitty?" whispered Katy, craning her neck.

"There," said Tetyana, taking a step forward and pointing at something on the ground with her gun barrel.

I bent down to look.

"Paw prints," said Katy.

Tetyana shook her head. "Look at what's next to it."

I pulled out my phone and swiped to the photos I'd taken earlier by the snowbank near the tracks.

"It's the same boot print," I said, as I enlarged the image and compared it to the footprint next to the paw marks on the ground.

"The psycho gravedigger," whispered Katy. "He's here."

"Resume search," said Tetyana, her steely eyes darting back and forth, on full alert.

In stealth mode, we scoured dilapidated building after building.

The first three structures were locked with rusty bolts that had looked like they hadn't been touched for ages. One swipe of our Glocks was all it took to break them open, but the buildings were empty. There was nothing inside, but broken furniture covered in cobwebs.

But the closer we got to the center of the village, the stronger was the smell of smoke.

"The church," whispered Katy. "That's where the paw prints are headed."

Tetyana nodded.

"That's the only building with a chimney."

The church was a few yards in front of us, but it was out in a wide-open space. We would make easy targets if anyone was waiting to ambush us.

Tetyana pointed with her chin to a small shack that was the closest structure to the church. It was open on one side, like one of those garden sheds where you'd pile firewood and store lawn equipment.

"Our next stop," she said. "Watch my back."

After a quick scan of the area, she scrambled over, keeping low. Katy and I scurried behind her and slammed ourselves against the wall.

"Look what I found," said Tetyana, pointing her gun to an alcove in the shed.

"A snowmobile!" cried Katy, as she spotted the vehicle parked under the crumbling wooden awning.

"Shh…" I said.

The Ski-Doo had been painted all white. Someone had painstakingly covered the brand name in white paint as well. Whoever did this was looking to camouflage that machine.

"It's an old model," said Tetyana, leaning in to take a closer look.

"That's one way back to civilization," I said, a hint of hope rising in me again. "Especially if that freight train doesn't show up."

Tetyana touched the metal pipes in the back.

"Frozen cold. No one's used it recently."

"We'd have heard it if they had," I said. "These machines are loud."

Tetyana opened the gas cap in front of the driver's seat and peeked in.

"Hard to say without turning the engine on, but I'd say the tank's nearly empty."

"If they have a Ski-Doo," I said, looking around, "they should have a few jerry cans of gas."

But a quick glance told me there was nothing much else here other than the snowmobile and a pile of wood cuttings.

We now knew this place was inhabited.

By whom?

How many were there?

I examined the open space between us and the church.

The church looked as forgotten as the other buildings surrounding it, but we were certain that was our destination. The smoky smell was coming from its direction.

"Someone's in there," I said. "Real people. Not ghostly women in white gowns."

"It was flesh and blood that shot you with that arrow," said Tetyana, making a face.

Katy frowned. "There's something about that church," she said. "I feel like it holds the key to everything."

I nodded. "I'd bet this is where they brought Theodore Henry."

After waiting ten minutes to make sure no one was watching us, Tetyana turned to me.

"I'm going in. Cover me."

She darted out into the open.

My heart leaped to my mouth.

I aimed my gun forward, and I swiveled around, scanning the buildings, the woods, the open area. The ten seconds it took Tetyana to cross the open space felt like ten hours.

When I was sure she was safe, I turned to Katy, ignoring the trickle of sweat running down my back.

"No, you next," she said before I could ask. "I'll watch your back."

With a nod, I mimicked Tetyana's movements, crouching low to the ground and dashing to the church wall nearest to the shed. Katy followed soon after.

The three of us stood quietly, our ears against the old wall, listening for sounds of life inside.

But it was quiet. There was no crackle of fire or even a mew from the kitten.

"The main door is around the corner," I whispered. "Let's go in."

We were at the door within seconds. Tetyana banged the lock open, while Katy and I kept watch, our backs to her.

I heard the lock break and the door creak as Tetyana pushed it open.

"All clear," said Tetyana's voice in my ear.

Katy and I walked inside, stepping backward, our eyes watching, ears alert.

Once inside, I kicked the door shut, and swiveled around.

Chapter Twenty-four

I t was dark inside.

The inside of the church was one large open hall. The high ceiling was gray with age and the walls were peeling.

The only light came from the narrow windows and the enormous fireplace at the far end.

The logs in the fireplace were burning, but the flames were low. Someone had strung a copper wire across it on which hung an old-fashioned black kettle. A wide brick chimney ran along the church wall toward the roof.

So, that was where we saw the smoke coming from.

Compared to the chilly air outside, it was toasty in here.

Next to the hearth was the podium and altar, all still intact, despite their age.

"Someone lives here," I said, scanning the space.

"Here, kitty," came Katy's voice.

I turned to see her step up to a huddle on a gray blanket on a nearby pew. The kitten was nestled on the folds of the blanket.

"How did she get in here?" I asked.

"There must be another entrance," said Tetyana in a low voice. "Or an open window. Stay alert."

I glanced around to see if there were any signs of the missing gold baron. But something told me we were alone, except for the cat.

The pews were aged, and parts of the wood had cracked, but they looked clean. They sat in rows all the way to the front of the church, waiting for a congregation that would never show up.

Compared to the other buildings we'd walked into, this place had been wiped clean. Whoever lived here had taken care of the building.

There was something else.

There was a sacred silence among these four walls. It was hard to imagine a brutal gravedigger who had no qualms tossing a dead body and a kitten on a rail track would make this place their home.

Tetyana and I stepped gingerly along the wall toward the altar, checking behind every pillar and peeking into every pew, nook, and cranny along the way, while Katy searched for a second entrance.

"Behind here," whispered Tetyana when we had worked our way to the front.

A false wall, about ten feet high, stood behind the podium.

We stepped around it, our guns at the ready. That was when we saw it.

"A side door," said Tetyana, rattling the doorknob. It was one of those small medieval-sized entrances that looked like it had been built for a child.

"A cat flap," I said, bending low to examine the leather flap at the bottom. It was insulated and fit right into the square opening. "The kitten must have slipped in through here."

"Storage," said Tetyana from behind me.

She was checking the space behind the false wall. A narrow corridor spanned the width of the building and along it were three wooden doors. They stood open, barely hanging on to their hinges.

"Lots of blankets, and bedding, and old shirts," said Tetyana as she peeked inside, using her flashlight. She paused and moved something using the tip of her gun barrel. "We know it's a man who lives here."

I walked over to see what she'd found.

"What's that smell?" I said, sniffing the air. There was something else mixed in with the moldy, musty odor of this old building and the smoky fire.

Tetyana nodded. "Something chemical."

"I smelled it in Theodore's cabin when I went to look for him," I said. "It was faint, but I'd recognize it anywhere. It was like nail polish remover mixed with disinfectant."

Tetyana stared at me.

"Nail polish remover?"

"His room didn't smell like that last night," I said.

Following my nose, I walked up to the third closet. The smell was stronger there.

Inside was a pile of well-used painting supplies. Old rags, paint palettes, tubes, brushes, and half a dozen bottles of various sizes. None of the bottles had labels on them.

I picked up one which contained a whitish liquid and twisted the cap open.

"Paint thinner," said Tetyana, her eyes flitting across the supplies. "That's what you smelled."

I held the bottle to my nose.

"Be careful," said my friend, watching me warily. "Sniff too much of that and you'd be puking all over the place like Tank."

I stopped and stared at her, suddenly realizing the clue I'd overlooked.

"I know what I smelled in Theodore's cabin."

"What?"

"Chloroform."

"Chloroform?" said Tetyana, staring at the bottle.

I shook my head. "This is turpentine, but it reminds me of chloroform."

I put the cap on the bottle and placed it back.

"You know what this means, don't you?" I said. "Theodore's door wasn't locked this morning. Someone went in, drugged him while he was sleeping, and he'd have gone out like a light."

Tetyana frowned.

"He's a small man," I said. "Once he fainted, it would have been easy for anyone to carry him out through the open dining car door. The question is who did it?"

"I know you're starting to trust that bumbling sasquatch," said Tetyana, still frowning. "Tank best fits the description of a person who could have pulled off that trick."

But the more I considered it, I felt Tank didn't have the mental capacity to take part in any of the convoluted activities we'd seen so far. He got confused with simple instructions.

For the tenth time, I wondered why Theodore Henry, with all his resources, would have hired that young man to do an important job.

Tetyana gave me a stern look like she was reading my mind.

"He could be the best actor north of the sixtieth parallel," she said.

"Okay, what's your theory?" I asked.

"Tank chloroformed the old man, carried him from the cabin, out of the train, and dumped him at the edge of the woods for someone to pick him up. Then, he goes to Katy blabbering about losing his boss, giving time for a third party to move Theodore. The train crew was knee deep in their mechanical mess up front, and all the windows in the train were shuttered, so no one would have seen anything."

She snapped her fingers.

"That's an easy ten-minute job for Mr. Tank—"

"Guys?" said Katy, her voice coming from the other side of the false wall. "Come, see this."

We whipped around and dashed over.

"What is it?" demanded Tetyana.

I stomped up the podium to where Katy was, the thump of my boots on the hardwood floor echoing across the hall.

"Is this what you saw the other day?" she said, pointing at something.

I stepped up to her and froze.

She was staring at half a dozen paintings that were leaning against the wall behind the altar.

I kneeled next to them. None of the paintings had frames, like they'd just been finished and were waiting to be packaged.

"They look exactly like the ones in Theodore's room," I said, as I inspected them one by one. "Look at this signature at the bottom. The cross. I saw it in all three paintings in the cabin."

"I think we found our artist," said Tetyana.

I looked up at my friends.

"Do you remember that upside-down cross scar on Jim Johnson's neck?"

Katy took a sharp breath in.

"Are you saying this artist is also the psycho gravedig—"

Tetyana put a hand up to shush her.

"What?" whispered Katy.

"Did you hear that?" said Tetyana.

I strained to listen.

A noise was coming from the outside. Footsteps scrunching on the snow.

My heart ticked a beat faster.

They were heading toward the side door.

Chapter Twenty-five

"**B**ehind me," whispered Tetyana, checking her Glock and aiming it at the side door.

Katy and I stepped up behind her and raised our weapons.

My pulse was pounding, and Katy's face looked pale. Tetyana looked cool and collected, but I imagined her heart was racing too.

Were we finally going to meet the person who placed the dead body on the tracks?

I was sure they were the same person who shot that arrow and had kidnapped Theodore. They had a lot to answer for, I thought as I stifled the anger unfurling inside of me.

The footsteps got closer.

Whoever it was, they were dragging their feet, lumbering along as if they were hurt. Either that, or they were carrying something heavy.

The ground outside was solid with only a few inches of new snow at the most, so it wasn't like they were trudging feet deep in the white stuff. It had to be something else.

I exchanged a quick glance with Tetyana.

Could it be Theodore Henry?

She shrugged, as if to say she was confused too.

Something knocked against the wood.

We stiffened, our fingers on the triggers.

Whoever it was, they were having trouble opening the door. Then came a loud wheezing from the other side.

The door cracked open an inch.

I stopped breathing, all my focus on the interloper.

The door widened further, and an ancient walking stick poked through the opening.

I raised my eyebrows. I hadn't expected that, but I held my position.

The opening grew larger, letting more light inside this dark recess of the church, and the wheezing got louder.

Suddenly, a man's outline appeared at the threshold.

We stared at the apparition.

It was a stooped, old man in a red lumberjack jacket, his thinning gray hair tied back into a ponytail.

The crook of his walking stick had got entangled in the door handle. He had his head down, as he wrestled to pull his stick away. I suppressed the urge to step up and open the door for him, like I would have done in any other circumstance.

But these weren't usual circumstances.

He still hadn't noticed us facing him, lined up in the shadows behind the door.

Normally, Tetyana would have leaped on the intruder, maybe even tackled him to the ground, but she kept a steady hand on her gun, scanning behind him for unexpected companions.

He finally freed his cane and stepped inside. He stopped when he saw us, his brown eyes narrowing and his shoulders tightening.

But there was no fear behind those eyes. First alarm, then curiosity.

He was elderly, and his only weapon appeared to be that beautifully carved walking stick. I lowered my gun, feeling silly to be aiming a sidearm at an old man who had trouble breathing, let alone walking.

But Tetyana kept her weapon up, her gun only five feet from his face. He didn't flinch.

I wondered if he could see well.

The four of us stood by the door, staring at each other for another minute. I was about to ask who he was when he spoke.

"I thought you'd come," he said softly. He had a gentle singsong voice that made me think of storytelling by a campfire.

"Who are you?" I asked.

He dropped his shoulders and leaned against his walking stick.

"Isn't that what I should be asking you?" he replied, his face neutral. "What are you doing in my home?"

"Anyone with you?" snapped Tetyana, her tone harsh.

He sighed and shook his head.

"I live alone," he said.

"Is that right?" said Tetyana, suspicion in her voice.

"I've lived by myself for a long time. As you can see, there's no one else here."

He turned to Tetyana, looked her squarely in the face, and spoke in a calm voice. "Are you here to kill me?"

I holstered my weapon and motioned to my friends to lower theirs.

"No, we're not here to shoot anyone," I said. "We didn't mean to intrude in your home. We're looking for someone."

I pointed at the kitten who was now washing herself in front of the fireplace.

"It was your cat who led us here."

He nodded, like that made all the sense in the world.

"Would you like to know where we found her?"

He raised his head and locked eyes with me.

Though his eyes were wrinkled and kind, there was a seriousness, even a sternness behind them. He looked like a man who had lived a thousand lives, one who carried a million memories, and was done with taking things as they were. There was a fighter inside this old man.

"She comes and goes as she likes," he said.

My mind whirred.

The paintings in Theodore's cabin and those leaning against the wall next to the altar were done by the same artist. There was a connection between this man and the train, between him and Theodore's disappearance, maybe between him and everything that had happened.

"Who else lives in this village?" I asked.

He raised his arm and pointed his cane at the closest pew. That was when I noticed the blue and green paint splashed across his callused fingers.

He was the painter.

But was he the gravedigger too?

"Let an old man sit, would you?" he said, before turning around and limping over to the bench and sitting with a loud groan.

The three of us positioned ourselves in front of him.

"What is this godforsaken place?" said Tetyana.

"It's my home," he replied.

"Are there others here?"

"I stay away from people as much as I can."

The kitten came over and stepped up to the man. A semblance of a smile crossed his face as he picked her up and cradled her. The cat purred loudly.

He still hadn't asked us who we were. It was like he knew. I hadn't forgotten the first words he spoke when he saw us.

I thought you would come.

What did he mean by that?

"How do you live here all by yourself?" said Katy. "How do you find food and water and all that, especially during the long winters?"

He looked at her with a gentle smile.

"My people have lived here for thousands of years," he said to her. "I know how to live off the land."

"What about your family?"

"All gone. Many years ago."

"I'm sorry," said Katy.

The man looked down at the cat again. He was stroking the top of her head with one hand, but I noticed his other hand lay by his side, twitching.

Were those nerves? Or a palsy of some sort?

"Sounds like you expected us," I said. "How did you know we were coming?"

"I had a hunch."

"Do you know how we got here?"

"Of course."

"How?"

"There's only one way strangers find their way here."

"So, you know we came on the train that's stuck in the valley beyond the woods?"

"How else would you find this place?"

He was correct, if not cryptic.

Tetyana let out an exasperated sound. When I turned around, she put her hands up as if to say, *you take care of this.*

She stepped up to the small side door, double-checked the lock, and started patrolling the church, checking the windows.

I turned my attention back to the old man.

"The three of us were on board the train from Black Eagle Town," I said. "There was a special passenger on that train. Do you know who it is?"

He merely looked at me, but didn't answer.

"Theodore Henry," I said, wondering if we'd get anything out of him. "Have you heard of that name?"

"Everyone in Alaska has heard of him."

"Do you know why the train is stuck?"

"Sounded like you had some engine trouble."

"Engine trouble?" cried Katy. "The whole thing blew up!"

The old man shook his head, making clicking noises. "That was a dangerous thing to happen. I'm really glad you're safe."

Katy and I exchanged a glance.

How could he be so serene in the face of this news?

"But we stopped because of something else," I said, watching him carefully. "We'd just crossed into the valley when the conductor noticed an object on the tracks."

The man had his eyes down, his wrinkled fingers still stroking the cat who'd snuggled on his lap.

"It was a dead body," I said, leaning in, wishing he'd look up so I could see his facial expression better. "Someone placed a corpse on the tracks. It was a miracle the crew spotted it and stopped just in time."

Silence.

"Soon after we found the body, it disappeared. Someone dragged it away. Now who would do a thing like that?"

No response.

"When we went to look for it, someone fired an arrow at me. Any idea who that would be?"

I half wondered if he could hear well. I bent down, so I could get to his level.

"Do you know what's going on here?" I asked, feeling my voice harden.

He finally looked up and locked eyes with me, his face a picture of calm, despite the insane story I just shared.

I stared back into those eyes, wishing I knew his name, his story, and most importantly, his connection to Theodore Henry.

He shook his head, sadly.

"That's what happens when you disturb bad spirits," he said, in a low voice. "They come after you with a vengeance."

Chapter Twenty-six

I stifled a groan.

Please, no more ghost stories.

Tetyana scowled from the other end of the church. If she had her way, she'd have her gun at the man's throat, forcing him to speak the truth.

There had to be another way to get him to talk.

Besides, he could barely stand, and he was surrounded by three armed women. He wasn't going anywhere fast.

I put out my hand.

"I don't believe I introduced myself. My name is Asha Kade and I'm a private investigator."

He didn't raise an eyebrow. He didn't comment or even introduce himself, just took mine with his paint-splattered hand.

I pointed at my friend.

"This is Katy. She works with me."

I gestured at Tetyana, who had opened the main door and was scanning the grounds now. "That's my security expert, Tetyana."

He nodded.

I put a hand on my heart to show him I was sincerely trying to make a connection.

"I own a bakery in Harlem. We cater to celebrity events, and whenever my clients need help to solve their problems discreetly, they call me."

I didn't want to complicate matters by bringing in Madame Bouchard and her potential relationship with the richest man in this state. That had no bearing to solving this puzzle, other than informing us that Theodore Henry had powerful connections.

The old man gave another nod, but looked like he didn't care either way.

"Theodore Henry was worried someone was poisoning him. All he asked us for was to serve his meals on the train. This was supposed to be an uneventful trip."

Katy leaned closer to the old man, reached toward the kitten and rubbed her ears. The man didn't move away or object.

"The train was held up and someone kidnapped Theodore," I continued. "Do you know where he is?"

A flash of what seemed like sadness crossed his face. Then, he gave an imperceptible shake of his head.

"We're trying to figure out what's going on," I said. "I think you know a lot more than you're sharing."

He stared at the floor.

We waited.

"You heard the train's boiler blow up from here, didn't you?" I said.

He stroked the kitten absentmindedly, but didn't reply.

"It felt like a mini earthquake," said Katy. "You couldn't have missed it."

"We lost a life in that explosion," I said. "This is serious."

Still no answer.

It was a full half a minute before he said anything. When he looked up, his eyes were cloudy and his face was sorrowful.

"Would you take some advice from an old man?"

"Of course," said Katy.

"There's a freight train that comes this way once a week. Should be here tomorrow afternoon around four." He paused and regarded us gravely for a moment. "If I were you, I would get on that train and head home."

Katy let out a gasp.

"We can't leave just like that," I said. "We have a job to do."

"You said you'd take my advice."

"You seem sure about the train," I said, narrowing my eyes. "We were told it's highly unreliable and gets delayed, sometimes, by days."

"I set my clock to it."

We stared at him.

Had Dwayne and Robin lied to us? Why would they fabricate something like this? Or was it the old man who was making things up? Was he really the psycho gravedigger?

He couldn't have physically carried out any of the activities we'd seen so far, even pull on a bow and shoot that arrow.

"What about the Ski-Doo?" I said. "There's one in the shed behind the church. If the freight train doesn't come, that could take us to the nearest outpost, right?"

"Low on fuel," he replied, shaking his head. "Good for ten or so miles at best. I had been meaning to get a few gallons next week, but it keeps slipping my mind. But it's not like I go anywhere these days..."

He trailed off.

I gave him a close look.

He sounded sincere, but it was hard to believe anyone who'd been living this remote lifestyle wouldn't have a decent amount of emergency rations, including gas cannisters.

"What do you have to lose by telling us what's really going on?" I asked. "Why aren't you telling us the truth?"

I paused, seeing that twitch come to his hand again.

"The truth?" he said with a loud sigh. He looked down at his cat and muttered. "The truth depends on who is speaking, isn't it? This is why I don't get involved."

"Involved in *what*?" I asked. "Is this a ransom kidnapping? An act of revenge? Is someone upset this private train cuts through this valley? Is this a land dispute gone bad?"

"Whatever it is," he said. "This has nothing to do with you. You're not even from around here."

I wanted to shake him. Instead, I curled my hands into fists and thrust them into my pockets.

"I feel your energy," he said, looking at Katy first, then me. "You're good people. You mean well. You're trying to do your job."

Katy and I nodded.

"Then take my advice. Get on the freight train as soon as it comes this way. Go back to the big city. And don't ever come back."

Why did he want us to leave so badly?

"You're on a fool's errand," he said, giving me a hard look. "You made a mistake by accepting this job."

"You seem keen to get rid of us," said Katy.

"It's for your own good."

Oh, really?

I turned and pointed at the paintings lined against the wall by the church podium.

"Theodore Henry has similar paintings in his train cabin. They have the same signature as these. How did Theodore get his hands on your paintings?"

The old man looked up and gazed at the canvases, his eyes hazy. I thought I saw tears, but couldn't say for sure.

"Did he steal them from you?" I asked, softening my voice.

By the way his face contorted at those words, I was sure Theodore hadn't acquired those paintings through legitimate means. It was just the kind of swindling he was apt to do.

"If Theodore took them from you, I'd be happy to talk to him. Negotiate a deal for you. Get them back, if that's what you want. But we need to find the man first and I think you know where he is."

He turned to us, his face etched in sorrow.

"What's done is done. I don't want my paintings back. I'm an old man who doesn't have a lot of time to live."

He paused and frowned, like he was thinking. He turned back and looked at Tetyana, who was guarding the main door, then back to Katy and me.

"If it makes you ladies feel safer, you can stay in the church for the night. There's enough space here for everyone on the train, if they want to come. Stay here, get some rest, then, get on that freight train tomorrow. All of you."

His eyes were pleading.

"Listen to an old man. You'll only regret—"

He didn't get to finish.

A thundering roar outside made us all jump.

Chapter Twenty-seven

Tetyana bolted out of the church.

"Katy, stay with him!" I hollered, pulling out my Glock.
I dashed toward the main door.

"Lock the door!" I yelled, before sprinting down the steps after Tetyana.

The roar was coming from down in the valley. It was the whine of an engine, a mechanical rumble that echoed through the village.

It didn't sound like a train.

Or a car.

It was more like an airplane, starting its engine, getting ready for take-off.

Just below the town was an open corridor that cut through the woods toward the valley. This could have been a passageway that conveyed the gold from the mine up the mountain to down below, ages ago.

The snow was even more packed here and the risk of stumbling and rolling to the bottom was high. At least it's snow, I told myself, trying not to hyperventilate. Hard-packed snow was safer than loose gravel, or so I hoped.

Tetyana was several yards ahead of me, making a beeline down the slope, staying close to the trees on the side to get more traction.

I doubled my speed and kept on my friend's tail, trusting her to find the most secure route.

If that was an aircraft, it could be our only means of rescue.

I hadn't seen anything resembling a plane overhead. Was there an airport nearby?

Unlikely.

Then again, I hadn't expected to discover an abandoned mining town inhabited by a mysterious painter and his cat in the middle of nowhere either.

Ahead of me, Tetyana had slowed down, her approach more cautious. The sound of the engine was louder now, almost deafening.

Suddenly she stopped and slunk into the woods.

Did she see something?

I slowed down and slipped behind the nearest tree. From here, I could see my friend's silhouette between the branches. She was observing something intently, her Glock gleaming in her hand.

I crept through the woods toward her, but my heavy breathing gave me away.

"Stay back," said Tetyana in a low voice, not even looking up.

"What is it?" I whispered, sidling up to her.

She pointed with her chin.

A lake.

It was a pristine glacier lake, frozen now, the kind you'd see on upscale brochures for exclusive winter vacations with outrageous prices.

And there it was.

A blue and white Cessna, its body gleaming under the Arctic sun.

It was a six-seater with short, flat skis attached to its wheels. It was parked at the edge of the lake, the roar of its engine reverberating across the open air. Its rotor blade was rotating so fast, it was a blur of blue.

I peered through the trees.

I made out the vague shape of a man's silhouette in the pilot's seat.

This was an unusual place to land a ski-plane. The lake was surrounded by the bleak tundra landscape with no signs of human habitat or activity. There were no fishing lodges or hunting shacks nearby as far as I could tell. A science expedition would have passengers.

This man was alone.

Too many bizarre events had taken place in this valley and the old man's evasive answers hadn't reassured me.

Tetyana and I exchanged a glance.

"Theodore Henry could be trussed up like a chicken in the back," she said.

I nodded.

"Whatever we do next, we can't do anything to that machine," I said in warning. "It could be our only way out."

We waited, hidden in the shadows, watching the plane and the pilot, my heart racing, and my brain trying to think of the next best step.

The rotor blades spun faster, and the engine whined louder.

"He's taking off," I said. "We have to stop him."

"Roger that," said Tetyana, taking a step closer to the end of the tree line. I stepped up next to her.

We fired our weapons at the same time. The blast of gunfire echoed across the frozen lake, the sound ringing in my ear.

We had our guns aimed upward and away from the aircraft. That had been a warning shot.

The pilot peered through the window. I imagined their shock, as they wondered if they'd really heard gunshots.

He cut off the engine, slowing the rotary blades.

Tetyana stepped out of the tree line, aiming her sidearm at his door.

"Tetyana," I called out, but she was already out in the open. If the pilot had a weapon, which I'd bet all my money on, she was vulnerable, even with her Kevlar vest.

The plane's door opened, and I caught the glint of a black handgun.

I wanted to yell at my friend, but instead, positioned myself behind the nearest trunk. My eyes were on the pilot. Any sudden moves, and I would shoot.

"Get out!" shouted Tetyana. "Put your weapon down!"

The pilot jumped down, slammed the door with one hand, while holding his weapon forward, pointing directly at my friend.

He must have been in his mid-thirties.

He was clean shaven, and his eyes were hidden behind aviator glasses. Unlike most men in this part of the country who wore hunting jackets and camouflage pants, he had on office khaki pants and a bomber jacket.

"Who the hell are you?" he hollered, his voice echoing across the lake.

"I said, put your weapon down!" yelled Tetyana right back. "Or you're a dead man!"

"You first!" he shouted.

Tetyana didn't budge.

They stood thirty feet apart, staring each other down, both with enough firepower to kill each other in an instant.

I scanned the lake, hoping the gunshot hadn't alerted any of the pilot's friends, if he had any close by. The last thing we needed was a gunfight in the middle of this valley. There would be no one to take our bloodied bodies other than the wolves.

I looked from the pilot to my friend, in exasperation. This wasn't how we solved problems.

Think, girl, think.

I racked my brain. There was only one way out of this stalemate.

I holstered my weapon under my vest, put my hands in the air, and stepped out of the tree line.

"Ahoy, there," I hollered.

The man spun around, his weapon pointing directly at me.

Tetyana didn't hesitate. All she needed were those two seconds of distraction.

She jumped on him like a panther grabbing her prey. His glasses fell and crunched under him. He elbowed her, making her double up, but she held on.

She kicked his gun from his hand. It flew across the lake and slammed into a snowbank, but she lost her own weapon in the tussle.

He grabbed her by her jacket collar with one hand, ready to strike her with the other, but she blocked him and punched his face instead. The two rolled on the frozen lake, punching, jabbing, and kicking.

My heart pounded inside of me. Tetyana had never lost a fight, and I'd only distract her if I joined in.

I lunged toward her weapon and picked it up. Then, I darted over to dislodge the pilot's sidearm from the snowbank.

There was something urgent I needed to check.

I dashed over to the plane, scrambled in, and scoured the inside. My heart raced at the thought of finding Theodore Henry, but there was nothing other than an emergency kit and a large duffle bag on a backseat.

Outside, I could hear the loud grunts and yells as Tetyana and the pilot scuffled on the ice. Unless he had military grade training, he wouldn't get far.

With shaking fingers, I pulled the duffle bag open and rooted through it. It contained a winter jacket, men's clothes, a handful of energy bars and a dozen packages of water purification tablets. After checking under the seats and in the back for false compartments and finding nothing, I jumped back down.

Tetyana and the pilot were still grappling.

"Stop it!" I shouted.

I aimed my gun, trying to get a direct line at the pilot's head, but they were moving too fast, fighting for the upper hand. Tetyana got him in a choke hold, but the man bucked like an angry bull, loosening her grip.

He wasn't giving up without a struggle. I didn't dare pull the trigger.

Suddenly, Tetyana slammed the man's head on the ice and kicked her knee on his back. I winced to hear the thud of his head hitting the frozen ground.

"Hey!" I shouted. "Stop or I shoot!"

He stopped struggling and turned to give me a glazed look.

Tetyana pulled him up to his knees roughly. They were both bloodied and bruised.

"You put a gun in my face like that again, buddy," growled Tetyana, "and you get treated accordingly."

I stepped around her and faced the pilot.

"Who are you?" I asked. "And where is Theodore Henry?"

He gave me a numbed look, squinting with his swollen eyes. A red-hot flash of anger crossed his face. He spat out snow from his mouth.

"Who the hell are *you*?" he barked.

I ignored the question, just like he did mine.

"What are you doing here?" I snarled back.

He scowled in reply.

Suddenly, Tetyana spun her head around as if she'd heard something.

"Did you hear that?" she said to me. "Someone's by the woods."

I turned around, my heart speeding up again, wondering who else was hiding on the mountain.

That was when a howl came from behind the tree line.

Chapter Twenty-eight

The pilot gave a startled look in the direction of the woods.

"Jacob," he gasped.

Two figures emerged from the tree line. A man and a woman, the man slightly stooped and the woman taller with a halo of red hair.

Katy?

She was with the old man from the church, who was hobbling with his cane, one hand on her arm.

The pilot stopped struggling and watched them, his mouth open.

"You know him?" I asked.

The pilot didn't answer.

The three of us waited silently for them to approach. The old man stopped within ten feet of us, making Katy halt.

"What was that howl?" I said. "Sounded like a wolf."

"Best way to get my voice across the valley," said the old man, his eyes on me, looking fiercer and more alive than when we were inside the church.

I had told Katy to remain inside with him. He couldn't have coerced her to come, could he?

Katy turned to me. "He said you could be in trouble, and to bring him here."

She patted her waist discreetly. She still had her weapon.

I nodded.

"We did fine," growled Tetyana at the old man. "We don't need your help."

He pointed his cane at the pilot.

"Let him go. He's done you no harm."

But Tetyana didn't loosen her grip.

"How do you know each other?" I asked.

The old man thumped his cane on the snow.

"Why are you treating him like a criminal? Didn't I tell you? You're not involved in this. Release him."

"Not until you tell us what the heck is going on," snarled Tetyana, maintaining her hold.

"Is this how you treat everyone you meet?" said the old man, turning to her.

"Heck, yeah—" started Tetyana.

"We've had a pretty rough forty-eight hours," I said, before she could finish. We didn't need another fight on the ice. "Theodore Henry has gone missing, our train engine just blew up, one man's dead, and we're stuck here. We're looking for answers. Can you understand that?"

"Shoving your guns in our faces and manhandling us isn't going to get you any answers," replied the old man.

I had the pilot's weapon, and the old man was holding on to Katy just to walk. They weren't threats. Not for now, anyway.

I turned to Tetyana and nodded.

"We can let him go."

Tetyana swiveled the pilot around roughly.

"Hands on head," she snarled.

He complied. I wondered if it was because of the old man's presence or the fact that he was outgunned.

Tetyana patted him down before pushing him away from her.

The pilot stumbled but caught himself. He stepped up to the older man and turned around, touching his swollen lips where my friend had pummeled him.

Katy stepped away from the men and joined us. Tetyana and I still had our weapons drawn. It was clear who had the advantage.

The two men stood close, side by side, like they were protecting each other, watching each other's backs. Almost like father and son.

The pilot towered over us, even Tetyana who, at six feet, was tall for a woman.

With his piercing blue eyes and crew-cut brown hair, he looked like someone you'd encounter in an elevator in an office tower. The older man was much shorter, wrinkled with age, and clearly someone who had spent most of his days in the wilderness, alone.

I wondered how they were knew each other, and what their connection was to Theodore Henry.

I didn't have to reach far to find a more disparate group of people who'd come together. My own family, including Katy and Tetyana, came from all four corners of the planet, but we were tight. We'd fought together, gone through hell together and now, we'd die for each other.

Something told me the bond between these two men was just as strong.

What was this peculiar duo doing out here in the middle of nowhere, hanging out near an abandoned mine?

The pilot glared at Tetyana while the older man gazed out at the lake, his face stoic.

"Who are you?" I asked, for what felt like the hundredth time. "And what are you doing here?"

"Who the hell are *you*?" spat the pilot, glowering my way.

I sighed. It seemed like we were always giving information, never the other way round.

"We came on the train from Black Eagle Mine," I said. "On our way to Anchorage."

"What the heck were you doing on the train?"

The old man glanced at the pilot. I thought I caught a warning look, but it was so fleeting I couldn't say.

"There was an incident on the tracks," I said, watching the pilot closely. "Our train is now stuck, and one of our most important passengers has gone missing."

"The engine blew up too," said Katy. "And someone shot an arrow at Asha."

The pilot frowned.

"How did you find the mine?" he asked.

He was evading our questions again.

"We followed the cat," replied Katy.

The young man's brows shot up.

"The cat?"

"We found it on the tracks with the dead body," said Katy.

He stared at her, his face slowly turning pink.

"And you?" I asked, thinking it was our turn. "What were you doing, flying out here?"

He stared at me silently for a moment. His color was returning, and it looked like he was thinking. He was buying time, trying to come up with the best answer to my question.

That meant he was going to lie.

"He brings my weekly supplies from town." The older man spoke before the pilot answered.

"That's an expensive grocery delivery service," said Tetyana, thumbing at the plane behind us.

"Only way to get around here," replied the older man. "I'm glad he comes my way because I'm getting too old to hunt like I used to, but I've still got to eat."

"You haven't told us your name yet," I said.

"Jacob King."

"You're an artist?"

"Among many other things."

A gravedigger too?

I turned to the younger man.

"Care to share your name?"

"Matt Ryder," he growled.

"You look familiar," said Katy, squinting at Matt, her forehead scrunched. "I feel like I've seen you before."

Matt shrugged and looked away.

"Plenty of people who look like me. I'm just a regular Joe."

A regular Joe who flies to one of the most remote lakes in Alaska to deliver supplies to a lone painter who lives in an abandoned mine?

Strange. But Katy was right. I'd seen that face before. Or those features.

But where?

Matt was good-looking in the conventional sense, someone you'd expect to be an actor, a singer, a quasi-celebrity of sorts.

Perhaps I'd seen him on television?

"This isn't the only delivery I make out here," said Matt, with another shrug. "There are other communities up north, you know."

"What supplies do you bring?" I asked.

"Water purification tablets. Fruit, lettuce. Toilet paper. Ammunition—"

"Ammunition?" said Tetyana, perking up. "To keep the grizzlies away? Or for something else?"

"For my hunting rifle," said Jacob. "Only way to survive up here is to stock up during the fall. Moose, deer, caribou. If I can bag one animal, I have dry meat for the winter."

I looked at his cane. This was a man who wheezed when he shuffled. I couldn't imagine him stalking prey in the wild. Then again, someone shot an arrow my way only a few hours ago.

Was it Jacob King?

Or was it the man who called himself Matt Ryder?

Something was off with their story.

Chapter Twenty-nine

“And what are you people?” said Matt, his mouth twisted into scorn. “The Three frigging Musketeers?”

“We’re a private investigation firm,” I said, ignoring the insult. “From New York.”

He took a sharp breath in.

Katy was still looking him over, like she was trying to recall where she’d seen him before.

I had misjudged people before. I wasn’t sure if Matt was friend or foe yet, but the vibes I was getting were definitely not friendly.

I pointed at Tetyana.

“This is my security expert. You’ve seen her in action. I wouldn’t make any stupid moves while she’s around, if I were you.”

Matt glared at Tetyana for a moment and turned back to me.

“What were you people doing on the train?”

“Theodore Henry hired us to escort him to Anchorage,” I said.

Matt’s eyes widened.

So, this was news to him.

But we were going around in circles again. I still had to find my client.

“Have either of you seen him?”

The two men exchanged a glance.

"Everyone has seen Theodore Henry at one time or the other. He owns half the state," said Matt. "The man's everywhere."

"Do you know why anyone would hold up the train and kidnap him?" I said.

Jacob let out a heavy sigh, his wizened face looking even more weary than before.

"I've spent my whole life trying to not get involved with other people's business. If others choose to self-destruct, that's their problem. I can't watch out for everyone."

He was speaking in riddles again.

He paused, his eyes looking at something in the distance.

"I learned a long time ago not to put my nose in other people's affairs because I'm the one who gets burned," he said in a somber voice.

He turned back to us.

"I already gave you my advice. I suggest you take it."

Wait for a freight train that others have said was unreliable? No, thanks.

I turned to Matt.

"We need to contact the authorities."

Matt merely stared at me, a numb look on his face.

"We need to use your plane," I said, realizing he hadn't understood my request. "There are more people in the train and the sooner we get everyone to safety, the better."

He shook his head.

"That's not possible."

"Why not?"

"I've got mechanical problems of my own."

"What kind of problems?"

"Propeller's giving trouble. I barely made it here. Need to fix it before I can take that bird up again. I was trying to figure it out when you two came out guns blazing, like bloody pirates."

My stomach sank. Seeing the plane had given me hope, but that was fading away quickly.

"It was working fine when I saw it." Tetyana frowned.

She took a step toward the aircraft.

Matt jerked his head up.

"You touch my plane and you're dead," he yelled, his face turning dark.

"You have a radio in your plane, don't you?" said Tetyana, ignoring his threat.

"Sure, I do."

"Why are we sitting here having a tea party when we can call for a rescue operation?"

"Because SATCOM doesn't work down here and VHF needs line of sight," snapped Matt, shooting her a nasty look.

He waved his arms in the air.

"Do you see a receiver or a tower anywhere near here? Do you? If I can't get that plane up in the air, there ain't no one to talk to. End of story."

Tetyana cocked an eyebrow. "I'll double-check."

He gave her a hard look.

"You a pilot?"

"I've flown."

"Cessna?"

"Copters."

Matt shook his head.

"Just because you flew a chopper doesn't mean you know crap about single engine turboprops. You touch my plane and something happens, I swear to...."

He looked so furious, even Tetyana stopped in her tracks.

Was there something in that plane he didn't want us to see? Something I missed?

Tetyana and I exchanged a glance.

"A check won't hurt," she said, turning around.

Matt took a step toward her, but I whipped my gun his way.

"Hey!" I said. "Stay right where you are, mister."

Matt stopped, his face turning purple.

"That plane was remodeled from scratch," he shouted after Tetyana's back. "I'm the only one who knows how it works. You take one screw out and you mess up the whole dang prop. Do you have a death wish?"

"Is the propeller issue that bad?" asked Katy.

Matt spluttered. "Go on, then." He waved his arms. "Go on and fly it if you want. Go on a suicide mission. Your call."

I held my aim, but didn't reply.

He glared back at us, chest heaving.

My mind whirred furiously, looking for signs of lies. A twitch of the eye. An unblinking stare. But he appeared outraged.

Tetyana could change a tire and hot-wire a car, but she wasn't a plane mechanic. But I also wasn't going to take Matt's words as is.

We waited along the lake shore as she stepped into the aircraft.

I kept my eyes and my weapon aimed at Matt. Katy shivered, her chattering teeth the only sound I could hear as we waited. While we were dressed for this weather, staying still in these temperatures wasn't doing us any good.

Matt and Jacob stood side by side, quietly, watching Tetyana rumble around inside the plane.

Matt's scowl remained intact, but he had given up trying to fight us. One stern glance from Jacob and he'd stepped back.

I wondered how much these two men were involved in the dead body on the tracks and the arrow that shot my way.

Matt was perfectly capable of doing it. While Jacob was weak and fragile, he was cagey. I didn't trust either of them. They could be part of a bigger team, people we hadn't met yet.

If that was the case, we'd have to be careful about our next steps.

I shook my head to clear it, feeling like I was trying to put a puzzle together when half the pieces were missing.

It was a good ten minutes before Tetyana jumped down from the Cessna, a sour expression on her face.

"No dice, huh?" said Matt as she walked back toward us. He was gloating.

Tetyana shook her head.

"We have to take it up, over the range. Then, maybe we can get a signal," she said. "If the plane can't be fixed, and that train doesn't come we siphon the gas from the plane into the snowmobile and drive to the nearest outpost."

Matt's eyes bulged.

"You planning to mix aviation fuel with regular gas? What the hell are you thinking?"

Tetyana shrugged. "I've mixed worse things before."

"I think it's an excellent idea," I said. "How far is the closest settlement or station?"

"Forty miles south," said Jacob in a quiet voice.

"Should work fine," said Tetyana. "Though the fuel mix could mess up the Ski-Doo engine."

Matt let out a raspberry. "You're mad. Might as well hike all the way to Anchorage in the dark and pray not to freeze to death."

"That's a final option," said Tetyana with a nod. "I haven't ruled that out."

He rolled his eyes. "You're suicidal."

"But we have to find Theodore first," I said. "That's our priority."

I turned to Matt. "How long will it take to fix the propeller?"

He stared at me, a strange look on his face, like he hadn't heard me.

"How long—"

"I heard you," he said in a huff. "Don't rush me. I'll need a day at most and full daylight."

"So, what are you waiting for?" barked Tetyana.

He gave her a livid look. "You stupid city folk," he spat. "You call yourself investigators?"

Jacob turned his eyes toward the sky.

"We're far up north," he said in his gentle voice. "It gets dark early. In a couple of hours, it will be pitch black."

Katy gave a shudder and rubbed her hands. "God, I can't wait to get out of here."

Jacob raised his eyes to her.

"Remember the freight train. It will come."

My stomach knotted again. *Why was he so anxious to get rid of us?*

The scar on the dead man's neck flashed to mind. The same cross that was on his paintings.

Theodore Henry was somewhere on this mountain, and these two had something to do with it.

I was sure of it.

Chapter Thirty

I was about to usher everyone up the slope, when two figures materialized by the tree line.

Tetyana and I spun around, weapons aimed forward.

"Ahoy there!" shouted a female voice I recognized. "It's us!"

"Robin?" I said, lowering my gun.

"With Dwayne," said Katy.

Jacob and Matt stared at the father and daughter hurrying toward us. Dwayne's limp got more pronounced as he tried to keep up with Robin.

Something was wrong.

Robin broke into a run as she got closer. Without acknowledging the two newcomers or the ski-plane behind us, she turned to me.

Katy opened her mouth as if she was about to tell her about the strangers, but I put a warning hand on her arm. I wanted to see how this played out.

"We need to get out of the train," said Robin, panting heavily.

"Why?" I asked.

"What happened?" said Tetyana.

"A bad hailstorm's on its way. The train's no good."

"How so?" I said. "The back carriages weren't affected by the explosions."

"The explosions didn't help. Everything's hanging by a thread. Windows, shutters, doors. The dining car door doesn't close anymore. The hinges got blown out."

Dwayne limped up to us, his face dark. His eyes scanned the plane, then Matt and Jacob.

"Who are you?" he said, turning to the older man. "Did you two just fly out here?"

Jacob shook his head.

"I live in town. The church building."

"Didn't know anyone stayed up there," said Dwayne, his brow furrowed.

"Now you do."

Dwayne turned to Matt.

"Delivery service," said the pilot. "Flew in just now but I have mechanical trouble."

Dwayne let out a heavy sigh.

"Got mechanical issues too, but mine are much bigger than yours."

Matt raised an eyebrow. "Are you the train conductor?"

"Engineer."

He turned to his daughter.

"Robin here's the conductor. But we have no train to conduct anymore. It's pretty much dead on the tracks."

Katy gave a shudder. "With a dead McNamara in it."

Matt gave a start.

"Recognize the name?" I said, narrowing my eyes.

"From Black Eagle Mines," he said, speaking deliberately. "Everyone knows him around these parts. He's... dead?"

"Burned to a crisp," said Tetyana.

A strange look crossed his face, like he was struggling with his emotions.

So, he knew Connor well.

I turned to Robin and Dwayne.

"Where are the others? Tank, Stella, Doctor Wilson?"

"Still inside," said Robin. "They're staying put till we get back. We said we'll come looking for you."

"Who's watching the train?"

"Tank," said Dwayne. "But we can't stay the night in there. The roof's going to leak once the storm hits. We need to find a place to stay before it gets dark."

I nodded.

Dwayne let out a sigh.

"Just wish I could dial nine-one-one and get help. Right now, all I want is to get away from here."

"If a hailstorm's coming, I need to secure the plane," said Matt, looking up at the peak where dark clouds were gathering. "If you folks want a plane that will still work tomorrow, I gotta tarp it."

"Right this way, then," said Tetyana, giving him a mock bow. "I'll come with you."

Tetyana followed him to the aircraft, her gun at the ready.

We watched as Matt pulled out a tarp from inside, unfolded it, threw it over one wing and tied it with rope. Tetyana stood close by, her steely eyes on the pilot.

Jacob stirred.

"You're all welcome to stay at the church tonight," he said, turning to us.

"That would be a fine thing, sir," said Dwayne. "Can you fit eight?"

"It's not the Notre Dame, but there's space for you all and a cat."

My eyes flitted around this strange and raggedy group, as we stood by the lonely, frozen lake at the bottom of this snow-capped mountain range.

Here we were, huddled in a circle, trying to figure out how to survive another day.

We had all come together as if by happenstance. Yet, I wondered if this gathering had truly been a coincidence.

We trundled up the mountain from the lake and entered the abandoned mining town.

It took forever to get up the slope, though Tetyana, Katy, and I could have run up in five minutes or less. But we let Jacob and Dwayne set the pace.

It was getting dark anyway, and there wasn't much we could do at the moment other than find shelter.

The church was ten yards ahead of us. Jacob and Matt were in front, with Tetyana at their heels. She had her weapon drawn, her face stern.

Stumbling behind them were Robin and Dwayne, with the father holding on to his daughter's arm for support.

Katy and I were at the rear, our weapons out, our eyes open, ready for more surprises to come our way.

I didn't know who or what I was looking out for anymore.

If Jacob and Matt didn't dump that body on the tracks, who did? Was that person still out there? Was it the same person who tied the body to the tree and shot the arrow?

I looked up at the crew staggering ahead of us, the knot in my stomach tightening. Maybe there was no one else on the mountains. Maybe it was one of them.

But who?

And, why?

Why would anyone put their own survival in jeopardy with these precarious actions?

"Night's coming," I said, looking up at the sky. "It isn't even four in the afternoon."

"That's Alaska for you," said Katy. "Thank goodness it isn't the dead of winter because then we'd have got twenty-four hours of darkness."

She shivered. My friend was rattled, and I couldn't blame her.

My mind went to the folks still on the train.

I didn't like the idea of leaving them alone. I wondered how they were coping back there.

Stella, I imagined, had holed herself up in her cabin, terrified. Doctor Wilson, I was sure, had stationed himself at the dining table closest to the liquor cabinet. I wouldn't have been surprised if he had drunk himself to a coma by now.

We would need to traverse the woods and escort them here soon.

We were almost at the church.

It was a relief to see the metal cross on top and get a waft of the wood smoke from the fireplace inside.

This was where we'd spend the night, huddled together like a bunch of refugees fleeing disaster, except we had no idea where the danger was coming from.

Or from whom.

Matt and Jacob entered through the main doors with Tetyana right behind them. Robin was holding the door open for her father. Katy and I were twenty feet from the main door, when she clutched my arm.

"Did you see that?" she said.

"What? Where?" I asked, swiveling my head.

After all that had happened, I was seeing shadows everywhere too.

"Near the shed," she said, pointing at the ramshackle structure behind the church where we had discovered the snowmobile.

"Male or female?" I whispered.

"No idea, but I'm sure I saw something move."

"Let's check it out." I said. "Tetyana can manage the others. None of them are armed. Jacob's too old to fight, and Robin can help Tetyana if Matt acts up."

Katy drew back.

"You want to go to the shed now? In the dark? By ourselves?"

"It could be Theodore Henry."

"It could also be the psycho gravedigger."

She had a point.

Between Katy and me, we held three semi-automatic weapons, in addition to the Tanto knives in our boots. Plus, there were two of us. Psycho gravedigger or not, we couldn't hide like cowards forever. "Time to find out who it is," I said.

Chapter Thirty-one

Katy and I waited for Dwayne and Robin to enter the church.

"Why I come on these trips with you, I don't know," whispered Katy, as we treaded lightly toward the shed, clutching our weapons.

"You'd die of boredom if all you did was keep accounts all day, every day," I whispered back.

"I'm an excellent financial manager," she said. "I do a great job for your bakery, thank you very much—"

"Shh," I said. "Eyes on the shed."

I looked around me. It was the time of day when it was no longer day, but it wasn't night either. It was the time when the twilight played tricks on your eyes.

We waited quietly watching for any sound or movement, but the mountains had gone quiet again.

I considered my choices.

One option was to sprint to the shed without knowing what lay behind that structure. If someone was there, and if they were armed, I'd be running straight into fire.

But the last thing I wanted to do was sit on my bum in that church all night, waiting in fear, wondering if a bogeyman was roaming outside.

It was time to confront it.

"Cover me," I said.

"Roger that," said Katy from behind me. There was a trace of panic in her voice.

My friend had a tendency to complain during our missions, but she always came through when I needed her.

I did another quick scan.

Then, sucking in a deep breath of the frosty air, I dashed toward the shed, my heart hammering. I slammed against the wall, knowing for sure whoever was behind the wall had heard me now.

I waited.

That was when I heard it.

Katy was right. Someone was here. On the other side of this wall.

A groan. Then, heavy but slow breathing.

Theodore Henry?

Another groan.

No, it was someone else.

I stepped quietly toward the edge of the wall, my weapon cocked and at the ready.

Soon it would be pitch black and I didn't want to fumble around in total darkness. I didn't have time.

I swung around the wall, screaming, "freeze or I'll shoot!"

Doctor Wilson?

A quick glance around the shed told me he was alone.

The physician was sitting slouched on the cold ground, propped by the snowmobile, barely awake. He was in his woolen overcoat, and in between his thighs was an open bottle of vodka.

The strong smell of liquor permeated the air.

"Doctor Wilson?" I said, bending over.

He opened his eyes and gave me a groggy look.

I pulled the flashlight out of my back pocket and shone it into his face.

He blinked and covered his eyes with his hand.

"Turn that thing off," he grunted. His voice was raspy, the kind you hear from lifetime smokers.

I shone the torch around his body to make sure he wasn't harmed, or worse, shot by that arrow-slinging bandit in the woods. But there were no visible wounds or tears on his clothing.

He looked fine, except he had drunk himself into a near stupor.

"I said, turn that thing off."

I turned the torch away from him and stepped back toward the wall.

Katy was by the church, probably worried about what had happened to me. I didn't want her to call Tetyana, as she had her hands busy as it was.

"All clear!" I called out.

Katy rushed over, crouching low. As soon as she got to arm's reach, I pulled her behind the wall.

"Oh, my goodness," she cried as she caught sight of the drunken man on the floor, barely able to keep his head up.

"Are you okay?" she said, stepping up to the doctor, her face scrunched in concern. "You'll die of hypothermia."

She turned to me.

"We need to get him inside immediately."

The doctor groaned.

"No... Not going anywhere. Just let me be..."

As we watched, he brought the bottle to his lips and took a slug.

I remembered pouring him a shot of the same drink when we were catering in the train. That was an expensive brand, one Theodore had exported from Russia. I couldn't remember if it had sixty or seventy percent alcohol, but it was high enough, I was surprised the physician hadn't turned into fumes already.

I squatted next to the doctor.

"How did you get here?"

Doctor Wilson turned his tired red eyes my way, hardly able to focus.

"Crawled here," he mumbled, sounding like it took all his effort to speak.

"Where are the others?"

He shrugged. "How do I know? In the train, last time I saw."

I gave a silent prayer, hoping Stella and Tank had made the intelligent decision to remain where they were. If they were wandering around like the doctor, we'd have a bigger rescue operation to contend with.

Katy kneeled next to the doctor and reached for the bottle. He pulled back with a shocked look, like she had tried to stab him.

The man needed serious help.

"The temperatures are dipping fast," said Katy. "In a few hours it's going to be very cold. You can't stay out here all night."

"Let me be," said Doctor Wilson, cradling his bottle. "I deserve to die, anyway."

My eyes narrowed.

"Why do you say that?"

He gave me another unfocused look.

"Because I killed him," he said, pulling his jacket tighter around him.

I looked at him in alarm.

"Who?" I said. "Who did you kill?"

He shook his head from side to side.

"I murdered a man and no one even knew."

Chapter Thirty-two

"Who did you kill?" I asked again.

"The boss," spat out the doctor. "Who the heck do you think I'm talking about?"

Was he referring to Theodore Henry?

He gave me a wild look. He was fully awake now.

I rubbed my forehead. Was he so drunk he'd confessed to a crime he never even committed?

Something bitter came to my throat. Did the doctor murder Theodore right in front of our eyes and I never saw it coming?

"How did you do it?" I said, hearing my voice harden. "And where is he now?"

He gave me an accusing look.

"Why are you asking me all these questions? How the heck am I supposed to know where Theodore went?"

"You said you killed him," I said, reaching deep inside to summon every ounce of patience in me. "That would mean you know where his body is."

"Yeah, I sure killed him," he said in that raspy broken voice, staring glumly at his bottle. I wondered if he'd even heard me. "All I had to tell him was he had cancer. After that, he was off to the races."

Was he hallucinating?

Katy shot me a confused look.

I wanted to shake him by the shoulders, but I knew that wouldn't help.

"Doctor Wilson," I said, looking him in the eye. "How exactly did you kill Theodore?"

He took another swig of his bottle.

"I told him he had cancer," he said, slurring his words. "I told him so because I wanted the bastard to die."

"Doctor Wilson," said Katy, leaning in and placing a hand on his arm. "Does Theodore have cancer or not?"

Tears rolled down the man's cheeks.

"He believed me," he said, turning his tear-stained face toward my friend. "I was his doctor, after all. We even shaved his head. I gave him a bunch of pills and that dratted wheelchair. The man swallowed it all. Hook, line, and sinker. He was sure he was in his last days."

"Why did you lie to him?" I said.

"To kill him."

I wondered if there was even a figment of truth in this delirious story. The more likely explanation was the strong drink had muddled his brain. It was time we got him into the church and under a warm blanket, and pry that bottle from his hands.

The doctor tapped his head.

"It's all up here, I tell you. All you have to do is tell a man he has three months to live, and if he believes you...." He trailed off.

"He will die," finished Katy.

"Slowly but surely he will die."

"Psychological warfare," I said, shaking my head. "It goes against every oath you took as a physician."

He gave a hollow laugh and took another swig of his drink.

"So, you didn't actually kill him, did you?" said Katy.

"I might as well have."

"Why did you do it?" I said.

He stared at me, his eyes stronger and more focused.

"Because if there's any man in this state who deserved to die, it was him."

For a moment, he looked more sober than I'd seen him since we met.

"The man's a swindler, a backstabber. Would have cut his mother's throat if he could make a buck from it."

"What did he do to you?" I asked.

He turned away with a heavy sigh and looked out into the darkness.

Katy and I both had our flashlights out, which provided the only illumination in the shed. I wished I could shine mine on his eyes to see his expression more clearly, but I knew that would shut him up.

I wondered how Tetyana was faring inside the church. A pale-yellow light was flickering through the high windows of the building. Someone had lit a candle or several. At least, I hadn't heard gunshots or panicked yells.

I wondered how long this peace would last.

"Where's Theodore Henry now?" I asked, turning back to the doctor.

"Your guess is as good as mine," he replied with a nonchalant shrug. "I doubt you'll find him alive."

He was babbling. None of this made any sense.

I sat back, a sudden realization hitting me.

"If your diagnosis was a lie, how were you planning to keep it from the medical personnel at the cancer clinic in Seattle? They would have figured it out soon enough, wouldn't they?"

Another hollow laugh and another swig of his bottle.

"What are you? FBI detectives?" he said.

I imagined he had downed an entire bottle of vodka since we started the journey, but something told me this man was more sober than anyone else in the group.

"What are you trying to tell us?" I said, watching him carefully.

"Theodore Henry was never supposed to arrive in Seattle."

Chapter Thirty-three

"Help!"

The terror-stricken cry reverberated through the old mining town.

Katy and I sprang to our feet.

I stared into the darkness, my heart pounding.

My eyes swept the ground, but I could no longer see anything. Our flashlights were tiny pinpoints in a sea of midnight black.

The candlelight still flickered through the church windows but there was no sign of a commotion, no noise coming from the building so that I wondered if they had all fallen asleep.

The sound had come from outside.

I was sure of it.

Was that Theodore Henry?

I wondered if my mind was playing games with me, but Katy had heard it too.

"Do we holler back?" said Katy in a hushed voice.

"That could be a decoy. If someone's in trouble, we don't want to alert whoever is doing this to know we heard it."

"It came from that way," she whispered, pointing upward. "Up the mountain."

We stood silently, faces turned up, ears strained, hoping for another sign that would give us the location of the yell.

Nothing.

"I swear it was a woman," said Katy. "Stella's the only female not inside the church. Maybe she walked out of the train and got lost."

But my mind flashed back to the first time I met Theodore Henry at the Black Eagle Mines. We had been waiting for him at the corporate headquarters when Tank rolled him out of the executive elevator.

We had just arrived after getting shuttled in four flights, including one on a tiny single engine turboprop in which we had barely fit.

This was one reason Theodore had been adamant on taking his new train to Anchorage.

I'd thought the train and railway line he'd been tinkering with after retirement were mere rich man's toys, but he told us the last thing he'd wanted was to get manhandled from one plane to another.

I'd already read several articles about Theodore with photos of him in his wheelchair, so I hadn't been surprised to see the small-framed man with a shaven head being rolled our way.

It was his voice that had startled me. That high-pitched voice. If I'd heard him without seeing him, I'd have expected to meet a woman, not a man.

"Could have been Theodore too," I said to Katy. "Remember how he talked?"

"If that's him, it means, he's alive."

Katy was right. The cry had come from above us, like someone was stranded high on the mountain.

"Come on," I said, gesturing at the doctor. "Let's take care of him first, or we'll have another dead man on our hands."

My adrenaline was back at its peak, and my mind was racing a million miles a second, but the Arctic night chill sank into my bones through the layers of shirts and vest.

I could only imagine the havoc these temperatures were wrecking on the doctor's body.

Doctor Wilson groaned and tried to push us away, but between Katy and me, we hauled him to his feet despite his protests.

He was a heavyset man. While Katy and I were fit, it was a struggle to get him out of the shed. I was considering bringing my gun out and prodding him in the back with it, when he started to move.

Flanked by us, he shuffled forward, clutching his bottle. While my eyes were focused on the ground ahead lit by our torches, my ears were on alert for another shout for help.

We had only got a few feet from the shed, when the eerie cry echoed across the mountain slopes again.

"Help!"

We froze.

The church door banged open, and a tall, athletic frame was silhouetted at the threshold.

"Tetyana?" said Katy.

She jogged toward us.

"Hear that?" she hollered as she got close.

"It came from up the mountain," I said, and then pointed at the doctor. "We found the good doctor in the shed, a little lost. We need to get him inside first."

"I'll take him," said Tetyana, pushing me aside and grabbing Doctor Wilson on one end.

I ran up ahead and looked inside the church.

All the candles on the altar had been lit, and the fireplace was burning bright, giving a cozy glow to the ancient building.

The group had transformed the pews into cots, and were now lying in uncomfortable cramped positions, huddled under the blankets we saw in the storage rooms in the back. They were covered from head to toe, so it was hard to make out who was who.

The sound of a sonorous snore came from one pew. That had to be Dwayne, I thought. He'd gone through enough trauma over the last couple of days I was sure he'd passed out as soon as his head hit the bench.

We pulled the doctor inside, bundled him into the bench closest to the fireplace, and covered him with two blankets. That was the best we could do for now.

There were others who needed our aid more urgently.

Tetyana, Katy, and I stepped outside and Katy closed the church door with a gentle thud.

I turned to my friends. "Ready for a midnight hike?"

Our flashlights were turned off and I could no longer see their expressions, but I knew they were with me, especially Tetyana.

We crept along the church wall to the end where the ground sloped up.

It was going to be difficult to pinpoint the location in the dark. Getting up the icy, craggy slope was going to challenge us all, but we weren't going to leave anyone in trouble behind.

We stopped and listened for a moment, letting our eyes adjust.

"Help!"

The three of us swiveled around, our weapons in the air. But we were pointing aimlessly at an inky blackness.

We waited with our backs to the church, our eyes gazing up and into the dark void, feeling the presence of the mountain looming above us but seeing nothing.

My mind whirred, trying to recall what the terrain looked like from that afternoon. The slope went up gradually so we wouldn't need climbing equipment, but a hike in the dark would still be a dangerous endeavor.

"I don't remember seeing trees or bushes from up here onward," said Tetyana. "Which means no cover. If someone's waiting up there, they can take a good shot at us, even in the dark."

"How do we even know which way to head?" said Katy.

I racked my brain, trying to remember the layout of the buildings, when I realized we had an answer.

I shuffled to the left, feeling my way in the darkness. I moved little by little until the side of my boot hit something solid. I bent down and felt it.

"Guys," I called out in a low voice, turning back to the church wall where I knew my friends were standing. "This way."

There was one way to get up the mountain without getting lost or anyone seeing us.

And I'd found it.

Chapter Thirty-four

The pipeline.

During daylight, it had looked like an ancient mechanical snake that wound its way from the mining shaft up the mountain down to the valley below.

"We follow this up," I whispered to my friends. "We can't get lost, and we don't need flashlights."

"What if the psycho gravedigger's up there?" said Katy.

"If anyone's waiting for us, they'll have something coming for them," said Tetyana.

"What if there's another dead body up there?" said Katy.

"I'll lead the way," said Tetyana, stepping ahead of us. "If I stumble over a dead body or anything else, so be it. You can stay in the church if you want."

"I'm not staying behind by myself," spluttered Katy.

"Why don't you go in the middle?" I said, knowing my friend preferred to be sandwiched in between me and Tetyana, especially when we were stalking around unknown territory.

I heard her boots crunch on the snow, and I fell into step behind her.

There was a waning moon in the sky, half covered by the clouds, giving some light but creating uncanny shadows that made me believe the enemy was nearby, ready to pounce on us.

After a while, all I could hear was the heavy breathing of my friends and me.

The air around me felt slightly warmer, partly because I was sweating from the hike, and partly because of the low storm clouds that had gathered over the peak.

That wasn't good.

It meant we were going to get a dump of snow at a moment's notice. The only good thing about that was we wouldn't freeze to death. That is, if the snow didn't bury us or this gravedigger didn't kill us first.

We kept trudging, an uneasy quietness settling among us.

My breath got shallower the higher we climbed. Exhaustion from the day's events was slowly creeping into my bones.

The rusty pipeline was a godsend. It was comforting to feel the tacks sticking out of the metal, knowing all we had to do was follow it down to get back to the church.

A hundred years ago, this hill would have been teeming with gold diggers seeking their fortune. If we had been hiking during the day, this would have been a much simpler task.

But we were here now, when darkness absorbed everything, with a potential madman waiting for us at the top.

I swallowed my fears and kept my thoughts to myself.

The last thing I needed was for Katy to panic. She was being a good sport. I knew she had qualms about having come with us and would rather be in her New York apartment telling a bedtime story to Chantelle.

Every time I got a call for my services, she seemed to forget the last trip and insist she join. Most of my jobs started innocently enough—find a runaway girl, identify a poison pen writer, cater to a mining industrialist on a scenic train ride through Alaska.

But these missions always finished unexpectedly, with us teetering over a dangerous precipice, fighting for our lives and the lives of my clients.

It happened all the time. I wondered how this trip would end.

I glanced behind me.

All the way down the mountain slope, I could see the yellow light emanating from the church windows, looking spooky from the distance.

My thoughts wandered over to the people sleeping in there. I felt for Robin and Dwayne. Neither had said it, but I could see from their faces they regretted taking on this job.

Doctor Wilson's confession had barely sunk in. I wasn't sure how much I could rely on his story given his state, but why would anyone make up such an outlandish tale?

Jacob came across as a soft-spoken old man, but he wasn't telling us everything. He was protecting himself and he wasn't as innocent as he looked.

But it was Matt Ryder I distrusted the most.

There was something about him. I made a mental note to check that plane again, first thing in the morning.

"Almost there," said Tetyana in a low voice, from up front. "Watch for mine debris."

I was too tired to answer. Plus, I didn't want to make any more sound than we already were.

I peered through the darkness. Now that my eyes had adjusted, I could make out the outlines of equipment abandoned by the pipeline.

What are they? Pans, shovels, an oversized wheelbarrow?

"Stop," said Tetyana.

Katy and I stepped up to her and flanked her.

The pipeline disappeared into the mouth of something big and gaping.

The mine shaft.

We were standing at an angle. The slope was steeper up here. From what I remembered, the shaft was only halfway up the slope, and the peak was still several miles above us.

"Do we go in?" whispered Katy.

"Let's do a recon first," said Tetyana.

She turned to me. "Stay and guard the entrance. We won't be long. Shout if you see anything."

She turned to Katy. "You're with me. Keep your weapon at the ready."

"Sure thing," said Katy in a hushed tone.

I watched as they treaded carefully around a rusty mining wagon, lying on its side.

A bone-chilling howl cut through the air and made me jump. I clutched my heart. The distant howl echoed across the mountain.

Wolves.

I swallowed.

They'd be more scared of us than we were of them. At least, that was what I told myself.

Trying to calm my heart rate back to normal, and feeling silly at being startled so quickly, I turned back to the gaping entrance.

Someone had placed a long beam of wood next to the shaft, like a stepping-stone of sorts.

I stepped up to it and peered inside.

I was looking into a long and narrow tunnel that seemed to go on forever. I imagined the miners of long ago blasting this entrance with dynamite.

There seemed to be a space between where the tunnel began and the entrance ended, but since everything blended into dark shadows, it was hard to tell.

I wondered how safe it would be to enter the mine with the rock shifting over the ages. I'd have been surprised if anyone had reinforced this structure after the original workers had abandoned it decades ago.

If Theodore was inside, he'd have more than a kidnapper to contend with.

Did someone bring him here?

I took a step closer, wishing I could turn my flashlight on.

"Theodore Henry?" I called out softly.

I stepped back startled, hearing my echo.

I stepped onto the wooden beam.

"Anyone here?" I said.

Nothing but my own voice returned to me.

The scrunch of footsteps made me turn.

A dark shadow loomed behind me.

"Tetyana?"

I'd barely looked back when I felt the hand on my shoulders.

"Hey!" I shouted, whipping my arm up to smash my Glock on their face. But it was too late.

I lost my footing and stumbled into a deep abyss.

Chapter Thirty-five

I screamed and clawed at the air.

The craggy rock scraped against my back.

Then, just as suddenly as it had begun, it ended. I fell with a thud on a hard surface.

It took a few seconds to catch my breath. I felt around me, my eyes trying to focus, my heart pounding like my chest was about to explode.

The sound of something made me look up. There was nothing but a dark void above me.

"Hey!" I shouted angrily. "Who the hell pushed me?"

Silence.

"Help!" I hollered. "Tetyana! Katy! Can you hear me?"

No answer.

I stood up shakily. My upper back hurt from scraping against the rock during the fall. It felt like an angry cat had dug its claws in and swiped my back in one fell swoop.

What did I fall into?

A cold sweat broke out as I remembered the dark and narrow space between the tunnel and the entrance. I'd stumbled right into it.

Correction.

Someone had pushed me in.

Someone who knew this shaft well enough to know of this chasm. Someone who had been waiting for us up here.

I whirled around, reaching out blindly.

Where am I? In a well? A trench?

Wherever it was, it was pitch black, and I was alone. But I hadn't fallen for long, or far. I tried to do a quick calculation in my head, but my brain felt woozy.

I shook my head to clear it. I'd stumbled down ten feet at most. The feeling of having plummeted into an unfathomable abyss was only my fear talking.

My heart in my mouth, I felt the ground with my feet, cautiously trying a few inches in all directions. The last thing I wanted was to plunge farther down, into the depths of this old mine.

But the ground was rock hard and smooth. This had to be part of the shaft, perhaps a portion of a tunnel carved out for transporting the goods a long time ago.

Where's my gun? My flashlight? Did I drop them on top?

Swallowing something bitter that came to my mouth, I put my hand around and felt through the darkness.

A wall.

A craggy, stone wall someone had roughly cut or dynamited through the heart of the mountain. I felt around it, taking one step at a time.

It was disorienting. I wondered if I was going to lose my way. Then, I remembered there had been no echo when I'd called out for my friends. I felt the tightness around me. This was a small, confined space.

That was when I realized what the wooden beam on top was for. It was the bridge over this chasm, but someone had removed it, conveniently, just before we had come up in the dark.

Evil, I thought, gritting my teeth, my emotions veering from fury to terror and back again.

I was mad at myself for not having been more careful. I'd crossed continents and oceans to die here, in this black hole in the ground?

"Tetyana!" I shouted, trying to suppress the panic bubbling inside of me. "Katy! Help!"

"Asha!"

A flood of relief went through me.

That was Katy, screaming my name.

"Asha!"

"Down here!" I hollered. "Watch out for the hole!"

There was a commotion above, like someone was scrambling around near the shaft.

"I'm right at the entrance. Look down!"

"Asha?" came Tetyana's calmer voice. "What the hell happened?"

"Someone pushed me in," I shouted. "Watch your backs!"

Suddenly, a beam of light shone down. I covered my face as the light crossed my eyes.

"Hang tight," came Tetyana's voice.

"Are you okay?" said Katy, her voice filled with worry.

"Nothing broken," I said, watching their heads bob back and forth only ten or so feet above me. "It's a shallow cave of sorts." I paused. "Hey, can you shine your torch down here? Pan it across the hole."

Katy moved her flashlight around the well.

I spotted my gun and pounced on it.

"Can you try the other end?" I said, my eyes sweeping the space, looking for my flashlight.

"There," said Katy, shining the spotlight on a small black object five feet away from me. "To your left."

I bent down and grabbed it.

I turned it on and examined the space.

"It's a well," I said, checking the walls to see if there were any entrances to other tunnels or caves within this hole. Above me, I could hear the rumble of something heavy being moved around.

What's Tetyana up to?

"How did you fall?" said Katy. "You were supposed to stand at the entrance."

"Someone pushed me in," I said.

"My fault," said Tetyana, popping her head in. "We should have never split up."

"I shouldn't have turned my back," I said, gritting my teeth. "Entirely my mistake."

Tetyana turned to Katy.

"Cover me and keep a sharp eye out."

Katy sprang up and disappeared from view, and Tetyana turned her attention back to me.

"Go to the farthest part and flatten yourself against the wall."

I slipped to the far end and huddled against the stone.

I hoped to goodness Katy was staying close by and keeping her eyes open. We couldn't have another one of us disappear.

Not in the middle of the night.

Not here.

"Watch your head," called out Tetyana as she pushed something long across the crevice.

It was the wooden beam. The one I'd been standing on, only moments ago. She had turned it around and was tilting it into the mouth of the well.

Loose gravel began to fall in. I covered my head with my hands and kept my eyes on the floor.

"Stay back," shouted Tetyana, as the beam swung and fell onto the ground with a thump only a few feet from me, raising a cloud of dust in the air.

I waited for it to settle.

"Come up slowly," called out Tetyana. "Beam's icy and slippery."

It was better than nothing.

I holstered my gun, switched off my torch and thrust it into my back pocket, making a mental note to bring a headlight the next time. But next time, I scolded myself, I wasn't going to stand with my back to the mountain like that.

Glad I had gloves on, I grabbed on to the beam that now lay in a slant across the well and pulled myself up onto it. Inch by inch, I climbed up, doubled over, gripping the wood with both hands, thankful for the deep tread on my winter boots.

I didn't have far to climb.

When I got to about eight feet, Tetyana's long arms reached down to pull me up. I held on to her and leaped up the beam. I fell to the ground, panting and shaking, more with fright than exhaustion.

My heart was still pounding, but I was out of the hole.

"Oh, my goodness, Asha," came Katy's voice. "You could have died."

"Only if you'd left me down there," I said, my chest still heaving. I sat up, pulled my torch out and shone the light around.

The person who'd pushed me in had vanished.

I gazed down the slope at the faint yellow light coming from below. Could anyone inside the church have followed us up here?

Impossible.

We'd have heard them, and I'd kept an eye behind me every few seconds as we climbed up along the pipeline.

Whoever it had been, they knew this mountain well, well enough to crawl up in the dark or hang around here and push me in just at the right place.

The only person who fit that bill was Jacob, but he used a cane and got out of breath simply walking a few steps.

Impossible.

No one inside the church could have done this.

Then again, I had taken everyone's word for who they were, but any one of them could be lying.

Or, was this the action of a stranger we hadn't met yet?

Someone prowling the mountains for their next victim?

Chapter Thirty-six

"When I find out who pushed me in," I said, "I swear I'll have their head."

"Did you see anything?" said Tetyana.

"I was at the entrance calling out Theodore's name," I said. "That was a mistake. I heard footsteps, but I thought it was you. That was when I felt a hand on my shoulder."

"Small hands? Big hands?"

"Didn't register. I wasn't expecting the push, and I didn't see the hole, so I stumbled straight down."

I swallowed the feelings of guilt coming up. I'd made a grievous error that could have got my friends into trouble too.

Katy stepped up to me and flashed her torch on my face, my shoulders, and my arms.

"No blood? No cuts?"

The scratches on my back stung, and a bump was growing on my head, but I didn't have time to think about my injuries.

"I'm good," I said, rustling up a smile for my friend. "Still standing and walking."

I turned to Tetyana.

"I bet Theodore Henry is inside the mine."

"We will come back at daylight," she said, shining her torch inside. "There are too many variables right now. If we go in, I want us to be able to come out safely."

Katy gave a gasp.

We turned to her.

"Poor Stella and Tank," she said. "We've totally forgotten them."

"I don't like them being stuck alone in the train either," I said. "We have to get them into the church."

Tetyana nodded. "Lead the way down," she said. "I'll take the rear this time."

I turned around and walked back to the pipeline. If Theodore Henry was imprisoned in the shaft, he'd have to wait. I only hoped he would be alive when we returned.

The longer Stella and Tank were on their own, the higher the risk we'd find them harmed or dead. Whoever was on this mountain wasn't fooling around, I thought as a shiver ran down my back.

Our descent was faster.

This time, we had our flashlights on and swiveled them around to make sure our path was clear, and no unwanted interlopers were hanging out on the slope.

We hastened our pace, treading silently. When we reached the town, we hurried into the church to see if anyone was missing.

The candles were still flickering, but the fire had died down.

It seemed like everyone was fast asleep on the benches, buried under blankets in human-shaped bundles. Dwayne's snores were loud, but the noise didn't seem to be keeping anyone up.

We stepped around them, looking at the feet jutting from under their covers to identify them. All were accounted for. It was time to get the final two in the train to safety.

"Let's go," said Tetyana in an urgent whisper. "I don't like us hanging out in the woods for too long."

Tetyana took the lead, heading back toward the train tracks like a bloodhound would find their way home.

We moved fast through the woods. In the dark, the forest looked sinister, but the thought of more people facing danger propelled us forward.

It was a relief to get out of the woods and onto the valley where the tracks were.

The locomotive now looked like the empty hull of an ancient steel monster.

Disabled.

Useless.

As much as I had disliked Connor McNamara, I felt a twinge of sadness, knowing his charred body lay within the engine car.

"It's so quiet," whispered Katy, as we hurried to the dining car door which lay wide open.

Robin was right.

The train was a wreck. The door was barely holding on to the hinges.

I jumped up the steps, shining my torch in front of me.

I was about to call out Stella's name, when I realized what we'd come to.

"Oh no," said Katy, putting a hand over her mouth.

"Frigging hell," said Tetyana, as she scanned her flashlight around the dining car. "A hurricane blasted through the *inside* of the train."

"This place was intact after the explosion," I said, staring at the overturned tables and the crystal glasses smashed on the carpet. "Something happened after we left."

"Someone raided the train," said Tetyana, stepping gingerly around a chair lying on its side.

A cold shiver went down my back as I realized what we might find. I didn't want to discover human casualties in here.

"Stella Green?" I hollered, my heart ticking fast.

Silence.

"Tank?" I shouted.

Making sure not to step on the broken glass, we threaded our way through the dining car into the kitchenette.

It was my turn to gasp out loud.

Someone had pulled out every drawer and flung the contents onto the floor.

"Why would anyone do this?" asked Katy as she stepped up to an overturned fruit bowl, the fruit smashed on the ground like someone had stepped on them.

"Stella Green!" I shouted, my stomach sinking with every step I took toward the sleeping car.

Please let them be alive.

Tetyana yanked the shower doors open and shook her head.

We kept moving.

If we'd thought the dining car and the kitchen were a jumbled mess, we hadn't been prepared for the sleeping carriage. It was like a tornado had ripped through each of our rooms.

All the cabin doors had been flung open, and someone had ransacked each one of them.

"Stella?" I called out as I stepped into her room.

It was empty.

"Tank?" shouted Katy from behind me. "Where are you?"

We went from cabin to cabin, checking inside the closets and toilets, but they were all in the same condition.

"They were looking for something," I said, surveying the clutter.

"What is it?" asked Katy.

I shook my head. I wished I knew.

"The storage car," said Tetyana as she stepped toward the end, her weapon at the ready. We followed her to the last train carriage.

"Geez!" exclaimed Tetyana.

Whenever Tetyana got unsettled, I knew things were bad.

I stepped inside the luggage compartment.

They hadn't spared our bags. Books, clothes, and shoes lay strewn all over while the emptied bags had been stacked at one end. It was like someone had meticulously gone through them, one by one.

One thing was clear.

The train had been turned upside down, but there was no one here any more.

"Oh no," said Katy. "They kidnapped Stella and Tank too."

Chapter Thirty-seven

"Someone was searching for something they think is on the train, and they're willing to kidnap or kill to get it," I said.

"What were they looking for?" asked Katy.

I shook my head. "I wish I knew."

Something was nagging in the back of my mind, something I saw in the private cabins just a minute ago.

"Wait, I missed it," I muttered, as I turned around and stepped back into the sleeping car with Katy and Tetyana at my heels.

I peeked into each room, shining my light on the beds, along the walls, and inside the now wide-open washrooms and closets.

It was when I got to Theodore's cabin that I realized what I'd been looking for.

"The paintings!" I said, swiveling my torch around the small space.

Theodore's wheelchair was lying against the bed. His pill bottles had been turned over, their contents scattered. The bedsheets had been ripped off and his clothes were littered across the floor.

I'd been so shocked at seeing the chaotic scene, it hadn't registered at first.

But I noticed it now.

"Someone took them," I said, shining my flashlight on the wall they had been leaning against, only that morning.

"Why would they mess up the whole train to find those paintings?" said Katy. "They're huge. They didn't have to rip the sheets off or mess up the kitchen like that."

"No," I said. "They were looking for something else, something much smaller. Maybe they found it. Maybe they didn't."

I turned to my friends.

"There's a clue here, staring in our faces. We're just not seeing it."

"Wait," said Tetyana. "How did they carry the paintings up the mountain or wherever they took them, anyway?"

I was about to answer when a loud thud on the roof made me jump.

Tetyana sprang up, her weapon aimed forward.

The thumping got louder, like someone was throwing rocks at the train.

I pointed my gun at the ceiling and whirled around wildly, my heart hammering.

What now?

Without a word, Tetyana dashed toward the dining car. Katy and I ran after her.

It sounded like an angry family of giants were stomping on the roof.

"Hail!" shouted Katy.

I spun around to face her.

"The hailstorm, remember?" she yelled over the din. "Robin said it was coming this way. Dwayne said he'd planned for us to get to the next town before all this hell broke loose."

Tetyana lowered her weapon. She was at the opened dining car door, a dejected look on her face.

"Like we need this crap now," she said as solid rocks of ice, the size of golf balls, rained down.

"Better now than when we were up at the mine," I said, reaching over to the nearest window and pulling up the shutter to look outside.

Rocky pellets mixed with sleets of icy rain clattered all around, deafening us.

Suddenly, a flash of lightning lit up the sky, followed by a roar of thunder.

As we watched with our mouths open, the tree, the same one we'd taken shelter under after the boiler explosion, caught on fire.

"Oh no!" cried Katy.

The branches withered and curled in the heat. The snow melted fast, but had no effect on the fire that was now engulfing the trunk. My eyes went to the trees next to it, sweat rolling down my back.

"Is this the start of a forest fire?" I said. "We need to warn the others inside the church."

"The ice rain will reduce the chances of that spreading," said Tetyana, pointing through the window. "Look, the tree's almost vaporized but the others haven't caught it. It's localized."

We peered through the hailstones raining down at the burning skeleton of the massive tree.

It had taken all but a few minutes to destroy something that had probably stood in that spot for decades, maybe even a century. If this had been summer, the consequences of that one lightning strike would have been disastrous.

"These are baseball-sized rocks," said Tetyana, looking up at the ceiling where we could hear the hail battering the metal roof.

Another flash of lightning cut across the dark sky, blinding us for a second. Then came the thunder, louder and longer than the explosion we'd heard when the boiler blew up.

I withdrew from the window to take stock. It would be impossible to trundle through the dark woods now. We'd slip and slide to our death, if we didn't get incinerated by a stray lightning bolt first.

"Hey!" shouted Tetyana.

The wind had suddenly cut sideways, ramming the hail into the carriage through the open door.

Tetyana jumped down the entrance.

"Get back in here," shouted Katy. "You'll get hit on the head."

But our friend was focused on her task. She reached over and grabbed the edge of the metal door hanging on its hinges. Then, keeping her head down as the stones pounded her, she backed up the steps slowly, gripping the door by its side.

Inch by inch, she pulled the door back into place.

"Rope!" she yelled.

I whipped up the closest tablecloth.

"Good enough," said Tetyana, as she snatched it from my hands. Katy and I held on to the door as she slipped the cloth around the handle and tied it to the nearest steel bar.

The hail was still hammering on us, but the sound was muted.

"We're not going anywhere in this," said Tetyana, rubbing her head and wincing.

"Are we sure we want to spend the night here, guys?" asked Katy, a slight note of panic in her voice.

"We're better off inside here, than tracking through the woods right now," I said.

Katy gave a visible shudder.

"Poor Stella and Tank," she said, shaking her head. "I feel like we're abandoning them."

My stomach sank at those words.

We'd abandoned Theodore Henry too. What a mess this mission had turned into. I kicked myself for not having foreseen these events.

Then again, how could anyone have imagined any of this happening in their wildest nightmares?

"What are we going to do now?" said Katy, looking at the chaotic mess around us.

Tetyana reached over to the nearest window, checked its latch and pulled down the shutter.

"We're going to secure the train," she said, her lips in a thin, grim line.

Chapter Thirty-eight

"Stay back!"

I jerked awake, my heart pounding.

It was dark, and I was lying on something soft. For a second, I couldn't figure out where I was.

The sound of something metallic crackling came from somewhere.

Static.

I whirled around blindly.

Where am I?

Then came a shout, hollow and loud, like someone was screaming through a megaphone.

"I said, stay back! We're armed."

That was Katy's voice.

That was when I remembered. We were inside the train.

I scrambled out of bed and jumped toward the door to see Tetyana dashing through the entrance to the dining car. I ran after her, my heart racing.

Katy was on her watch shift in the dining car up front, while Tetyana and I had retired to our cabins to nab a few hours of sleep until our shifts started.

Are we under attack?

Katy shot us a frightened look as we rushed in.

Tetyana already had her gun in her hand and was whirling around.

"Where are they?" she hollered.

"I... I saw something outside," stammered Katy, pointing through the window which faced out to the woods.

She had her sidearm in one hand and the train engineer's megaphone in the other.

Tetyana had dug it out of the rubble in the engine room earlier. She had handed it to Katy with strict instructions to watch for any movement nearby and alert us immediately.

"What did you see?" I said, looking out the window that opened up to the woods, behind which lay the abandoned mining town.

"I swear I saw a shadow by the trees."

Tetyana and I peered out for a minute, our eyes scanning the area.

The hailstorm had stopped within a half hour, but the ice rain was still coming down. It was hard to see anything, and even harder to make out a shadow behind the line of trees.

Did Katy imagine the shadow?

I watched the rain come down, shuddering to think of the skating rink that was forming around the tracks, one we'd have to navigate tomorrow, hopefully without breaking our necks.

No one in their right mind could be outside in this weather.

Even a crazed killer.

"Are you sure you saw someone?" I said, turning to my friend. "Was it a man? Tall? Short?"

Katy gave me a glazed look. Her eyes were red and lined, like she was ready to drop at a moment's notice.

"I saw something move."

"Sure it wasn't the Sasquatch?" said Tetyana, turning to her with a wonky grin. "You tend to see shadows everywhere, Kate."

I reached over and put a hand on my friend's shoulder.

"It's time for a break, hun. I'll take over."

I took the megaphone from Katy's hands.

"Get some rest," I said. "You need it."

I needed some too, but I wasn't going to say anything, or my friends would force me to lie down.

The adrenaline that had been coursing through my veins had subsided. For a while, it had been easy to forget the crushing pain in my back and the throbbing bump on my head.

But now, it seemed like all the nerves in my body had woken up and were crying out in pain. With little sleep, and the shock of confronting one madness after the other in this wilderness, I felt every jolt from the past forty-eight hours.

I shooed Katy off her perch and took over.

Tetyana nodded.

"We'll check first thing tomorrow morning," she said. "We'll find what or who the heck was hanging around out there."

"Could have been Matt," said Katy. "I don't trust him."

"I'm not sure it was anyone from the church," I said. "Nobody could have come out in the hail and ice rain."

Katy gave me a frightened look.

"That means there's a total whack job waiting to get us all."

I nudged her away from the table. "You get some rest. Tetyana and I'll finish the shifts and we'll face whatever tomorrow brings us."

With a dejected sigh, Katy turned around. Tetyana put a hand on her shoulder and ushered her back to the sleeping car.

I was alone in the dining carriage now.

I shifted on the table, trying to find the most comfortable position where I had a good vantage point of both windows that looked out to the two sides of the train.

There wasn't much to see in the pitch darkness and rain, but it was better than being taken in surprise while asleep.

I touched the comforting steel ridges of my Glock lying on my lap, thankful for our firepower and even more grateful the three of us had stayed together throughout this ordeal.

A shiver went through me, and I pulled my jacket closer around my shoulders.

It was getting cold fast.

The engine disaster had taken out power, light, and heat. We had got around using our flashlights so far. The spare batteries we'd packed in our bags were still there. Surprisingly, the person or people who'd turned our cabins inside out and pried open all of our luggage hadn't taken them.

They'd even left behind our spare ammunition. Like Tetyana, I'd buried my extra cartridge cases deep in my suitcase. We had removed them from their original packaging, but anyone who knew anything about firearms would have identified those cold gray utility boxes instantly.

But they had been left behind too.

Strange.

If this had been the work of desperate individuals looking for survival gear, our batteries and ammo would have been snatched up in a red hot second.

No. They had been searching for something else.

Something far more valuable.

But what?

I shivered again.

It seemed like the temperature was dropping by the second. I was glad I wasn't outside, being pounded by the pouring ice rain, but the cold was seeping through my layers.

This was going to be a long shift.

After a half an hour of shivering on the table, trying hard to not fall asleep, I looked around for something warmer to huddle under. Even a tablecloth would do, I thought, as I peered around the dark car.

That was when I spotted it.

Chapter Thirty-nine

C onnor's jacket.

It was draped over his chair.

The man had been a stickler about everything, a pain of a passenger who loved to throw tantrums and abuse everyone around him.

I jumped off the table and stepped up to his chair. I plucked the jacket and wrapped it around my shoulders.

It was a warm, fur-lined winter jacket specially made for this region. I wasn't a fan of the fur, but it would have to do. Given Connor had been an extra-large size, and I was an extra petite, it acted like the perfect comforter for me.

With Connor's jacket draped over my shoulders, I trundled back to my watch position.

I settled back on the table, shaking out my tired and frozen limbs.

My mind was warming up again. I desperately wanted to figure this puzzle out. Our lives depended on it.

Something told me all the pieces were there, clearly laid out in front of us, except we weren't seeing things for what they were.

What am I missing?

Keeping one eye on the window, I racked my brain.

I'd been in sticky situations before, but never in my life had I imagined I'd be stuck in the middle of an ice-coated valley in one of the most remote regions of Alaska.

Miles away from civilization.

I pulled the jacket down to cover my cold knees, before I resettled myself on the hard table.

"Ouch," I muttered as something stabbed my thigh.

As I pulled the jacket flap away, it hit the table with a clunk.

What was that?

I touched the flap and felt something hard inside. I reached into the left pocket. It wasn't deep and there didn't seem to be much.

First came a rustle of paper, then came something pointy at the bottom. It was jagged, and it moved, like it was in pieces.

It wasn't a gun. That, I was sure of.

Against Tetyana's strict instructions, I turned on my flashlight, and switched it to the lowest setting. Then, I reached into the pocket to pull everything out.

The crumpled piece of paper came out first.

It was a printout of Connor's flight from Anchorage to Seattle. I recognized the flight number from the travel itinerary Theodore had shared with us.

Doctor Wilson's slurred words flickered through my mind.

Theodore Henry was never supposed to arrive in Seattle.

What did he mean by that?

I reached into the pocket again to pull out that clunky jagged thing that hit against the table. I fumbled around. I could feel it but couldn't reach it.

But it was there.

Placing the flashlight on the table, I took off the jacket and turned the pocket inside out, expecting it to fall out. But nothing came out.

That was when I saw what he'd done.

Through my flashlight's pale light, I examined the stitches at the bottom. The thread was in the same color as the jacket, like Connor had concealed a part of his pocket. Whatever I was feeling had been secured behind those stitches.

Why would he do this?

I pulled the Tanto knife out of my boots and got to work. It took a while to get through the thread as I didn't want to damage whatever was inside. Feeling slightly guilty for having the light on against my security expert's advice, I plucked the stitches out, one by one.

After pulling the last thread out, I put my knife on the table, and pried the false opening. Something soft touched my fingertips.

I plucked it out.

It was a small velvet pouch, like the ones Katy liked to carry whenever she wanted to change into nicer jewelry for an after-work party.

I pulled on the drawstrings of the pouch. Inside was a white cloth-like tissue, the type you'd find in a box that held a fine Montblanc.

I took out the tissue gingerly, pulling it out of the bag, and turned the pouch upside down.

Six translucent crystals fell into my lap.

My eyes widened.

I stared at them, mute and immobile, but my brain was buzzing.

Diamonds?

I turned my torch one setting higher, picked up a stone and held it to the light. It was rough, yet to be cut and polished. I was no lapidarist, but I was sure these weren't cubic zirconium.

My heart beat a tick faster.

Are these really diamonds?

Is that what they were looking for?

How much were these worth? How did they end up in a false bottom in Connor's jacket?

I fumbled in my pocket to pull out my phone, but remembered we had no internet connection here. With a resigned sigh, I scrunched my forehead, trying to recall all the research I'd dug up before coming on this trip.

Alaska wasn't diamond country.

That prestige was held by Canada's Northwest Territories. Canadian diamonds were popular for their high-quality clear stones that weren't steeped in blood, unlike the blood diamonds of Africa.

But did someone discover diamonds here?

If anyone had found these precious stones in Alaska, the media would be abuzz, talking about it nonstop. But I hadn't come across anything that even hinted at such a discovery, other than how Alaskan prospectors jealously regarded their counterparts across the border.

Did Connor McNamara dig up these diamonds at the Black Eagle Mines? Did he keep it a secret from his employer and friend?

Or were Theodore Henry and Connor McNamara in on this together, but had kept it quiet from everyone else?

I tried to put myself in their shoes.

Knowing the way they operated, I would expect them to keep things under wraps until they got confirmation of these stones' value. They'd leak the news out slowly to build intrigue and anticipation.

Then, and only then, would they talk about it with great fanfare, with a mega marketing campaign to hype up their value. I could see them exploit the romantic notion of finding diamonds, of all things, in Alaska, to its hilt.

So what were these doing in Connor's jacket? Was Theodore carrying his own stash? Was that why he was kidnapped?

There had to be a miner at Black Eagle Mines who knew about these stones. I suspected neither Theodore nor Connor had gone down those shafts for ages. That meant someone else was aware of them.

Who were they? What did Connor or Theodore do to make them keep this a secret?

I had so many questions, but no answers.

I turned the stones in my hands, wishing they could tell me their story.

"Why the hell is the light on?"

I jumped a foot high.

Tetyana was standing by the threshold of the dining car.

A warm flush crept up my neck. I was supposed to be the watchdog on duty, and here I was, flashlight turned full on, and I hadn't even heard her step up to only ten feet from me.

"What are you doing up?" I asked, trying to mask my guilty face.

"Not getting any sleep tonight," she said with a resigned sigh, strolling over, rubbing her forehead. "I swear I'm going mental. My brain's going nonstop."

"Mine too," I said. I picked up the biggest stone from my lap and held it up. "Especially after I found these."

Tetyana came closer and peered at the stone. She grabbed her own flashlight from her pocket and turned it on.

The stone twinkled in the light of our two torches.

She let out a low whistle.

"Is that what I think it is?" she said in a stunned whisper.

"This is the linchpin," I said, waving the stone in front of her eyes. "This explains why everything's going berserk around us."

Chapter Forty

Tetyana and I took turns keeping watch, every three hours till dawn.

I'd handed the stones to Tetyana for safe-keeping.

She was the battle-hardened warrior in our team. Whoever wanted them would have to put up a good fight, and few people won when they dared to take her on.

She tucked the velvet pouch in the breast pocket of her Kevlar vest. I knew she wouldn't take it off for a shower if she could get away with it, but none of us were going to get showers soon.

Or sleep.

Or food.

The rain stopped close to dawn, leaving a thick sheath of ice around the tracks. Icicles had formed overnight on the tree branches and along the outside of the train, looking like rows of translucent daggers.

Angry storm clouds still hovered overhead, threatening another downpour. I just hoped it wouldn't hail again.

A shudder went through me as I realized Matt's ski-plane had been moored by the frozen lake, exposed to the elements. That plastic tarp wouldn't help against those baseball-sized rocks that came raining down.

There goes our ticket out of here, I thought. The freight train was still a question mark, even more so in this harsh weather.

The snowmobile could be our only option, if we could get the fuel from the plane in it and get it to work. Even then, it wouldn't guarantee a smooth ride to the nearest outpost. It was a risky proposition.

I stirred and sat up.

There's always a way.

Think, girl, think.

"Breakfast?" came a voice from the doorway.

I turned to see Katy standing by the door with a small plate in her hands.

"You guys made me sleep through the night," she said, coming over.

"One of us has to be alert," I said, with a smile.

"Peanut butter and jelly," she said. "Everything else is splattered and stomped on the floor."

"You didn't scrape this butter off the ground, did you?"

"Some things were spared by the psycho gravedigger."

I took the sandwich gratefully.

Katy leaned against the table, a conspiratorial look coming over her face.

"Tetyana told me about the diamonds," she whispered, as if there would be anyone else to hear us. "That's why the psycho turned this place upside down, didn't they?"

I nodded.

"The only reason they didn't touch the peanut butter and jelly jars was because they were sealed." Katy pointed at my sandwich. "Guess they didn't expect unopened bottles to contain the diamonds. They left them exactly where I put them last."

That was when it dawned on me.

"Hey, Katy, does this strike you as the work of an amateur?"

"Amateur?"

"A professional would have found the stones. I mean, I did."

"Sure, but—"

I gestured around the dining car.

"Right now, it looks like a crazed Tasmanian devil raised hell through the train."

"I was thinking the same."

Katy and I spun around.

It was Tetyana. She came over, eyeing my sandwich.

"Thinking the same about what?" asked Katy.

"This wasn't the work of a professional," said Tetyana. "Unless they wanted to make it look like it wasn't."

"That would require some planning," I said, breaking my sandwich in two and handing a piece to Tetyana.

"Exactly," said Tetyana, taking it from me and leaning against the wall.

"Exactly *what*?" said Katy.

"Think about it," said Tetyana, taking a bite. "They dug a body from a recent grave and dumped it on the tracks to stop a train to kidnap a mining baron. All calculated to happen just before a hailstorm. A strategic plan, but their methods were messy."

"Who would do that?" said Katy.

"Whoever it is, they planned this in advance," I said. "They knew of Theodore's itinerary. They knew the stones would be on the train. They just didn't know where. I think I have an idea who that could be."

"*Who?*" blurted Katy.

"Anyone who came on the train with us," I said. "They could be in cahoots with the two people we met on the mountain."

"Are you saying everyone on the train is now a suspect?" said Katy, giving me a wide-eyed look. "Dwayne? Robin? Stella? The doctor? None of them look like professional jewelry heist thieves."

"They don't exactly tattoo it on their heads," I said.

"This is so twisted."

"Stella is a geologist," I said, still sorting this out in my head. "She knows all about precious stones, right?"

"It can't be her," said Katy, shaking her head. "She was the most shocked when everything went haywire. Didn't you see? She was so frozen, she could hardly talk."

Katy was always so trusting.

"She was with me in the kitchen when the boiler blew," she continued. "She was telling me how much she liked to hike up here and said she was going to give online dating a try and settle down in Alaska. She was opening up to me. She looks aloof, but she's nice."

"Her doctorate thesis was on precious metals in this state," I said, trying to recollect my research. "She would know more about mining, probably more than the old veterans in the company."

"I just can't imagine her being a gravedigger or a kidnapper," said Katy. "Maybe she knew about the find. Maybe that's why she and Connor were going to Seattle. To get the stones valuated while Theodore got his cancer treatment."

Tetyana was now peering out the window, a frown on her face.

"You have a point," I said to Katy. "This could have been a legitimate find and the company execs were just trying to find a market for them in the city, when someone ambushed the train. It was someone who knew about the discovery and wanted to steal the—"

"Hey!" shouted Tetyana.

I jumped down from the table, my heart racing.

Tetyana slammed the window open, her Glock pointing out.

"Stay right where you are!" she hollered.

I rushed to the window just in time to see a man emerge from the woods. Tetyana must have caught his silhouette from behind the tree line.

"I told you there was someone hiding back there," said Katy, joining us.

"Tank?" I said.

"Hands up!" hollered Tetyana.

With a shocked look, Tank raised his arms in the air.

"Watch him," said Tetyana, as she stepped away from the window and marched toward the door. She untied the knot and pushed it open.

"Approach," she called out, aiming her Glock at his head.

A panicked expression overcame Tank's face. He took a hesitant step forward, as if he wished he hadn't left the safety of the woods.

"He's limping," said Katy, as we watched him navigate the icy ground toward the tracks. "What happened to his face?"

I peered at him. "My gosh. Looks like he barely survived a bar fight."

Chapter Forty-one

T ank wobbled across the icy ground.

Tetyana waited until he was within six feet from the train and jumped down. He took a startled step backward, slipped, and came crashing down on his back.

Tetyana skated across the ice toward him, grabbed him by the collar and pulled him up, her weapon at his head.

"Please don't hurt me," cried Tank, his hands shaking in the air. "Please let me go."

He was blubbering, tears running down his face.

I dashed toward the open door and popped my head out.

"Hey, Tetyana," I called out. "Let him come in."

She frisked him before shoving him roughly toward the door.

"Get in."

Tank didn't need to be told twice. He stepped into the train, trembling. Tetyana came after him and shut the door.

"You can put your hands down," I said.

"Are... you sure?" he stammered, glancing at Tetyana's gun that was still pointed at him. He was shivering so badly his teeth were chattering.

"Sit down, Tank," said Katy, pulling a chair for him.

He landed on it heavily, placed his arms on his thighs and slouched over like he was about to throw up. I wondered if we should rustle up a bucket for him.

I leaned over and examined the black eye and the bruises on his forehead.

"Where were you last night?" I said.

He looked up, his eyes moving anxiously from me to Tetyana and back.

"What happened?" I asked again, in a softer tone. "You can talk to us."

"I... we... this is a crazy place," he stammered. "When do we get out of here?"

"Spotted another ghost in a white dress, did you?" said Tetyana. She pointed at his face. "Did she give you a big whooping?"

"What?" he said, looking at her in surprise. "No... no. Something's going on here. Just please make it stop."

"Who hit you, Tank?" said Katy.

"I don't know. It was dark. I couldn't see."

With a heavy sigh, he slumped again, head down, and rocked back and forth. Tetyana gave an impatient hiss and shook her head. I knew what she was thinking.

Pathetic behavior for a hired bodyguard.

"Hey, Tank?" said Katy, pulling a second chair next to him. She sat down and put a hand on his arm. "You can trust us. Tell us what happened."

"I... d... don't know," he stuttered.

"What happened after we left to find Theodore? Start from the top."

He looked up at her with a pained expression. Katy tilted her head like a psychologist trying to coax a patient to open up.

"It was... Dwayne and Robin...."

"Yes?"

"Dwayne and Robin went looking for you about a half hour after you left," he said. "They said a bad storm was on its way. Said we couldn't sleep in here and they were going to find a place for us to sleep at night."

"What happened after they left?" said Katy, her hand still on his arm.

"Doctor Wilson took a bottle from the liquor cabinet and sat on the steps. He sat there drinking, and staring out into the woods. Didn't talk to me or anything."

"What about Stella?"

"Doctor Green locked herself up in her room. I was so scared, but she didn't want to talk to me either. I sat by her door. I didn't know what else to do...."

He rubbed his face as if in frustration, then winced and touched his swollen forehead gingerly.

"What happened then?"

"About ten minutes later, I heard someone call out from the woods," he said, pointing out the window. "I thought it was Doctor Wilson, so I went to look. But he was gone and someone was shouting."

"Shouting?" I said. "Are you sure it wasn't the doctor?"

"Sounded like someone else." Tank looked up miserably. "I had no idea who it was, but it wasn't Doctor Wilson. They were shouting *help, help.*"

Tetyana and I exchanged a glance.

Was it the same person who lured us up the mountain? Had they played the same game with Tank? Or did he just make that up?

Those bruises on his face looked real enough.

Tank wiped his nose with his sleeve.

"I ran back in and banged on Doctor Green's door. I told her someone needed our help."

"Did she come out?" said Katy.

He shook his head.

"I knew I should go out and look, but there was no one. I walked up and down the tracks and I tried to follow a trail inside the woods too, but I saw nothing."

He sat up, animated.

"And then, and then, I heard a plane. I swear I heard a plane. You gotta believe me."

"We believe you," I said.

"I was sure it landed somewhere nearby. I tried to find it. I walked and walked, but the woods got really thick, and then I couldn't even find my way back...."

His shoulders slumped again.

"What did you do?" said Katy.

"I kept walking for hours. I was shouting your names too. Did you hear me?"

We shook our heads.

"There was a major storm last night," said Tetyana. "You'd be dead from hypothermia if you stayed outside the entire night."

She leaned toward him, scowling.

"Tell us the truth, Tank. Where were you really?"

"I'm telling you the truth," he said, his voice several notches higher.

She glared.

Tank spluttered.

"It... it got dark real fast. I thought I could take shelter under a big tree. I think I fell asleep because I woke up and someone was there."

"Someone?" I said.

He nodded. Tears were rolling down his face again.

"Couldn't see anything, but I felt it. They started hitting me. I don't know why. Then it started to hail, and they were gone. I thought it was a nightmare, but man, I felt every hit."

"What did they look like?" I said. "Did you recognize them?"

"It happened so fast. They just punched me in the face." He gave me a frightened look. "I didn't have time to think, and then the hail started. It was crazy. Lightning too. Brutal. I couldn't stay in the woods. So I ran and ran until I came to this strange place, halfway up the mountain."

He shuddered, and took a raspy breath in, like he was trying to contain a sob.

"It was like a ghost town or something. Everything was locked up, but I found a cabin. A shed. I crept inside and took cover. I think I passed out there."

"Why didn't you go into the church?" I said.

"Church? What church?" he replied, his brow furrowed. "It was hailing so bad, I wasn't looking around. I crawled into the shed and stayed put."

He turned to each one of us.

"I know this sounds like crazy talk. I swear I'm not making this up. I don't know what's going on, but something's out there trying to get us all."

We stared at him for a minute. Unless he was a superb actor, it seemed like he was telling the truth.

I gestured around us. "Any idea what happened in here?"

Tank jerked his head back and glanced around him, as if seeing the chaos for the first time.

His jaw dropped as his eyes swept over the overturned chairs, the broken glass, the liquor cabinet opened wide with its contents strewn all over the place.

"The storm did this?" he said.

"The storm didn't come inside the train," I said. "But someone came in looking for something. Do you know who that would be?"

His face turned pale. "Someone smashed this place up? Why?"

"That's exactly our question," snapped Tetyana.

He looked up, fear etched on his face. "Where's Doctor Green? I left her alone. What happened?"

"We were hoping you could tell us that," said Tetyana.

With a loud groan, Tank put his head into his hands.

"I failed. I told Mr. Henry I've never been a bodyguard before. I told him I'm not the man for the job, but he said he didn't trust anyone else."

"Why did Theodore Henry hire you?" I said. It was the question on everyone's minds.

Tank looked up.

"Mr. Henry is my uncle."

Chapter Forty-two

M*r. Henry?*

"Do you address all your uncles formally?" I asked.

"He told me I have to be professional on the job, so I thought...." Tank paused and shook his head. "Look, I didn't even want the job. He told me if I took it, he'd pay for college. My football scholarship fell through. That's the only reason..."

Tank looked down with a sigh.

"He knew I didn't have any training, but he said I looked like a bodyguard. Besides, he couldn't trust anyone anymore."

He looked up, his face scrunched.

"He told me he hired you for the train ride, to protect him. Said his lawyers recommended your firm."

We fell silent for a minute, absorbing this news.

"How old are you, Tank?" I said.

"Nineteen, why?"

Theodore Henry had hired his own nephew, an untrained teenager who looked like a linebacker, to watch his back. That explained Tank's erratic behavior.

He pointed a shaking finger at us.

"He told me you were going to keep him safe. Doctor Green too. Where's everyone? Why aren't you looking for them?"

"We're doing our best," I said in a subdued tone. "We're grappling with many missing pieces, but I promise you we'll find your uncle and we'll find Stella."

He gave me an earnest look.

"What about Doctor Wilson?" he said, his voice cracking. "What are you going to do about him?"

"He's safe and sound," I said with a thankful sigh. "He's with the others in the church."

Tank's eyes bulged.

"The church? But I found him this morning." He looked like he was about to hyperventilate. "That's why I came here looking for you."

I narrowed my eyes.

"What do you mean you *found* him?"

"He was near the shed this morning. I swear it was him. I thought he was sleeping, but someone got him too."

A chill went through me.

Tank looked at us, all color drained from his face.

"Doctor Wilson's dead," he said.

⁂

It took us longer to hike through the ice glazed woods. Once we reached it, I stared at the ghost town through the pale early morning light.

The church simmered in the foreground, eerily quiet. The front door remained closed. There was no movement and there was no yellow light seeping through those aging windows. I wondered if anyone was still inside.

Then again, daylight was streaming through the grounds, which meant it was impossible to see any remnants of candlelight.

Tank hadn't been lying.

Doctor Wilson was lying facedown, with his legs splayed out, only twenty feet from the shed. A frosty steam rose from the hard glacial ground around his prone body, a reminder of the ice storm from the night before.

"Check his pockets," I said to Katy as I picked up the doctor's limp wrist.

Tetyana crouched across from me to inspect the body for bruises, bumps, or blood.

Tank was standing behind us, teeth chattering from the cold, shuffling his feet nervously, and rubbing his hands to stay warm. He'd refused to walk over and check the church to see who was inside, giving me a terrified look when I asked him.

Either he was petrified or was keeping a surreptitious eye on us. By the way he glanced from side to side like he was expecting something to jump out of the woods and devour him, he looked more afraid than anything else.

Doctor Wilson was still clutching the bottle of vodka in his hand, but his grip had loosened now. I double-checked his pulse on both wrists and on his neck.

There was nothing.

I studied his half-turned face. It was as white as the ground he was lying on.

"I'd say he's been here for a few hours," said Tetyana.

Why on earth would he leave the warm church and stumble out in the dead of the night?

I let out a defeated sigh.

"Either he walked out last night, which I don't think he did, even given his state." I frowned. "Or someone lured him outside."

"Look what I found."

Tetyana and I turned toward Katy, who was squatting by his feet.

Katy extended her arm toward us, her palm turned up.

"Check this out."

She was holding an opened yellow plastic bottle in one hand and a small pile of white tablets in her other hand.

"Pills?" said Tetyana.

"It was in his coat pocket," she said.

"Wait," I said, scrunching my forehead. "Where have I seen that bottle before?"

"In Mr. Henry's cabin," said Tank, speaking for the first time since we left the train. "He has a stack of these in his room."

Katy turned the label toward us. "Well, what do you know? This belonged to Theodore Henry."

I raised an eyebrow. "What was Doctor Wilson doing with it?"

"He was his doctor, wasn't he?" said Katy. "Maybe he kept an extra stash for his patient, just in case."

"In his coat pocket?"

Katy shrugged.

"What are these?" said Tetyana, taking a pill from Katy's outstretched hand and sniffing it.

"Vicodin," said Katy, squinting at the label. "A strong painkiller."

"Not over-the-counter medication, then?" I asked.

Katy shook her head. "This is serious stuff. You have to be in killer pain to get a prescription for these."

I looked at the bottle of alcohol in Doctor Wilson's hands.

"If he'd been mixing vodka with these pills," I said, "and he'd walked out in the middle of the freezing storm last night, that would have done it."

"That's plain suicide," said Tetyana.

"He would have known better than to do that, even if he'd been dead drunk, wouldn't he?" said Katy. "He was a doctor, after all."

"Either that," I said, "or someone brought him out of the church and let him die out here."

Tank gave us a wild, childlike look.

"Someone did him in last night?"

"Hard to say," I replied. "We should talk to the others."

Katy slipped the pills back into the bottle and twisted the cap shut. We stood up, one by one, wiping the damp snow from our clothes.

"What do we do with Doctor Wilson's body?" asked Tank.

"We don't touch him," I said.

I pitied the medical examiner whose job it would be to remove him in these temperatures. The last thing I would want to do was to rip a dead body off an icy surface.

"The cold will preserve the body as is," said Tetyana. "Best to leave him where he is, so the authorities can determine the cause."

The sound of a heavy door creaking made us spin around.

Someone was opening the church door.

It was Matt Ryder.

Chapter Forty-three

"Ahoy, there!" called out Matt.

No one replied.

He jumped down the church steps and walked our way, hands thrust in his pockets, like he was ambling into a coffee shop.

We watched him approach us in stony silence, our arms crossed. Even Tank.

Matt slowed down halfway, noticing the animosity on our faces. That was when he saw Doctor Wilson's body.

He stopped and gaped.

"What happened?"

"He's dead," I said.

"What the hell...?"

"My question, precisely," said Tetyana. "Last time we saw him, he was on a church pew near the fireplace under a warm blanket. Any idea how this happened?"

Matt put his hands on his face and rubbed his eyes like he couldn't believe what he was seeing.

"Oh, man," he said. "I... I don't understand."

I frowned. A warning flag went up, but I couldn't figure out why.

Tetyana took a step toward him, her hands on her hips.

"What did you do? Kick him right back out, after we left?"

Matt gave her a shocked look.

"What?" he said. "What are you talking about? I didn't even see him. I didn't get up until a few minutes ago."

"Is that right?" said Tetyana.

"I was dead tired, I passed out. It was so cold last night...." He was spluttering now. "I thought you guys stayed in the train."

That was when I realized what I'd missed.

He hadn't asked who the corpse belonged to. The doctor's face was turned away from him. I'd have expected Matt's first question to be who the dead man was.

Had he known the physician before? Had he recognized his coat? It was a small world up here, a place where according to Dwayne, everyone knew what everyone else had for breakfast, after all.

"Where are the others?" I said.

Matt turned to me and blinked rapidly, like he was trying to think.

"Everyone's still inside, dead to the world."

"The doctor's the one who's dead, Matt," said Katy, her voice hard.

With an angry hiss, Tetyana stepped past him and stomped toward the church.

"I'll go check," she said, as she marched away from us.

"It's not my fault," said Matt, giving Katy and me an indignant look. "I didn't know you brought him inside. I didn't hear anything."

"There was a hailstorm last night," I said. "Enough lightning and thunder to wake the devil. And you're saying you slept through it all?"

Matt spread his arms wide.

"Look, I don't know what's going on. I'm as much in the dark as anyone else." He squared his shoulders and gave me a pointed look, like he'd regained his confidence. "I got up to check on the plane and see if I could make it work, so we can get help. I'm trying to do my bit here, people."

Throwing his arms up, Matt swiveled around.

"Don't take off, you hear?" I called out as he slid down the slope, arms in the air for balance.

Katy inched toward me and dropped her voice.

"What if he flies off without us?"

I turned toward Tank.

"Don't make me go with him," he said, as soon as I looked his way. "I ain't going by myself anywhere. I swear this mountain is haunted. I'm sticking with you. You have guns."

"Where's yours?" I said. "You had one, didn't you?"

He shrugged. "Dropped it in the woods last night. Looked for it everywhere, but couldn't find it. I was trying not to get pounded by the hail."

I looked down at the doctor's body. We couldn't move him, but I didn't want to leave him alone here either.

Dwayne had warned us about coming into the woods, saying animals who'd normally hunt for food could resort to carrion after a long hibernation.

Those lonely wolf howls I heard up in the mountain echoed in my head. What did wolves eat?

I gave my head a shake, realizing it wasn't wolves I needed to be concerned about.

"Hey, Tank," I said, "do polar bears roam around here?"

He shook his head and hugged himself tighter. "Never heard of one near here. Seen them on ice floes out at sea."

We stood in a semicircle around the dead body, my brain furiously trying to figure out our next steps.

How did the doctor die? Was this suicide?

He had told us to leave him alone last night. He had been remorseful, thinking he'd killed Theodore.

Or was this murder?

I wanted nothing more than to interrogate everyone, but I was now sure everyone was lying to us. No one was behaving how I'd expected them to.

I sighed.

We couldn't stand out here all day and night until someone came with a CSI kit.

"So, what's the plan?" said Katy.

"Our priority is to find a way out of here and alert the authorities," I said. "The longer we hang around on the mountain, the more people are going to get in trouble. Worst case, Tetyana and you can take the snowmobile to get help while I stay with everyone here."

"I don't want us to split up," said Katy, with a nervous look. "I'm with Tank on this. Think it's best we stick togeth—"

A loud roar made us whirl around.

"The plane!" cried Katy.

The sound of the propeller spluttering came from below us.

"Tank," I said. "Go inside and tell Tetyana we're going to the lake." I gave him a hard look. "Now!"

With an unhappy nod, he shuffled off.

"Let's go, Katy!" I shouted, as I pulled my Glock out.

Chapter Forty-four

The slope was icier than the day before.

Katy and I stuck to the rusty old pipeline, sliding along it, knowing we could grab it if we tumbled down. The last thing I wanted was either of us to break a leg.

The sound of the plane got louder as we got closer.

"I swear he's going to leave us behind," said Katy, panting hard. "He's just the type to do something like that."

I doubled my speed and stumbled out of the tree line onto the shores of the frozen lake, my heart in my mouth.

The plane was still where it had been parked the night before.

Even from where I was, I could see the hail dents on the wing, but the propeller was rotating fast and the whine of the engine was growing louder. The tarp was lying on the ground like Matt had hastily pulled it off and threw it down.

He was in the pilot seat, headphones on.

"He's buckling up," cried Katy.

"Hey!" I hollered, as I dashed toward the aircraft.

"What the heck are you doing?" I shouted, aiming my gun at him through the glass door.

Matt opened his door and gave me a dark look. I stepped up to him and pointed at the propellers.

"Thought you said they didn't work," I yelled.

He gave a shrug.

"Should be good for ten minutes," he yelled back over the din. "All I need is to get over the mountain, make the call, and land back down."

I frowned.

Yesterday, he'd been adamant the plane wouldn't work without extensive repairs. Today he was almost blasé about it all. Another red flag went off in the back of my head.

"I'm coming with you," I hollered.

"No way," he shouted back.

I pointed my gun at his head. "You don't have a choice."

Matt's eyes widened, but only for a second. With an angry shrug, he pushed himself back into his seat and slammed the door shut.

I skated around the back of the plane and toward the passenger door. I yanked it open and jumped in.

Whether he liked it or not, I wasn't going to let him get away with the only means of transportation we had.

Matt was playing with the dashboard dials when I got in. He continued, ignoring me.

"Where's the seat belt?" I said, feeling around the seat.

"Don't have any," he said, not looking up.

I raised an eyebrow.

"What about a headset?"

"This is a bush plane. Not United fricking Airlines."

With a shake of my head, I looked around for anything to hold on to, but there was nothing. It was going to be a loud and rough ride. I settled back in my seat, my Glock tight in my hand.

Matt tinkered another ten minutes before taking off.

I knew the engine needed a warmup, but something told me he was buying time. There were no towers to call, no radios to tune to, but I waited, watching him carefully from the corner of my eye, my weapon at the ready if he tried any funny moves.

Then, without a warning, the plane wobbled across the icy lake, and within seconds we were in the air.

I breathed a sigh of relief. The engine sounded normal, and the propellers were working fine. But another and even bigger worry crossed my mind.

Matt lied to us. What was his game?

Suddenly, the plane dipped, sending me sliding toward the door.

"Hey!" I shouted.

I thrust my weapon between my thighs and grabbed onto my seat, my fingers digging into the cloth.

Another dip.

This time I caught sight of the ground. Far below us, Katy was standing by the frozen shoreline, hand over her eyes, squinting at the sky.

But there was something else.

Just before the plane slanted to the other side, I thought I caught a shadow near the tree line.

I wanted to shout to Katy, but she'd never hear me from up here.

The plane banked sharply to the right, pushing me against the door again.

I slammed my hand against the side so I wouldn't hit my head.

"Watch it!" I shouted.

A semblance of a grin crossed Matt's face.

"If you're looking for peanuts and a hot towel, you're stiff out of luck."

The plane tilted again. I held on, one hand on the dashboard and another on my seat. We were circling over the lake and rising fast.

My brain spun, wondering if I'd imagined that shadow near the trees below us. My stomach sank at the thought of Katy being by herself with all the strange things happening on the mountain.

I cursed myself.

Why did I leave her alone?

"Matt," I hollered over the din. "We have to get back. Katy's alone down there."

"Can't descend now," he yelled, turning a dial on the console. "Might not be able to get back up."

I craned my neck, but I could no longer see the ground, just the icy blue Arctic sky on all sides. I hoped to goodness that shadow had been nothing but my imagination running wild.

I turned to Matt.

"We're high enough. Try the damn radio!"

He started fiddling with the knobs on the dashboard. I hoped he was trying to get the communications equipment to work.

I stared at the array of dials on the console, wishing I knew what they were.

I could guess some of them, but that was all that would be. Half-calculated guesses I had no business making at this altitude. Not for the first time since I started my private investigation firm, I wished I had my flying license.

Suddenly, the plane lurched like we were about to dive into the frozen lake.

My body hurled toward the dashboard. I grabbed it with both hands just in time to stop myself from crashing.

I spun around and glared at Matt.

"What the hell are you playing at?"

The engine screeched loudly, a high-pitched whine like it was about to blow.

Matt pulled the plane up and I slammed back in my seat, my heart racing.

I'd been on small aircraft before in turbulent weather, but the skies were clear.

We were descending again, nose pointing to the ground.

Fast.

My stomach leaped to my mouth.

"We're going to crash!" I shouted.

Chapter Forty-five

M att's eyes were dead ahead.

Then, from out of nowhere, his right arm flung toward me.

I ducked with a yell.

His fist slammed across my chest and banged against my door.

"What the hell?" I hollered, punching his arm.

He pulled back quickly and clutched the wheel.

My heart raced.

Where's my Glock?

Just as I grabbed my weapon from the floor well, the plane banked sharply right.

Suddenly, I was propelled in the air. My head banged against the roof.

We were descending fast.

The engine was whining loudly.

I flailed my arms, desperately trying to get back to my seat, but it was too late.

Matt flung his arm across the passenger seat again and banged on the door.

This time, it flew open.

A hurricane force wind rushed into the cockpit, deafening me. I hung on to my seat with my fingernails, my heart pounding like mad.

"What the hell are you doing?" I shouted.

The plane tilted again, violently.

I didn't have a chance.

I fell through the door, screaming.

Freezing air rushed into my lungs. I clawed at the air but there was nothing, except for the thundering roar of the wind in my ear. I wanted to shout, but I'd lost my voice.

My stomach was somersaulting like a carnival ride gone haywire. I no longer knew which way was up or down.

It felt as though I fell through the air forever, when I heard a resounding crack, like glass splintering around me.

I felt the pain for only a second before I crashed through the ice and dove into the frigid water. I flailed around, as sheer panic seeped into every cell in my body.

My lungs screamed for life, but I couldn't breathe. I gasped for air but took a mouthful of the cold water.

I'm choking.

My eyes were screwed shut. I couldn't see.

I'm going to die.

Something sharp tugged at me.

What's that?

Suddenly, I was airborne. I landed with a painful thud on a hard surface, spluttering and gasping for air.

I tried to force my eyes to open, but the icy water had numbed my lids. I reached out blindly.

Am I still underwater?

Did someone pull me out?

My chest heaved and my lungs shrilled in pain. My whole body was convulsing.

Urgent voices came from nearby.

Shouting.

Yelling.

Then, I was moving on my back, like someone was pulling me by my feet, dragging me across that hard surface.

I heard my name. It was a familiar voice.

It seemed like an eternity when the dragging stopped.

Then, something soft fell on me. Soft and warm.

I fumbled at it.

What is this?

Did I die?

Is this what happens when you go for good?

A blurred face appeared in front of my eyes. I blinked and tried to focus, but my eyes felt like they had been stabbed with a dagger.

Who is this?

They were saying something to me. I saw a mouth move, and I heard sounds, but I couldn't hear the words.

Wait. I knew that face.

Tank!

I stared at him like a zombie.

My fuzzy brain tried to think.

What's he doing here?

Is he trying to smother me?

There was someone else. Someone or something touching me, rubbing my back, my legs, my arms. I twisted around to see a dim silhouette of a woman with a red halo around her head.

Katy!

I wanted to ask her what happened, but my lips were numb.

Something thundered above us. I'd heard that sound before. It was a deafening roar. Getting closer and closer.

I turned my head.

The plane. The Cessna I was in, only moments ago.

I vaguely remembered Matt's hand slamming the door open.

Did that really happen?

I was sure I'd closed the door properly, but I'd had no seat belt on. He pushed me out, and I'd free fallen all the way into the lake.

"Help me, Tank!" I heard Katy shout.

Someone was holding me up. Or trying to. I felt their arms tighten around my shoulders.

I struggled.

Tank's trying to kill me!

I thrashed around, pushing him away.

"Stop it, Asha!" came Katy's voice, firm and in control. "We're trying to keep you warm. Stop fighting us."

But it was the gunshot that stopped me.

It stopped all of us.

I craned my neck and squinted in the distance.

Tetyana!

She was standing a few feet from us, her arms raised, her gun in her hand, her legs apart, and her shoulders strong.

She was aiming at the plane, which was careening over us, the engine spluttering.

Her gun blasted in succession, the ear-splitting sound ringing in my ear. As I watched, she reached into her pocket for her spare ammo. Within seconds, the blasts echoed across the lake again.

A high-pitched whine came from the plane's engine. The propeller was slowing down, choppy. Inside, I imagined Matt fighting to take control.

Did she hit him?

The plane tilted back and forth dangerously.

I wanted to scream but my lips refused to open.

The Cessna was diving into the frozen lake.

"Watch out!" cried Katy.

Someone slammed me to the ground. I covered my head and flattened myself as the aircraft brushed over us, missing us by only a few feet.

I turned my face up to see the plane teetering above the lake.

Tetyana scrammed over, sliding across the ice. I wanted to shout at her. The ice wouldn't hold her, not close to the middle.

More shots echoed across the lonely landscape.

I didn't know who was shooting at whom anymore.

"Head down," said Tank's gruff voice. I felt a hand cover the back of my head and push me back to the ground.

The plane skidded across the ice and came to a stop sideways. For a moment I was sure it was going to topple over.

Tetyana was right next to the plane now.

She yanked the pilot side door open and pulled Matt out, hurling him to the ground.

Chapter Forty-six

I turned to Katy and pried my lips open.

"Back her up," I croaked, my voice hoarse, my words a cobbled mumble.

Tetyana had a knee on Matt's back, and her weapon was at his head. He was bucking under her, but she was in control.

I struggled to sit up, my brain feeling like it was filled with ice. Though my limbs still fell like jelly, I wanted to run over and help her, but Katy had a firm hold on my shoulder.

We watched as Tetyana pulled something from her back pocket. It glinted in the morning light that bounced off the lake's surface.

Handcuffs.

Within seconds, she had Matt cuffed and up. We could hear her angry yells as she pushed him toward us.

Katy pulled me up to my feet. That was when I realized I had on Tank's long overcoat.

The teen was standing behind us, rubbing his arms and shoulders furiously to stay warm, with only a thin shirt to cover his torso.

My hazy brain tried to think.

It was Tank who pulled me out of the lake. It was him who dragged me away from danger.

Is Tank the good guy here?

"You need to get inside the church," Katy was saying. "We need to get you by that fire and under some blankets pronto."

I turned to her, still in shock at how I'd survived the fall.

"I lost my Glock," I said.

Katy gave me a wistful look. "It's probably at the bottom of the lake now. Sorry, you were our priority."

"Matt tried to kill me. He pushed me out."

"That murderer dropped you in midair," said Katy, gritting her teeth. "Good thing we were down here to see it."

I wanted to ask her how long I'd been flailing in the water, how Tetyana and Tank got here so quickly, and how Tank had traversed the dangerous stretch of ice to pull me out, before I went under.

There had been no way I would have survived that plunge, weighted down by my winter gear and Kevlar vest.

That was when I remembered.

Our vests floated.

Tetyana had shopped for military grade vests in a secret online weapons and ammunition store accessible to only a few in the undercover world.

Don't ask, just put the damn thing on, had been her words when she'd presented them to us. I owed my friend my life.

Tetyana was shoving Matt over with the butt of her gun and was only a few feet away from us now.

I pushed Katy aside and stepped up to the pilot, my legs still shaking but my hands curled into fists.

I wanted to smash his face, but I knew throwing a punch in my weakened state was a remote goal. But my voice had returned. That was all I needed to get the fury roiling inside of me out.

I stepped up to Matt and screamed in his face.

"What the hell did you think you were doing? Who the hell are you? You good-for-nothing sick piece of a human being. You think I'll let you get away with it?"

Matt looked away, his face stony.

"Enough," said Katy, pulling me away. "We'll deal with him later."

"Forward," said Tetyana, kicking Matt's shin. "March."

We were only a few feet from the tree line when a sharp crack made us all whirl around.

Tetyana swore.

Matt let out an obscenity.

"Oh no," cried Katy, putting her hand over her mouth.

The ice beneath the plane had cracked open. A large circle of crystal blue water appeared around the aircraft.

The plane dipped, one wing slanting toward the water.

Then, with a loud bang, the Cessna collapsed to its side, its left wing crashing through the ice.

We watched in horror as it sank, getting submerged foot by foot, until only a few feet of the right wing stuck out from the surface.

That would disappear too in a matter of minutes.

There was nothing much any of us could do. We turned back and started our walk.

It was a raggedy group that crawled back up the mountain.

Tank and Katy held me on both sides, so I wouldn't lose my footing. Behind us came Tetyana pushing the handcuffed Matt in front of her.

My mind was a whirl.

Why did Matt try to kill me? What's he doing out here? Is he after the diamonds?

Why did Tank save me?

And what's their connection to Jacob? Who is Jacob, really?

Jacob was waiting for us by the church doors.

He gave one look at me, grabbed a blanket from inside and wrapped it around my shoulders. Putting an arm around me, he nudged me toward the fireplace, as Katy followed.

I watched Jacob warily from the side of my eyes. I now knew Matt's intentions, but the others were still a mystery. For once, I wished the bad guys would act like bad guys, so I'd know who was who.

To my surprise, Jacob rustled a clean shirt and pair of pants from his closet and handed them to me. I scooted toward the false wall behind the altar to change, thankful to get into something dry.

I pulled my Kevlar vest over Jacob's shirt, threw Tank's coat across my shoulders, and hurried back to the fireplace to curl up as close to it as I could. The last thing I needed was to contract hypothermia and become a burden on my friends.

Tank plopped next to me with a loud sigh, like he'd had enough for the day.

"The fire will help you," he mumbled, rubbing his arms.

I nodded, unsure whether to interrogate him or thank him.

I was grateful he'd hauled me out of the frigid water and spared me his coat. I took it off and placed it on the floor next to him. He promptly put it on and rocked back and forth like a child.

I stared at him, wondering if he was fully right in the head. Then again, he was just a teen, a kid in an overgrown body. I kept forgetting that.

I turned to Jacob. He'd plucked the kettle hanging on the wire strung across the fireplace and was pouring some water into a mug.

"Your delivery guy tried to kill me," I said, with a snarl. "He isn't who he says he is."

Without answering, Jacob handed me the mug.

I took it, feeling the warmth spread through my hands and my arms, but I wasn't about to drink it. I wasn't that stupid. I squinted at the liquid. It looked like water, but did it contain anything else?

Crushed pills?

Translucent poison?

"It's hot water," said Jacob, shuffling over to the nearest pew where his kitten lay sleeping in a nest of blankets. "You need to warm up."

"Sit," said Tetyana, pushing Matt onto a bench near us. "Talk."

We all turned to him.

Matt stared back at us, his eyes cold.

The easygoing, frat boy personality had disappeared. His confidence hadn't waned but there was something dark underneath this man.

"Who are you?" I asked.

He didn't answer.

"Why did you try to kill Asha?" growled Katy.

Silence.

"You waiting for your attorney to show up or what?" said Tetyana.

Matt glared at her, his eyes hard and his lips in a thin, harsh line.

"Do you want to do this the easy way or the hard way?" she said, leaning close, her weapon pushing into his ribs.

He didn't even flinch. He looked supremely confident he was going to get out of this alive.

My gut was sending warning flags again.

My eyes swept the church.

Something was missing.

No, *someone.*

Chapter Forty-seven

"Hey," I said, sitting up, startling Tank next to me. "Where's Robin? Where's Dwayne?"

"They were both gone," said Jacob in that soft voice of his.

"Gone where?" I demanded.

"When I woke up this morning, their benches were empty. They left their blankets behind and went out."

"Out in the cold?" said Katy, frowning. "Why would anyone do that?"

A shudder went through me at the thought of seeing them dead in a snowbank, just like Doctor Wilson.

"Didn't you hear them leave?" I said. "Why didn't you stop them?"

Jacob let out a weary sigh.

"I normally sleep lightly. But I'm tired. I fell asleep hard. I didn't see anything or hear anything."

How do people vanish into the mountain like this?

That made four now, five with Doctor Wilson.

Theodore Henry. Stella Green. Now Robin and Dwayne.

I looked at Jacob, who was cradling the kitten.

"What's going on here?" I said. "You're not who you say you are. You might as well tell us. It's not like you have the upper hand now."

Jacob looked down at the floor for a moment, as if contemplating something. He lifted his head slowly, his face looking even more ancient than before.

He opened his mouth to speak.

That was when the church doors banged open.

We spun around.

"Stella?" I said in surprise.

Stella Green was standing at the entrance.

The last time I saw her, she had looked frightened and timid. But now, the expression on her face was grim.

She had someone with her, and she was holding a gun to their head.

"Robin!" cried Katy.

Robin had her hands behind her, like they'd been tied. Her face was pale but expressionless.

Stella had one hand gripped on Robin's arm and the other pointing the sidearm to her head.

"What the hell are you doing?" yelled Tetyana, springing up. "Let her go."

"Stay back or I shoot right through her," said Stella, her voice low and controlled, with much more confidence than I'd heard her speak on the train.

Tetyana stopped, but kept her Glock aimed at Stella.

Stella's eyes didn't even flicker.

This was someone who knew she held all the cards.

I turned to Robin. There were no marks or bruises on her, and she didn't look frightened, but I recognized that expression. The look of someone dazed, in complete shock.

"What happened, Robin?" I asked. "Where's Dwayne?"

Robin's eyes met mine for a split second, then she quickly looked away. She stared ahead of her like a deer in headlights, as if unable to move or speak.

Matt was looking at Stella, his eyes softened and his mouth turned into a small smile. It was strange the way she looked back at him.

These two knew each other well.

I wondered who else was in on this racket. I kicked myself for not suspecting Stella sooner.

Stella and Tank were the last two people on the train before it got ransacked. Someone could have lured the teen into the woods with that cry for help, while Stella looked for those diamonds.

My mind raced.

Robin was no wallflower.

She was a tough woman who worked in harsh weather and held a manual job usually reserved for hardy men. While having a gun to your head would silence anyone, she wasn't one to give in without a fight.

How did she get cornered?

I flinched as someone stepped close to me.

It was Katy.

Something hard bumped against my lower back. I reached behind me.

Katy's Glock.

I was a better marksperson than her. I sent a silent thanks to my friend and gripped the sidearm tightly.

Tank was standing to my right, which meant there was no one behind us. I turned back to Stella, hoping we hadn't alerted her or anyone else to the exchange.

"So, this is all your nasty work, then?" I said.

She glared.

"How does it come to this? A renowned scientist threatening the life of an innocent woman?" I asked, keeping my voice level.

No reply.

Through my peripheral vision, I could see everyone inside the church. I was in a good position to take action, and I had the firepower now.

I took stock.

But our weapons were useless.

One wrong move and Robin could end up dead. Tetyana wouldn't hold back. But a gun battle in the middle of this old church would only mean one thing.

A massacre.

"Where's Theodore Henry?" I asked.

"None of your business," snapped Stella.

Jacob muttered something and looked away.

Was he part of this criminal cabal too? He stood slouched against a pew, cradling the kitten in his hands, eyes on the floor, his face a picture of sadness. Or was it remorse?

"You're just hired goons," snarled Matt. "You people know nothing."

"Is that right?" I said.

No one spoke. No one moved.

My brain spun madly, like a swirling typhoon.

Except for Katy, Tetyana and me, nobody knew of the diamonds we'd discovered in Connor's false pocket. That pouch was now hidden inside Tetyana's Kevlar vest.

We held the treasure they were seeking. It was something they would hunt us down for.

Kill for.

My eyes flickered to the back, where Jacob's paintings leaned against the wall behind the altar.

I gave a start.

The three paintings that had been in Theodore's cabin were here now inside the church. But with one change. All three had their frames removed.

My eyes swept the hall.

Whoever had ransacked the train was here.

There was no bogeyman in the mountains. The bogeyman was among us.

I turned to Stella.

"Whatever is going on here, Robin has nothing to do with it," I said. "She was just doing her job. Let her go."

Stella didn't even look at me, her eyes on Tetyana and the gun pointing her way.

"What do you want, Stella?" I tried again. "What do you want from us?"

She finally turned to me.

"You don't know what you've got yourself involved in," she said. "You have no power to make any deals with us."

"Why did you kidnap Theodore Henry?" I asked, undeterred by her hostile glare.

"You can ask him when you see him," she snapped.

A cold shiver went through me.

"Where is he?" I asked, keeping my face and voice stoic.

"How much did that man pay you to come on this trip?" said Matt with a smirk. "How much did you take to protect the sickest criminal in this state?"

"You're one to speak of criminals," I growled.

Matt shot me a condescending look.

"You're in deep with something so over your heads," he said. "You can't even imagine what you've got yourself tangled up in."

"Wanna bet?" I said. "I know you're looking for something."

Stella and Matt both jerked back.

"I've a darn good idea what game you're playing," I said. "Happy to share more, but not with a gun to Robin's head."

"Right," said Matt with a hollow laugh.

"I might even have evidence," I said. "Hard evidence of what you're looking for."

The room fell silent.

Stella stared at me unblinkingly.

"But first, let Robin go," I said.

Without any warning, Matt sprang up. Tetyana swiveled around and aimed her weapon at him.

"Stay right where you are, or you're a dead man," she snarled.

Matt stopped in his tracks, only ten feet from me. He glared, eyes blazing, his face slowly turning a tinge of purple.

I'd hit a nerve.

"So the old man told you, did he?" he yelled. "You're all in with him too?"

He took another step forward. I wondered what he'd have done if he hadn't been handcuffed.

"I said, back!" shouted Tetyana.

Matt stopped.

I didn't budge.

"It's clear as day to me," I said with a shrug. "You're petty thieves using violence to steal what you want from an old man dying of cancer."

"Enough!"

Stella's voice echoed through the church hall.

"Get those handcuffs off Matt Ryder," she growled, "or my next bullet goes straight into her head."

Stella pushed the end of the barrel into Robin's forehead, making her wince.

"Now!" she shouted.

Chapter Forty-eight

"No negotiations, no discussions," said Stella, back in control.

Tetyana glanced at me.

I didn't want to play with Robin's life. She was an innocent bystander, now minutes, if not seconds, from death.

"Give the handcuff key to Jacob," said Stella, her voice hard. "I don't want any of you near Matt except him."

What happens then?

Will they take our weapons and overpower us? How do we know Stella won't shoot Robin, regardless?

"Here's what we're going to do," I said, my heart hammering, hoping my next move wouldn't haunt me.

"You turn your weapon away from Robin's head, and we'll hand over the keys to Jacob."

Stella turned and glared my way.

"Fair's fair," said Katy, speaking for the first time since Stella walked in. "How do we know you won't shoot her, anyway?"

Stella turned to my friend and to my surprise, gave a shrug.

"Fine," she said. "Let's get on with it then."

I stared at her.

That had been too easy.

I racked my brain. There was something more going on here.

Robin's head was at a slant, away from the barrel of the gun that was thrust against her forehead. She looked like she was about to faint.

I wanted to make eye contact with her, ask what she knew about Theodore and Dwayne. I wanted to ask her if there was something we needed to know, something important we were missing, but she was staring at the floor like a zombie.

We'll rescue Robin first and ask questions later.

I turned to my friend and gave a curt nod.

With an angry hiss, Tetyana pulled the key from her pocket and threw it at the older man. It fell at Jacob's feet.

He bent over slowly with a low groan, picked up the key, and shuffled over to Matt.

"Now," I shouted at Stella. "Let her go!"

Stella pulled the weapon away from Robin's head.

I sighed in relief, but Robin didn't move.

"Get back, Robin!" shouted Tetyana.

Robin didn't even blink.

The handcuffs fell to the floor and Matt rubbed his wrists. He walked up to Stella by the door and shot me an impetuous grin, back to his cocksure self.

"Like I said, you people have no clue what you're dealing with."

"Robin," I said, ignoring him. "You're free to go. Get away from them now."

The last thing we needed was to have her taken hostage again.

"Come on over, hun," coaxed Katy. "You're going to be okay."

But Robin stood in her spot, flanked by Stella and Matt, her shoulders hunched, with the same weary expression.

Was she drugged?

"What are you going to do now?" I said, turning my attention back to Stella. "Ransack the train again to find whatever you missed the first time?"

"It wasn't there," she said, turning to me.

"What wasn't there?"

"I thought Theodore told you."

"Like he would," I said. "We're just hired goons from out of town, remember? Our instructions were to keep an eye out. He told us nothing about a dead body on the tracks, a potential train wreck in the middle of nowhere, or a kidnapping."

"Don't play with me," said Stella.

I racked my brain, thinking of how to keep the conversation going while one of us figured out how to pull Robin away from these two.

I hadn't forgotten what Stella had said earlier when I asked about Theodore.

You can ask him when you see him.

"I'm not playing," I said. "I'm just baffled by your methods."

I paused.

"Why did you take the paintings from the train, Stella?"

Her eyes narrowed.

I turned to Jacob.

"Why did you remove them from their frames?"

He didn't answer.

I took a step back.

No one moved.

I walked backward until I got on the podium and reached the altar. I bent down and picked up one of the three empty wooden frames next to the paintings.

It was made of cheap light wood, like something exported from a sweatshop in Asia.

I held it up.

"I always wondered why anyone would put these beautiful pictures in such cheap frames," I said. "Especially Theodore, who could afford solid frames for his pretty pictures."

Nobody replied.

I ran my fingers along the back and felt the grooves. Only a thick brown paper covered the back. The manufacturer had cut corners with this product.

I ripped the paper apart and gaped to see the hollow tunnel inside. I waved the frame in front of me.

"Did Theodore put something in here? Gold nuggets from the mine? Something else? Why would he do that?"

Stella and Matt's faces remained stony.

I turned to Jacob.

"How did your paintings get into the hands of Theodore Henry? That wasn't a coincidence, was it?"

He shook his head.

"I sold him a few," he replied.

"Why?"

"He said my work was important. They represent Alaska. He was going to take them to Christie's in New York after his medical treatment."

I raised my eyebrows.

What a tale. This story was more convoluted than I'd imagined.

I turned to Stella.

"Where's Theodore? Is he locked up somewhere? Or is he dead?"

Matt gave her a look. Stella stirred. Tetyana tensed up.

Stella still had her weapon in her hand. So did Tetyana and me.

"Seems like you're dying to see him," said Stella. "Why don't you come and see for yourself how he's doing?"

What was she playing at now?

Every bone in my body told me we were burrowing deeper into dangerous ground.

"Only if you can guarantee our safety and the safety of everyone else," I said.

Matt laughed.

"That was a rhetorical question, stupid," he said. "It's not like you have a choice."

That was when Stella cocked her weapon and pointed it at Robin's head again.

Katy let out a gasp.

"We made a deal," I said.

"I don't do deals," said Stella. "But you do have another choice."

"What's that?" said Katy.

"Do I shoot Robin now, or will you follow me out?" She glared at us. "Your call."

Chapter Forty-nine

Why didn't Robin get away from Stella and Matt when she had the chance?

She had to be drugged.

Why else would she stand like a statue in between the two people who had threatened her with her life?

That was when I realized.

Dwayne.

They must have her father somewhere. Probably with Theodore Henry. Tied up and silenced. If they had Robin's father, she'd do anything they ask.

"Weapons on the floor," said Matt, pointing to the ground. "Both of you. Now."

How quickly the tables had turned.

"I said, weapons on the floor," he hollered.

"Or what?" snarled Tetyana.

Matt raised his hand and mimicked firing a gun at Robin's head.

"Don't you dare!" shouted Katy.

Matt grinned.

"I'll give you another choice, ladies. Would you prefer Stella or me to shoot her?"

Robin's face remained expressionless. I wanted to punch Stella and Matt, put a gun to their heads and make them feel what she was feeling.

Stella pushed the barrel of her weapon against Robin's head, making her bend down even more from the pressure.

"You made your point," I said. "There's no need to hurt her. Tell us where Theodore Henry is, and we'll come."

"Put your weapons on the floor first," growled Stella.

I didn't have a choice. My only hope was they wouldn't search us. We still had our Tanto knives tucked inside our boots.

I bent down and put the sidearm next to my feet.

"Kick it this way," called out Matt.

I glared at him.

"Get it from her!"

Before I could move, someone came from behind me and swiped the weapon from the floor.

I turned around, startled.

Tank?

Only an hour ago, he'd saved my life and kept me warm with his coat.

"What's going on?" I said.

Tank pocketed my sidearm, his eyes down, like he was too embarrassed to look me in the eye.

"You too," snarled Matt, turning to Tetyana.

Tetyana dropped her sidearm to the floor and kicked it into the fireplace.

"What the hell?" shouted Matt.

Tank lumbered over, dragging his feet. Using a log, he pulled the weapon out of the fireplace. Then, he walked over and handed it to Matt, who grinned at Tetyana.

The way she glowered back at him, I imagined red lasers shooting out of her eyes.

I turned from Stella to Matt, then from Tank to Jacob.

Are they all in on this heist?

"Tank," called out Matt, pointing at Tetyana. "You're with her."

Matt stepped behind Katy and me.

"All righty, you two," he said, prodding my back with the barrel of the gun. "No funny games."

Stella turned around, her weapon still at Robin's head. Pulling her forward, she stepped on the threshold of the church.

Katy and I followed Stella out of the building with Matt at our heels. Behind us was Tetyana, her hands in the air, as Tank followed with my gun aimed at her back.

My head spun.

What was Tank's role? Why did he save me if he was going to turn on us like this?

"Along the pipeline," commanded Stella, as she walked over to the same spot we had used the night before to navigate up the slope toward the mine shaft.

Katy and I exchanged a glance.

Theodore had been inside the mine, all along.

If I hadn't fallen into that hole, we might have even rescued him the night before. Whoever had pushed me in had wanted to distract us.

I wondered who it had been.

Stella?

Tank?

Matt had been inside the church. He couldn't have run up that slope, unless there was another and faster way up. But if he'd come up using a mechanical pulley or some other contraption, we'd have heard him.

That meant it had to have been Tank or Stella.

Had Tank lied to us about that cry in the woods? He was a better actor than I thought.

But one thing was clear now.

Stella.

She was the mastermind of this operation.

She was highly intelligent, determined, and knew what she was doing. If anyone knew about diamonds, it had to be her.

Tank was merely following orders, a pawn. And Matt was her sidekick, a formidable one with valuable skills, but he was clearly not running the show.

It was Jacob I couldn't figure out. How did he get involved with this ragtag gang?

I felt for Robin. I hoped against hope Dwayne was still alive.

If Theodore Henry had been harmed or was dead, I'd failed at my job. Miserably.

But I'd feel much worse if an innocent person got hurt—someone who had nothing to do with the backstabbing, swindling businesses Theodore was involved in. All because I hadn't got my ducks lined up and figured this puzzle out sooner.

Katy and I trundled up the slope, staying close together.

My hair was still wet from the plunge in the lake. But with my heart pounding like a jackhammer and my adrenaline levels sky high, I didn't feel the cold.

I knew I'd pay for this later, but right now I had to think. And think fast. With every step up, my brain swirled faster and faster.

I sighed as I realized the ultimate and terrifying challenge we faced.

Even if we found a way out of this debacle, we'd still be stuck on the mountain.

I turned my head up to see how much more distance we had to cover when a furious roar came from behind us.

I snapped around.

Tank and Tetyana were facing each other, as if ready for a fight. Tank had one arm up in the air about to strike her.

"Tetyana!" I shouted. "Watch out!"

"Get her!" hollered Matt.

But Tetyana was ready. She jumped on Tank and crashed to the ground with him.

"Tetyana!" screamed Katy.

The two rolled down the slope. Stella yelled something incomprehensible from up ahead.

"Get off her, you brute!" I shouted, my heart racing.

I knew Matt wouldn't hesitate to take a shot at Tetyana, but not without the risk of hitting Tank too. I prayed he had a smidgen of sympathy toward the teen.

But Tank seemed to have got the upper hand all of a sudden. He grabbed Tetyana's arms and held her on the ground.

I stared, my mouth open.

Tetyana had been roaring like a lioness, punching and kicking. But then, in two seconds, she lay flat on the ground, face down, with Tank's gun pointed at her back.

"I got her!" shouted Tank, with a nod at Matt.

"What just happened?" said Katy. "How did he...?"

For anyone to take our friend down in hand-to-hand combat that quickly would have been impossible without military training.

My heart sank.

I'd made a big mistake. An unforgivable one.

Theodore Henry's choice for a personal bodyguard had always surprised me, but it all clicked into place now. Tank had the proper training, but had been hiding it until he needed to use it.

Like right now.

Matt turned around and glared at Katy and me.

"What are you waiting for? Keep walking, you two," he growled, waving his weapon in front of us.

We didn't move, our eyes still on Tetyana lying motionless on the ground with the gun at her back.

"Now!" Matt roared in our faces. "Start walking or she dies!"

Chapter Fifty

"You hurt one hair on her head, and I'll hunt you down!" I shouted at Tank.

He looked the other way, his aim not wavering from its target.

A smirk spread across Matt's face. He knew we were cornered.

I wanted to grab his shoulders, yank his stupid head down, and smash my knee into his face. But I knew that would only result in a trigger pulled.

I'd never be able to help Tetyana or get ourselves out of this situation with a bullet inside of me.

"Turn around and keep walking," sneered Matt. "Follow my orders and your friend might live."

His smirk had transformed into a hateful grin.

"Go!" he shouted, sticking the gun in my face.

I turned around, my back tense, my entire nervous system twitching, readying to hear a gunshot from below us. I gave Katy a side glance. Her face was ashen.

We continued our trudge up the mountain.

Tank had acted like a bumbling goof whose incompetence led to his boss getting kidnapped. Yet he was behind the crime all along.

I had seen things as I had wanted them to. Not as they were.

Nothing here was as it seemed to be.

I squinted up the slope. Stella was standing at the mouth of the mining shaft, holding on to Robin's arm.

Another hard prod came on my back.

"Faster," said Matt. "Someone special is waiting for you inside."

Special?

Would that be Theodore Henry?

Katy and I kept a slow but steady pace. What I really wanted was to race down and kick Tank and his gun off Tetyana.

My mind whirred at the unusual turn of events.

Maybe this was Tetyana's strategy. Play the subdued prisoner. Convince Matt to leave her and Tank behind. Then, she'd send the teen flying down the mountain before he knew what hit him.

My spirits rose.

If this was the case, Tank didn't know what he had coming.

Now the shouting had died down, an eerie silence had settled on the slopes. I could only hear my breathing and the heavy thud of my heart beating inside of me.

When we arrived at the mouth of the shaft, Stella had already disappeared inside with Robin. I turned around to take a final look at Tetyana when Matt raised the barrel of the gun as if to strike me.

"Keep moving," he snarled.

Katy went in first. She stepped on the wooden beam that was now placed across the chasm. I glanced down at the dark hole I'd tumbled into, only hours ago.

Balancing carefully, Katy crossed to the other side. I followed her, putting one foot in front of the other, as the memory of falling into that black hole still haunted me.

Several yards ahead of us, the thin light of a handheld torch moved back and forth. Was that Stella? There was only one way to go, and that was toward that light.

It took a minute for my eyes to adjust to the semi darkness. When they did, I realized we were inside a roughly cut, low tunnel.

On the ground were small rail tracks which ran the length of the passageway until they disappeared into the darkness at the far end. We passed a rusty mining cart left on the tracks filled with rock and dirt, an ancient shovel still sticking out from one end.

The torchlight swirled around the tunnel and landed on us. As if satisfied by what they saw, the flashlight turned back around.

Katy and I kept moving, feeling Matt's hostile presence behind us.

When we arrived at the end, Stella was waiting with Robin next to her. They were standing in front of a large iron door.

The sound of a mechanical whine began as we walked up. It seemed to come from the belly of the mountain, somewhere beneath us.

It got louder and louder, and soon the ground rumbled under our feet. Katy and I exchanged an alarmed look.

When the whining and shaking stopped, Stella pulled a handle on the door, exposing a room enclosed by iron walls. It was large enough to carry a few miners and a mine cart.

An elevator.

"Get in," said Stella.

I wondered how old this contraption was, if it would even hold us all. That didn't seem to concern our captors. Stella nudged Robin inside, and Matt prodded Katy and me in with the butt of his gun.

"Against the wall," he barked.

We took our positions on the far end.

As the elevator doors closed, Matt stepped away and leaned against the wall across from us, his weapon still aimed our way.

Through the darkness with only Stella's single flashlight for illumination, I stared at the others.

Stella and Matt stood silently with Robin sandwiched in between them. But there was no gun pointing at Robin anymore. Stella wasn't even holding on to her.

My eyes swept around the lift, which was moving at a snail's pace compared to any modern elevator I'd been in, its loud mechanical whine screeching in my ears.

I glanced at the rusty iron ceiling, looking for escape hatches or hidden exits, but the space looked airtight.

I wondered how far we'd plunge into the innards of this mountain. My heart beat a tick faster as I tried not to think of the unthinkable.

Was this how we were going to die? Deep inside an abandoned mine in a remote region of Alaska, a place few even knew existed.

The elevator stopped with a heavy shudder, throwing Katy against me. Matt pulled on a handle to open the doors, and Stella and Robin stepped out together as casually as if they were office workers stepping out for a cup of coffee.

Robin.

There was something strange about her behavior.

My stomach sank as I realized another option I hadn't considered before.

Had I been wrong about her too?

"Out," said Matt, waving his gun.

Katy and I stepped out, staying close to each other.

We walked into a cavernous and well-lit underground cave. A series of battery-operated lights had been placed around the space. Despite their brightness, the cave had a gloomy atmosphere.

"There you are," said a familiar voice.

It was Dwayne.

I breathed a sigh of relief. He wasn't tied up or dead. He walked up and pulled Robin in for a hug.

"You okay, Dwayne?" I said, peering at him, looking for visible wounds.

Without answering, he pulled his daughter to the side. When he looked at me, his eyes flickered, then he turned away.

What's going on here?

That was when Katy clutched my arm.

"Theodore!" she gasped.

Chapter Fifty-one

Theodore Henry was seated in a metal chair at the back of the cave.

His hands were tied to the arms of the chair with rope, and his feet were bound to the metal legs.

His eyes were closed, and his chin rested on his chest. It was cool down here, but the only sign he was alive was the sweat streaming down his face.

He looked like a man who knew death would come soon.

How did they bring him from the train all the way up the mountain?

My mind flashed back to all the strange happenings we'd seen so far. This was not the work of one or even two individuals.

This required team effort.

The question was who was in this bizarre squad.

Was it all of them?

"Thank goodness, you're alive," said Katy, stepping toward Theodore. "We thought you were dea—"

Matt grabbed her by the shoulder and pulled her away.

"Stay back," he growled.

"Tie them up," said Stella, turning to Dwayne and Robin.

They shot her an alarmed look.

"Is that necessary?" stammered Dwayne.

"Absolutely," said Stella. "They're too much trouble. Get the rope and tie them up."

Robin shook her head. "You do it."

Stella glared at her.

"This was your idea," said Robin, thrusting her hands into her pockets.

I gawked at the father and daughter. So, they were in this too.

With an irate sniff, Stella picked up the extra piece of rope lying at Theodore's feet and moved toward Katy.

I watched her, my heart pounding, my brain whirling, trying to think how we could get away from this dungeon without getting killed.

Stella's face didn't show hatred or even anger. She looked frustrated, like she was upset she'd been forced to deal with us.

This wasn't personal.

Katy, Tetyana, and I had been unfortunate bystanders who'd interfered with her plans.

It was Matt who looked angry. He kept his eyes and his weapon aimed our way. The determined expression on his face told me he wouldn't hesitate to pull that trigger.

I considered our options.

If we fought back, he could shoot. If we didn't, we'd get tied up and be left to rot in this cave. I wasn't sure how Tetyana was managing outside with Tank. I couldn't rely on her right now.

We didn't have any choice.

Except one.

My mind flashed to the conversation Katy, Tetyana, and I had the morning after we discovered the diamonds in the train. These were amateurs. If they had been professionals, none of us would be alive right now.

There was one trick that might just work. It was a tip David had given us during our Saturday Krav Maga martial arts class. I only hoped Katy remembered it too.

I took a deep breath in and let it out. My mind needed to be clear if I was going to get us out of here alive.

"Who are you people?" I said, as Stella began to tie Katy's hands. "This has nothing to do with us. Why don't let us go?"

"What I want to know is who *you* are?" said Stella, shooting me an accusing look.

"I own a bakery in Harlem. From time to time, we help our clients out. This was a simple job. We didn't expect any of this," I said. "If you let us leave now, we won't say anything to anyone."

"How do hired caterers carry guns?" said Stella. "I think you know way more than you're telling us. What did Theodore share with you?"

Hearing his name, Theodore lifted his chin and squinched his eyes, but he didn't say a word. His face was haggard and etched in pain.

"I wish he told us what the heck was going on before he hired us," said Katy, moving her shoulders back and forth, as Stella worked on a knot behind her.

Good. She got it.

"What did he hire you for exactly?" said Stella, her curiosity overcoming her.

"Theodore Henry was suspicious someone was out to get him. He asked us to keep an eye out," I said. "I just didn't realize it was you he had to watch out for."

Stella stopped and scowled my way.

Then, she moved toward me with the remaining rope.

"Theodore was certain someone was poisoning him," I said, wriggling my hands as she slipped the rope around them. "He wanted us to serve him his meals, so he'd feel safe, but I guess you had other plans, didn't you?"

"Stop moving," said Stella as she tried to grip my wrists together.

Stella was no career criminal, and I doubted she had any physical training. I kept my hands as far apart as I could, but I needed a distraction, a bombshell that would stop her in her tracks.

I craned my neck to look at her.

"You're looking for the diamonds, aren't you?"

Stella let go of my hands and stared.

Matt jerked his head back in surprise.

Excellent.

"How do you know about the diamonds?" said Stella, her eyes narrowing.

"Why else would you go to these extremes?" I said.

My hands were still bound. I wiggled my wrists gently, and an enormous rush of relief went through me as I felt the slack.

Now, I just had to wait for the right time.

I pointed at Theodore with my chin.

"You kidnapped him because you couldn't find the stones," I said. "But he never told you where they were, did he? He's a stubborn old man."

Matt and Stella simply stared, stunned expressions on their faces. Dwayne and Robin stood close, their arms around each other's shoulders, looking like they wished they could be anywhere else but here.

"That's why you ransacked the train," I said. "But you never found them."

I had everyone's attention now.

"Because we know exactly where they are," I said.

Hushed gasps went around the room.

"Where?" cried Stella.

Ignoring her, I turned to Matt.

"You put the dead body on the train tracks, didn't you? When did you do it? A day before the train was due?"

Matt and Stella exchanged a nervous glance. The two of them were standing close to each other now, their arms rubbing, looking like a couple. I wondered how and where the bush pilot had met the scientist.

I felt like I had barely scratched the surface of this mystery, but I kept going.

"It was also you who shot that arrow our way, to keep us out of the woods, wasn't it?" I said, my eyes on Matt. "You didn't realize we'd be on that train and you had to improvise. Did you get that bow and arrow from Jacob?"

Matt glared back.

I was hitting the right notes.

"You strategized your heist well, except you didn't prepare for us. We threw your plans into a loop, didn't we?"

I turned to Dwayne and Robin.

"You two were part of this all along. You blew up the boiler when you realized we were going to find a way out and contact the authorities. It was one way to make the train immobile, so you could find the stones and get away in the plane."

Dwayne flinched. Robin looked away. She wore the same zombie-like expression she had inside the church only an hour ago.

"You pretended to be a victim, Robin, but you're playing the game too."

"This isn't a game," blurted Robin.

"Of course not," I said. "This is serious business. How much are those stones worth? Several million? How were you planning to share it? Split it four ways? Five with Tank? Or six with Jacob?"

Silence.

I had no evidence to back any of my claims, but I knew the more I kept talking, the more chances we had of getting out alive.

Anything to buy us time. Anything to plot an escape.

I glared at Dwayne.

Connor McNamara may have been an unpleasant man, but I now knew he wasn't part of this cabal.

"Do you realize you killed a man in your attempt to stall the train? An innocent man who had nothing to do with this heist?"

"Connor?" said Robin with an angry huff. "You call him innocent?"

"He deserved to die," said Stella, her voice turning hard.

Next to her, Matt was shaking with anger. His face had turned purple, like he was about to explode.

Something about McNamara had triggered strong emotions in all of them.

Had that boiler explosion been accidental? Or had it been cold-blooded murder?

"You lied to us," I said, turning around and looking every one of them in the eye. "You planned all this to kill McNamara. You have blood on your hands. All of you."

"It's McNamara who has blood on his hands," yelled Matt, his eyes blazing with fire. "Don't you dare defend that sick dog!"

Chapter Fifty-two

A sob came from Theodore's corner.

His eyes were scrunched and his hands were curled, like he couldn't bear the pain. Tears rolled down his cheeks now, mingling with the sweat.

This wasn't just a diamond heist.

We had stumbled into something bigger.

I had to think fast.

Was that velvet pouch filled with rough-cut stones a red herring? A high-priced distraction from a cold-blooded killing?

The diamonds were still ensconced inside Tetyana's vest. Unless she was near death, or even then, I couldn't imagine our friend giving up the secret she was carrying with her.

But what did all this mean?

I turned to Matt.

"Why did you kidnap Theodore?"

A rustle from the back made me turn. Theodore was shifting in his chair, craning his neck to make eye contact with Matt.

He opened his mouth to speak, gave the pilot a pained look, and shook his head, grimacing as he did.

"It was a…" He coughed a dry and hollow cough, like he hadn't had water for several days. "It was… a long time ago."

"You let Connor get away with murder!" cried Matt, swiveling his gun around and pointing it at Theodore's head.

"I… I was a different man then," croaked the older man. "P… please believe me."

I looked from Theodore to Matt and back again.

This case changed direction so fast, my head spun.

I had to take stock again.

My eyes swept the room.

Stella held a gun which was pointing at Katy and me. Matt's sidearm was aimed at Theodore, albeit shakily.

Dwayne and Robin stood by Theodore's chair, their faces glum, like the weight of the world had landed on their shoulders.

Stella was the only person who looked in control.

She was watching me watching her, a stoic expression on her face, weapon at the ready. Though she might be lousy at knots, she was not one to lose her cool fast.

Unlike Matt.

"What's going on here?" I asked out loud, to no one in particular.

Robin turned to me.

"You're protecting the wrong guy," she said in a dull voice.

"How are you all connected?" I said.

Silence.

I tried another tactic.

"What I do know is you're all in serious trouble. You can be put away for life. I've been in this business long enough to know you aren't getting away with this."

"Connor McNamara's death was an accident," said Dwayne, rubbing his forehead, his voice strained. "Yes, I blew up the boiler, but I never expected him to run inside the engine room just that minute. He was ranting and raving and I didn't have time to warn him."

"My goodness," said Katy.

"The explosion was already timed. I didn't know what to do... but I swear I didn't mean for him to die."

"You lied to us," I said.

"We didn't know you three were coming on the train," said Robin. "You were poking around, looking for ways to contact the authorities, so we had to make sure the train couldn't move."

Her eyes flitted over to Matt, then to Stella.

"But we weren't planning on killing anyone," she said, her tone turning hard, almost accusatory. "That wasn't what Dad and I agreed to."

"I, for one, am happy that McNamara is dead," said Matt, through gritted teeth. "He deserved it."

He was boiling with anger. This was a man liable to shoot us all. We couldn't push him too far.

"If that sick dog hadn't died in that explosion," said Matt, his furious eyes on Theodore, "I was going to put a bullet through his head the minute all this was done. That was my plan."

Robin took a sharp breath in. Dwayne gave the young man a sad look.

So this was a surprise to them too.

"What did Connor do to you, Matt?" asked Katy, her voice softened.

I wasn't sure if the light was playing games with me, but I saw tears well up in his eyes.

"Like Robin said, you fools are protecting the wrong man."

He swallowed hard and turned to Dwayne and Robin, his face glistening with tears, but his eyes still blazing with fury.

"I know you weren't planning for anyone to die, but I was."

Dwayne and Robin stepped closer and clutched each other's arms, unhappy expressions on their faces.

"Why are you two here?" I said, turning to the father and daughter. "Is it for the diamonds? Is that what you want?"

Dwayne bent down and pulled up his right trouser leg. The steel rod glinted under the light. I'd seen his artificial leg before.

"It wasn't just me," he said, looking up. "There are many of us."

"What do you mean?"

"Some of us are long gone, but some of us are still alive."

He turned his gaze on Theodore.

"We got paid to stay quiet. He knew what was going on, but never said a word. Covered it up with layers of lawyers."

Theodore didn't reply.

His eyes were closed again, and his chin was slumped against his heaving chest. His mouth opened and closed as he took heavy, rasping breaths, like someone struggling with asthma.

I couldn't help but feel Dwayne was telling the truth.

"And all you wanted was your damn gold," muttered Dwayne, spitting on the ground.

Theodore raised his head and looked at me through weary eyes.

"No wonder you were worried someone was poisoning you," I said to him. "With a track record like yours, I'm surprised you're not already dead." I paused. "But someone was poisoning you, Mr. Henry, and it wasn't anyone in this room."

He gave me a hazy look.

"Your personal physician," I said. "Doctor Wilson confessed to us before he died. Did you know he gave you a false cancer diagnosis?"

Theodore jerked up in his seat. His eyes opened wide.

"He poisoned your mind," said Katy. "He made you believe you were dying."

Robin gasped. Dwayne looked at me in shock, and Matt stared at me like he couldn't believe what he'd just heard.

So, none of them knew.

I turned around to Stella.

"Did you know?"

She blinked, but her outstretched arm that held the revolver didn't waver.

The only reason Katy and I were alive was we had information she wanted.

I wondered what Stella's story was. She had a cool, business-like persona, unlike Matt, who looked like he'd burst into flames any moment.

"Enough!"

It was Stella.

"We don't have to answer their questions," she said, turning to Matt, and then to Dwayne and Robin. "We don't have all day. It's going to get dark out soon and we have to find a way out."

She looked at me, her eyes stony.

"You can ask all your questions to Theodore," she said. "You'll have enough time to get to know each other once we leave."

"You're going to leave us here to die when we can tell you where the diamonds are?" I asked.

Stella's face was cold.

"If you think that's why we went to all this trouble, you know nothing."

Chapter Fifty-three

The blood drained from my face.

That had been my trump card.

It was useless now, unless Stella was bluffing.

But one look around the room, and I knew whatever motivated all of them was much bigger than those uncut stones.

My mind raced.

There was no sign of Tetyana, and I didn't know if she was dead or alive. But I wasn't going to let anyone make this cave our coffin without fighting back.

"I have a team in New York who knows precisely where we are," I said. "They're tracking us. They know who hired us. They know we were on that train, and they also know who else was on it."

Silence.

"A train heist is one thing. Kidnapping is a whole other game. What will finish you all off for good is murder. Quadruple murder, if you bury us here."

I turned to Katy.

"What does that get you?"

"Multiple life terms," she said. "Or worse."

Stella blinked a few times, as if unsure whether to tell me to shut up or not.

"What did Theodore Henry do to you?" I asked.

She glared, but her lips were quivering.

"You could have found a job anywhere on this planet and have had an excellent career. Why choose Black Eagle Mines?"

"I'm done with your questions," she spat out.

I had reminded her of something deeply unpleasant.

"How does a smart scientist like you end up pointing a handgun at us?" I paused. "Whatever Theodore Henry did to you couldn't have been that bad."

Stella's eyes narrowed, and her chest heaved.

"Did he deny you a promotion you wanted badly? Were you getting fed up with the old boys' club? Must have been tough working with this crowd. Did it get to you, finally?"

She let out a disgusted hiss.

"Was it harassment? Is that it? Now you're on a vigilante mission? I'd be mad too, but kidnapping your boss and burying him in a cave is a bit extre—"

Stella's eyes burned. "How dare you!"

Gotcha.

I kept my gaze steady.

I suppressed the urge to look at my friend, who had been standing quietly beside me. Our backs were to the wall, and that was a perfect position to be in. Slowly but surely, I worked on the rope, twisting my hands, while I kept the conversation going.

"That man," said Stella, pointing a shaky finger in Theodore's direction. "He ruined a lot of people."

I nodded but didn't speak. Sometimes silence was the best response.

"Do you know how many suicides my village had, after he stole our land? We lived peacefully for years here, then everything changed."

Now we were getting somewhere.

"He expropriated your village?" I asked, my curiosity growing, despite our circumstances.

"He pushed us all out," said Stella, glaring at Theodore, spittle flying from her mouth. "He didn't care if we froze to death on the mountains. If Jacob and his village hadn't taken us in, fed us, and given us a place to stay, more would have died."

That was when I heard something.

A dull thud over my head. I felt it more than heard it, but nobody else seemed to have registered it, their full attention on Stella.

Was there another entrance to this cave?

I worked my hands faster.

"You're lying," I said. "You became an executive at Black Eagle Mine. Your work made Theodore rich. You didn't care an iota about your village or your people."

Stella's face went red. She turned the gun on me and hissed, like an angry rattlesnake ready to spring. For one short second, I wondered if I'd gone too far.

"You're so wrong," she said. "This man had all the connections and the cash. We sacrificed everything so he could mine his wretched gold."

She shook her head, now almost talking to herself more than us.

"He had the mayor and the city council on his side. Even the sheriff. All bought and paid for. One day, the sheriff's men came to our village, rounded us up and put us in school buses. I remember looking back at my home. Do you know what's there right now?"

"What is it?" I said.

"He built Black Eagle Mine's headquarters right on top of my village!" Stella spluttered. She waved her arms in the air, becoming more and more animated by the second. "My house... my family's home for generations, the one we left behind, was bulldozed to the ground."

She took a raspy breath in, like she was having difficulty breathing.

"My father, who'd lived off the land all his life, had to beg for a job in Anchorage, washing dishes. My mother cleaned toilets at a motel. We barely made enough to pay rent, let alone eat. My father died at forty and my mother died three years later. They died of shame and guilt."

She looked at Theodore, her voice rising several pitches higher.

"And you're wondering what this man did to me?"

The gold baron had resumed his slouched position as if to deflect all these accusations targeted at him.

"Keep your friends close, but your enemies even closer," I said, nodding. "You joined his company to get back at the man who did you wrong."

Katy wiggled her shoulders.

I glanced at her from the corner of my eyes and my heart leaped.

She's free!

She was holding the rope, but her wrists weren't bound anymore.

My turn to focus.

"But you know better than this," said Katy, taking over the conversation. "You could have gone to the courts. You could have used the legal system. Got a local politician on your side."

"Shut up," said Matt, glaring at her.

"There's still time for you to get what you're looking for," continued Katy, in an earnest voice. "You could get punitive damages. I'm sure there's—"

"I said, shut up!" shouted Matt. "Nothing's going to make up for what they did to us."

"What did they do?" asked Katy. "What did Theodore do to you—"

"Him and his best buddy, McNamara!" yelled Matt. "He killed my mother and got away with it all!"

Without a warning, he sprang toward the old man and raised his arm.

"McNamara strangled her like an animal!" he shouted. "And this is the man who got him off!"

Chapter Fifty-four

"Stop!" cried Katy.

But it was too late.

The sharp crack of Matt's gun hitting the old man's face made me cringe.

Theodore's head fell to the side. He was breathing heavily, but still alive.

Matt's arms released to his sides. He faced the floor, his chest heaving so much I wondered if he'd collapse too.

Whatever wound we'd opened up was raw. Still bleeding.

If I hadn't known him as the self-assured, cocky pilot who'd tried to murder me only hours ago, I'd have felt sorry for him.

That was when I noticed the bruises on Matt's hands. His knuckles were raw and ripped, like he'd punched something hard.

Tank.

Was it Matt who'd punched Tank in the woods that night? Why would he do that to one of his own team?

I shook my head to clear it.

I turned toward the rusty elevator, our only escape from this claustrophobic cave.

I strained my ears.

That strange dull thud had come from somewhere up the elevator shaft. It had been so muted I hadn't been sure if my ears were playing games with me.

With Matt hyperventilating next to Theodore, Stella's weapon was the only threat to us now. That and my tied hands.

Like a duck appearing to float serenely but paddling furiously underwater, I pulled at the rope, wiggling my hands behind my back, while keeping a stoic face.

How do we get out?

Do I jump on Stella and let Katy take care of Matt?

What about Dwayne and Robin? Will they fight back?

That would make four against two, two with weapons.

I gave a discreet glance at Stella. If I could disarm her, the rest should be easy.

We had to be careful though.

Every time I thought I had another piece to this puzzle, a seemingly errant piece got thrown in front of me. I was unsure of what puzzle I was trying to put together anymore.

The picture kept changing shape and color with every passing minute.

Maybe the diamonds weren't the main motive. Maybe they had nothing to do with anyone here.

Connor could have been double-crossing his boss. Or he could have been carrying them in his person with Theodore's permission to get them evaluated in Seattle. He had been Theodore's right hand, after all.

I looked at Theodore to see if he could give any hints, any clues to better understand what was going on.

He looked barely alive, but he was watching Matt, a strange expression on his face.

"It should have never happened," said Theodore in a raspy voice. "And it was a long time ago."

Matt snapped his head up and stared at the older man.

"Is there a time limit when you forget who killed your mother?" he spat.

Theodore didn't reply.

Matt turned to us, his eyes black pools of madness.

"You want to know why Theodore is here?"

Katy and I nodded, though I wished he'd look the other way. My hands were almost out of the rope, but I had to be careful not to drop it and give away my position.

"Theodore Henry bailed Connor McNamara out of jail and used his team of high-powered lawyers to get him off. There was nothing I could do. I was just a kid, but I knew what was going on. I stood on the streets watching the man who strangled my mother walk free, for years."

To my surprise, Theodore let out a sob.

Matt turned to him, his eyes flashing, his lips trembling.

"She was only sixteen when she had me. She raised me alone. She had nothing, but she did everything for me." He wiped a tear off his cheek. "It's not like she had much of a choice to do what she did, did she, after her family lost everything to your damn mine?"

He seemed to vacillate between extreme fury and hopelessness, one second gripping the gun like he was ready to shoot Theodore, and the next minute, shaking uncontrollably like he was fighting off a perilously high fever.

I kept my voice leveled and low. "What happened to your mother, Matt?"

He turned his angry eyes on me.

"She worked at the local bar. Not the kind you have in Manhattan. This is the kind of drinking hole they set up next to the mining camps. The type of hole you people wouldn't survive one minute."

So, Matt's mother had been a prostitute.

Like most who ended up in this field of work, I could imagine this had been her last resort. The only way she knew how to feed her child and get a roof over their heads.

Matt whirled around to the older man.

"She worked there every night," he said, tears streaming down his face. "That dog McNamara was one of her clients. Nobody knows what happened in that motel room above the bar that night, but they found her dead on the bed, strangled, left half-naked like a discarded piece of rotting meat..."

Theodore's sobs grew louder.

"This sick man," said Matt, pointing the weapon at his head. "He got his lawyers to bail his best buddy out. No time. He was out again walking, like he owned us."

The more I learned about Theodore, the worse it got. If what everyone was saying was true, I had made a terrible mistake.

They were right.

I had been protecting the wrong man.

A thick thread of anger was winding itself around my spine until all I wanted to do was whip that gun out of Matt's hands and smash it on the mining baron's head myself.

I swallowed hard.

Katy turned to Matt.

"There must be another way," she said. "They can dig up your mother's remains and do an autopsy. They can look for witnesses, get evidence, and redeem—"

"*Right*," said Dwayne, throwing Katy a disgusted look. "Y'all have no idea what it's like to live in a small town where those in power are closer than blood brothers."

"But the authorities—"

"Do you think we're stupid?" said Robin. There was no malice in her voice, just dejected helplessness. "Do you think we didn't try to help Matt?"

"We learned the hard way they don't care for the likes of us, a long time ago," said Dwayne. "We tried everything when Theodore took our homes. We talked to the mayor. We've tried to get lawyers to help, but when you're going against the biggest and most corrupt businessman in the state, do you think we had a fighting chance?"

Theodore was making strange sucking noises now. Whether he had cancer or not, he looked like a dying man in the last stretches of his life.

I pulled one hand away and relief flooded through my veins.

I held the rope tightly, trying not to tremble.

I was free.

Finally.

Chapter Fifty-five

"Do you have anything to say for yourself?" I asked Theodore.

Without answering, he turned to Matt.

"Why do you think I brought you here?" he said.

"You didn't bring me here," snarled Matt. "I came looking for you. I came to make you pay for what you did to my mother. Your pal's dead and you're next."

"No," croaked Theodore, shaking his head. "I'm the one who brought you here."

I narrowed my eyes. Did he even understand what Matt said? Had he already lost his mind?

There.

That thud again.

I felt the goose bumps on my arms. It was coming from near the elevator, right above my head, but there were no signs of it being operated. I wondered if there were more people inside this mine than those of us in this room.

No one else seemed to have noticed, their full attention on Theodore.

"I hired a firm that looks for missing people," the older man was saying, drawing his words out slowly, like it hurt him to speak. "I told them to find you, even if it took all my resources."

"You liar," growled Matt. "I knew who you were and where you were. I found this job to get close to you, to wait for the right time."

"Ah, your pilot job," said Theodore. "Which company did you sign up with?"

Matt stared at him mutely, as if he hadn't understood the question.

Dwayne turned to the old man, his brow knotted.

"Alaska Sky Delivery Services," he said.

Theodore nodded. "Do you know who owns that company?"

Dwayne's face turned dark.

Robin spat on the ground.

"I should have known," snarled Stella. "You have your fingers in everything."

Matt was silent, as if he was still trying to comprehend what he'd just heard.

"That wasn't a fluke," said Theodore. "I hired the firm to find you, but make it appear like you found them. I told them to give you any job you wanted in the state."

Matt's face turned purple.

"I don't need your charity!"

He straightened up like he'd been injected with a vial of venom. He took a step forward, his gun barrel pointing at Theodore's head, his finger on the trigger.

"Matt," Katy called out. "What happened to you was horrible, but don't do anything you'll regret."

"I'll never regret sending him or Connor McNamara to their graves."

He took another step toward the gold baron.

"You think you can silence me just like you did when my mother died. You treated her worse than a dog on the streets."

"I loved her!"

Matt froze.

A shocked hush fell in the cave.

We all turned to Theodore.

Theodore's eyes were on Matt. Matt's eyes bulged, but he stood still as a statue.

It was Robin who broke the ice.

"*What* did you say?"

"Do you know who I am?" croaked Theodore.

The younger man stared at him silently.

"How dare you speak about my mother, you sick animal? I swear to—"

Theodore shook his head. "I looked for you because... because..."

He broke into a dry, heaving cough. He looked brittle and vulnerable, tied up in that oversized chair, like a hapless victim. But I knew better now than to feel any sympathy for this man who'd manipulated so many people.

The more I heard, the more I felt Theodore Henry deserved everything coming to him that day.

Theodore recovered from his coughing fit and turned back to Matt.

"I went to the municipal court in January," said Theodore, tears rolling down his cheeks. "I signed a paternity action." He paused. "For you."

We stood stunned.

I looked at Theodore, then at Matt.

So, that was why Katy thought Matt's face was familiar. It wasn't something I would have picked up on, especially given Theodore's condition, but she was right.

This time, no one spoke for a long time.

The puzzle was finally coming together. There were still pieces missing, but I now knew how this all started.

"Theodore Henry," I said, looking at my client. "You're Matt's father."

Before I could do anything, Matt jumped on Theodore, his eyes blazing, and whacked the old man's head with the pistol.

The dull sound of the weapon smashing against Theodore's haggard head reverberated around the cave.

Matt raised his hand again.

"Matt!" shouted Katy. "You're going to kill him!"

Dwayne jumped in and pulled the young man away. Matt's gun fell with a clatter to the ground.

I eyed it.

I had to get my hands on it.

But Stella was watching me now.

"You don't need to do this," Dwayne was saying, holding the shaking young man at bay.

"When I die..." said Theodore, raising his head, seemingly not registering the trickle of blood running down his forehead. "You'll inherit everything I own."

"How dare you!" cried Matt, his face red in rage, his entire body shaking.

He probably felt like he'd been shoved inside a snow globe and shaken up.

"You don't have to believe my words," continued Theodore, his voice getting raspier and losing volume. "You'll know the truth when you're done with me. You can bury me alive. You can shoot me in the face. Lord knows, I deserve it. But I want you to know before I die that I loved your mother."

Matt pushed Dwayne away and turned a furious face to Theodore.

"Is that why you let her murderer get away?" he shouted.

"I was barely out of my teens when I met her," said Theodore. "I didn't know what I was doing."

"She was just a common village girl to you," yelled Matt, his voice cracking too. "You used her and dumped her, you sicko. Just like you did to everyone else in our village."

"I was wrong," said Theodore. "I know it's too late, but I was wrong."

The trickle of blood was getting bigger now. I wondered how long he'd last.

Matt's gun was still on the floor, calling out my name.

I took a discreet step closer to the weapon.

"I have more regret in my heart than you can ever imagine," Theodore was saying. "When Doctor Wilson told me I had terminal cancer, I knew what I had to do. I had to right my wrongs. I'm not asking for forgiveness. I just want to you to have a—"

"There's no redemption for what you did," shouted Matt, his voice echoing across the chamber. "You ruined all of us!"

Suddenly, the ancient elevator groaned.

We all spun around.

Someone had called it up.

Stella took four steps back, aiming her weapon at the lift.

I didn't know who would step out of those doors. It could be friend or foe, and I wasn't about to be taken by surprise again.

I didn't hesitate.

I leaped forward and scooped up the gun from the floor.

A rustle made me look up.

I swiveled around, just as a rope fell from the ceiling, right next to the lift. I'd been so engrossed with the conversation, and while I had been searching for hidden exits on the rock wall, I hadn't seen the hollow shaft by the elevator.

Loud gasps went around the cave.

A tall figure dropped down the rope, firefighter style.

Tetyana!

She turned her Glock at the room.

"Stay back, all of you!" she shouted.

Pulling Katy by the arm, I stepped backward, toward the elevator, my gun aimed at Stella, the only person other than Tetyana who carried a weapon in this room.

Stella whirled around, confused, pointing her sidearm first at Tetyana, then at me, then at Katy, and back again.

I was standing next to the elevator, by the rope that hung from the ceiling. I glanced up quickly to see a small opening right above my head. Inside were machinery, levers, old-fashioned pulleys.

How did she know to find this entrance?

"Asha, Katy!" hollered Tetyana, gesturing at us, but her eyes on Stella and Matt. "Get Theodore!"

Katy whipped around to her.

"But Tetyana—"

"Now! No debate!"

"I don't think that's such a good idea—"

Katy didn't get to finish, as the elevator doors clattered open.

Chapter Fifty-six

J acob.

What's he doing here?

He stepped out of the elevator and walked into the cave. He moved slowly, like a monk treading gently across sacred temple grounds.

He stopped in the middle of the room, halfway between Stella and us, while the old elevator doors rattled shut behind him.

He closed his eyes and stood still.

It was bizarre to see him, a shaman-like character in the midst of a potential underground gun battle. It would be risky to fire a shot now, without hitting Jacob. I wondered if that was his strategy.

With an exasperated sigh, Tetyana stepped toward Katy and me, without changing her aim or moving her eyes.

"What the hell are you two waiting for?" she hissed from the side of her mouth. "Get the fogey and get out."

Katy and I didn't move.

My mind was racing a million miles a second.

Who do we believe?

Do we rescue Theodore Henry, who'd done irreparable harm to these people? Or do we save this sad crowd who'd conspired against the gold baron, catching all of us in their revenge drag net?

The last person I wanted to defend was the reprehensible man who'd destroyed so many lives and ravaged an entire village so he could profit from the resources underneath.

He'd admitted to his crimes himself.

As far as I was concerned, he was no longer my client.

Then, a voice screamed from the back of my head. *But Matt pushed me out of a plane*, it said.

Stella turned to Tetyana.

"How did you get here?" she growled.

"It doesn't matter how I came down," snapped Tetyana, "but there's only one way I'm going up. In the elevator with my two friends and Theodore Henry. So, don't try anything funny."

"You still want to protect him?" said Stella, her eyes flickering my way.

I glanced at Matt, who was staring at Theodore, his eyes wide in shock, like he was still trying to come to terms with what he'd just learned.

Matt Ryder was in the center of all this.

He was the one who'd been harmed the most, the one who had the greatest need for vengeance.

I still didn't know how this raggedy team had got together to plot the train holdup and Theodore's kidnapping, but he was the mastermind. The others had their own grievances, but not enough to kill.

Suddenly, I knew what to do.

"Katy," I said as I stepped up to Theodore's chair. "Grab the other side."

She gave me a perplexed look, but came over and picked up the arm of the chair across from me.

Together, we dragged the old mining baron to the elevator. He sat still, his eyes closed, his head resting against his chest.

Tetyana pulled on the handle, and the elevator doors clattered open.

I turned my flashlight on and pushed Theodore into the elevator, making him jerk back and moan.

I bit my lip, suppressing the urge to tell him what little pain he was going through was nothing compared to what he had inflicted on the others.

His face was pale. He wouldn't survive for long. But the last thing I wanted was for Matt or Stella to do something they'd severely regret later.

"Stay right there," said Tetyana to Stella, as she stepped back toward the elevator.

"You're going to leave us here?" said Robin, a tremor in her voice.

Tetyana turned to Dwayne and her.

"Don't you think I know what game you're playing at?" she said to the startled father and daughter who were huddling in the corner of the cave.

To my surprise, Jacob turned around and walked into the elevator.

He's coming with us?

When he was in, Tetyana slammed the elevator handle.

The last image I saw was Matt's eyes, wide, staring at me with a dazed expression.

My stomach sank.

Part of me felt bad for them.

Katy spun around to face Tetyana and pointed at the old man.

"He's the one we should have left behind," she said in an angry whisper.

Tetyana shot her a confused glance.

I hushed Katy with my hand.

Jacob was standing in front of the door, his back to us, his face down.

I didn't know who he was, what he was up to or if he had reinforcements hidden in the mountain. We could explain all this to Tetyana later.

Theodore was gurgling. If I had to guess, Matt's punches had hit their target. He was probably bleeding internally.

"What about the others?" said Katy. "Do we just leave them down there?"

"They'll come out later. We don't have time for them right now," said Tetyana, looking at her wristwatch.

"What's the plan?" I said.

"We have a train to catch."

"A train?" said Katy in shock.

"The freight train?" I said.

"That's what he says," said Tetyana, pointing at Jacob with her chin.

"Knows the exact time it comes by too," she added.

The elevator door opened.

Jacob stepped out and started walking down the slope along the pipeline.

"What if he's lying?" whispered Katy.

"If he makes one wrong move, I'll have his head," said Tetyana, giving the man's departing back a grim look. "And he knows that."

Chapter Fifty-seven

Tetyana holstered her weapon as soon as we stepped out of the shaft.

Then, she bent down, pulled the wooden beam away, and kicked it down the slope, away from Jacob.

The log rolled down about twenty feet from him, but he didn't flinch. He didn't even look up.

"That should give us more time," said Tetyana, wiping her hands. "They'll have to work harder to get out."

I looked down at the chasm between the entrance and the cave. Unlike me, they knew of this hole, and they had daylight. They would be fine.

Let them come up with their own solution, I thought as I turned away and grabbed onto Theodore's chair.

Tetyana stepped ahead of us with her gun in her hand, while Katy and I pushed the old man in his chair down the tracks, step by step, using the nails sticking out of the pipeline for traction.

If we tripped and snowballed down, we'd hit Tetyana first, then Jacob. I kept a tight grip.

It took us a lot longer to descend than before.

It was near noon and the sun was out, glistening brightly on the pristine landscape around us, a vivid contrast to our dark moods.

"Where's Tank?" I asked as soon as Jacob was out of earshot.

"In the train," said Tetyana.

"Thank goodness, you got him in the end," said Katy.

"He got me first," said Tetyana. "Jumped on me real good."

"Last we saw, he had a gun to your back," I said. "We underestimated him. He had to have proper training from somewhere. I don't know anyone who could win over you in hand-to-hand combat."

"I let him."

"Why would you do that?" I said, frowning.

"He told me he could help us. He was talking to me while he was pretending to hold me down. Begging me not to kill him."

Katy and I stared at her.

"I had two choices," said Tetyana. "I could have beaten him easily, but he had a gun. So did Matt and Stella, and I didn't like those odds. Or I could wait for you all to disappear into the mine and see if Tank was telling the truth."

"Tough choices," I said.

She nodded. "Sometimes you gotta go with your gut. He turned out okay."

"You hate Tank," said Katy.

"I changed my mind," said Tetyana.

I stopped to catch my breath. Katy halted too. This was hard work.

My eyes swept the open terrain, and the abandoned town below. I peered at the tree line that bordered the coniferous woods from the town.

We three were armed again, and we still had our Kevlar vests on. But that wouldn't stop anyone from ambushing us, especially if they were hidden behind those trees.

"What did Jacob tell you?" I said, turning to Tetyana.

"Other than the train's coming?" she said. "Something about us protecting the wrong guy."

I looked down at Theodore, who seemed to have passed out in his chair.

"Guess who was evil enough to expropriate everyone's land and throw them out on the streets?" I said.

Tetyana raised an eyebrow and kicked the back of the chair.

"This gentleman?"

"He's no gentleman," said Katy.

"Jacob supposedly saved an entire village when they lost their homes to the mine," I said.

Tetyana turned to look at the old man from the church, walking several yards ahead of us now and well out of earshot. "He said some gibberish about everyone being connected. Couldn't make head or tail of it."

"Stella, Dwayne, Robin, and Matt all have good reasons to be angry at Theodore," I said. "All their families were victims."

"Dwayne was a teen laborer in the mine, so he got it doubly bad," said Katy. "They all wanted revenge on the owner of Black Eagle Mines. Even Stella."

Tetyana let out a low whistle.

"So, that's why you guys were acting so strange down in the cave. I thought it was all mumbo jumbo."

"Matt was about to kill Theodore when you came in," I said.

"What about this Matt Ryder?" said Tetyana, narrowing her eyes. "Can't figure the man out."

Between Katy and me, we shared what we'd heard with her. Tetyana stood by us, one eye on Jacob and another on the woods below, shaking her head, as if she couldn't believe her ears.

"You believe these stories?" she said when we were done.

"Verdict's still out," I said. "I say we take everything with a big grain of salt until proven otherwise."

"I second that," said Katy. "I don't trust anyone."

"Let's get this criminal down first," said Tetyana. "We don't want to hang out on these slopes for too long."

She gave me a side glance.

"If it had been me, and I heard all these stories, I'd have shot this man myself, you know."

"I want him to live to see the repercussions of his actions," I said.

We resumed our hike, but my mind was a whirlwind.

My stomach lurched to think we were rescuing the very man I wanted to leave behind in that cave and let nature take care of him. If those horrific tales were true, I would have done that unapologetically.

I'd killed before.

I had no qualms about getting rid of evil on this earth. But I also knew such actions should never be taken rashly. Every time I acted on impulse, more people suffered, including me.

We had to do the right thing.

The right thing was to notify law enforcement and tell them everything. Though justice didn't always happen the way I wanted it to, it was better in this country than any other place I'd lived in through my nomadic childhood.

At the very least, we had curtailed another murder on the mountain.

Compared to my dark ruminations, Tetyana's scowl, and Katy's thoughtful demeanor, Jacob seemed calm, floating effortlessly down the slope.

Every time the wind turned, a strange hum came from his way, like he was singing a hymn to himself.

I wondered who he really was.

Jacob was a withdrawn, mysterious man who spoke in riddles. Living in isolation for long periods could wreak havoc on your mental health. But he also seemed to know everything and everyone. I wondered if he was actually saner than any of us.

Jacob was waiting patiently for us at the bottom of the mountain, still humming to himself.

"Quite the happenings going on here," I said, as we got to talking distance. "Why didn't you tell us of this before?"

"I was trying to avoid anyone getting hurt," he replied.

I stared at him, unsure whether to believe him or not. Too many people were hiding too many things from us.

It took another half an hour for us to carry Theodore in the chair through the woods, all the way to the train.

The ice was melting, and the air was getting warm which was a good thing. Otherwise, we'd have never got back to the tracks without slipping.

It was a relief to reach the threshold of the tree line.

That was when I saw him.

Tank was standing on the steps of the dining car.

He had a Glock in his hand.

Chapter Fifty-eight

Seeing us, Tank jumped down from the train.

Tetyana motioned him to come and help.

Without asking any questions, he took Katy's place. Katy and I stepped aside, watching with wary eyes as they lifted the chair up.

Theodore looked like he was oblivious to all that was going on around him. Or was he alert, but pretending not to be?

Tetyana and Tank carried the old man up the steps and inside the dining car. They placed him close to where he had been sitting when all hell broke loose.

After he was settled, I walked up to check his pulse.

His heartbeat was strong, despite his sickly appearance. The trickle of blood had stopped and had congealed on his cheek, but he was still breathing.

Good.

We needed him alive so he could give a full confession to the authorities or to a court. I loosened the ropes on his hands and feet. He wasn't going anywhere fast.

As the rest of us huddled around Theodore's chair, contemplating him, Jacob stood next to him, hands folded in front, his eyes half closed, like he was meditating.

Theodore opened his eyes, like he knew we were watching him.

Jacob shook his head.

"Bad deeds never go unpunished," he said in his signature soft voice. "I told you that a long time ago, Theodore Henry, but you never listened."

Theodore pushed against the chair's arm and struggled to stand.

"Sit down," said Tetyana in a stern voice.

I wondered if I should tie him down again.

"My throat is parched," said Theodore, looking around.

I turned to Tank. "Get him some water."

"Let me make one thing very clear," I said to Theodore. "This wasn't a rescue mission. This was a civilian arrest."

He turned and looked at me, his eyes narrowed. Even in his state, I could see the slow anger burning in them.

"For the record, our contract is null and void," I said.

"Is that right?" said Theodore.

"I don't make agreements with criminals."

He let out an angry hiss.

"Don't worry. I won't be asking for payment for work done to date."

Another angry hiss. Holding on to his chair, Theodore got up shakily.

"I said sit down," growled Tetyana.

"Let him," I said. "He can't go far."

"Get me out of this chair, for heaven's sake," said Theodore in a shaking voice. "I need some fresh air."

Tank stepped up.

Leaning against his nephew for support, Theodore shuffled to the end of the carriage and popped his head out of the door.

"Watch him," said Tetyana to Tank. "And keep your eyes on the woods."

With a nod, the teen took position, his eyes gazing out to the tree line.

I imagined Tetyana had a good talk with him after we went down the shaft, but still, I wasn't going to put blind faith in any of them.

I gestured to my friends to join me at the end of the dining car.

It was time for a huddle to make sure we were speaking in one voice, especially in front of the authorities when they arrived.

If they ever arrived.

"How are you so sure about the train?" I said.

Tetyana looked down at her wristwatch.

"Jacob said it should arrive in half an hour."

"Dwayne and Robin said it got delayed by days, sometimes," I said.

"Jacob could be lying to us," whispered Katy. "I don't think we can believe him any more than the others."

"He heard it," said Tetyana.

"*Heard* it?" I said, cocking my ears. "I don't hear a thing."

"It's still miles away."

"You believe that?" said Katy.

"I heard it too," said Tetyana, nodding. "Something big is slowly rumbling this way."

Katy and I stared at her.

"Used to put my ear on the tracks when we were fighting the Russians. I could hear them from a distance," said Tetyana. "I left Tank on the train in case it arrived early."

"Wow," said Katy.

"They'll stop as soon as they see the stalled train on the tracks," said Tetyana. "When they do, we get Theodore inside and secure him first."

I glanced up at Tank, who was standing forlornly by the open door. He was leaning away from his uncle, like he didn't like being this close to him.

Theodore was holding on to the door with one hand and holding an opened bottle of water with the other. He was staring out at the woods, though I doubted he was looking at anything in particular.

He'd confessed to a series of serious crimes and had just introduced himself to a son who'd wished him dead since childhood. A son willing to kill him.

I couldn't begin to imagine what was going through his mind.

Jacob was standing in the middle of the dining car alone, his eyes closed, but he was humming again.

Something about that hum made me uneasy. It wasn't a soothing hymn, but a deeper and slower one that came across like a warning.

A warning for what?

Could things get any worse?

"Tank could turn on us at any time," I said in a low voice.

Tetyana shook her head.

"The man doesn't want to be here. He got roped in by Stella and Matt to be the bodyguard. It was all part of the plan."

"Why didn't Theodore hire a professional team?" I said. "It's not like he can't afford one."

"He supposedly doesn't trust anyone," said Tetyana. "When Stella and Matt hatched their plan and *voluntold* Tank to sign up, Theodore thought he'd found the perfect solution. Tank's his nephew and is built like a linebacker."

"Wouldn't Tank be loyal to his own family though?" said Katy.

"Sounds like old Theodore took his family for a ride too," said Tetyana. "Got them to invest their life savings in some dodgy gold stock scheme and they lost a lot. Theo isn't everyone's favorite uncle, that's for sure—"

She didn't get to finish.

"Hey, stop!"

We whipped around.

It was Tank, shouting.

Chapter Fifty-nine

"Don't shoot!" shouted a familiar voice.

It was Dwayne.

We dashed toward the open door and pushed Theodore and Tank aside.

The group we'd left inside the mine were emerging from the woods, one by one. Stella was at the lead, her sidearm pointing at us.

"Put your weapon down," shouted Tetyana as she jumped down the steps, her arms raised, her Glock in her hands.

"Stay with Theodore," I said to Katy before I stepped across the tracks and ran toward the tree line, following my friend.

"Weapon on the ground!" hollered Tetyana.

Stella glared.

I stepped up to Tetyana and stood next to her, shoulder to shoulder.

It was a bedraggled crowd that stared back at us.

Dwayne, Robin, Matt, and Stella.

They had planned a heist, a kidnapping, and possibly even a series of murders in Matt's case. But none of them looked like the hardened career criminals we'd fought off in our youths.

My mind swirled.

They weren't the only people present who'd tried vigilante justice to right old wrongs. We had been guilty of it too.

Tetyana, Katy, my fiancé David, myself, and everyone in my found family had fought back against those who'd haunted us and made them pay. Dearly. It was how we'd learned to hunt, to spy, to spar, to shoot.

No one moved.

There were two of us with weapons, against their one.

"You don't care what happens to us, do you?" said Robin, her face dejected, like she'd given up. "You're working for him, like everyone else."

"How much did he pay you?" said Matt. "Enough to look away from everything he did?"

Tetyana and I didn't speak. There wasn't much to say. We knew exactly how they were feeling.

Despite having a weapon, Stella's hand was shaking.

"Put your gun down," I said in a quiet voice. "You don't want to do this."

"So you can kill us?" she said, turning her reddened eyes on me. "So you can haul us all off to prison and make us rot in jail?"

Her and Matt's eyes flickered to someone or something behind us.

"He would like that, wouldn't he?" said Stella. "Theodore Henry always wins. He always gets what he wants."

"Stella, Matt," I tried again. "Killing your enemy isn't worth it. Whether the authorities catch up to you or not, you'll have to live with your nightmares for the rest of your life. It's time to let go."

Matt looked away, a disgusted expression on his face.

"Believe me when I say this," I said. "We were in your shoes once—"

That was when I heard the piercing whistle.

My heart leaped.

The freight train!

It was here.

Jacob was right, after all.

Another long and loud whistle echoed across the valley, then came a low rumbling sound in the distance.

Relief rushed through my veins. I'd never felt this happy to hear a locomotive in my life.

I turned back to Stella.

"Please put your gun down. Hand it over before they come, and we'll figure this out."

Matt's eyes flickered behind me again. From the hatred that flushed across his face, I was sure he was looking at Theodore.

"You've made your point," I said. "We know what happened. Don't do anything rash. Not now."

To my surprise, Stella dropped the gun and stepped back.

Thank goodness.

Tetyana sprang ahead and scooped Stella's sidearm up. I lowered my weapon.

Dwayne and Robin stood in place, their faces turned toward the approaching train. They looked crushed, like they were ready for whatever came their way, however devastating.

Stella no longer looked furious, but there was an undercurrent of simmering rage in her eyes.

But it was Matt who had the most peculiar expression. He was the only one not looking in the direction of the train. He was staring behind me, at his father, quiet agony etched on his face.

Without any warning, Stella grabbed Matt's hand. Facing us, she pulled him back, closer to the woods.

"Wait," I said, my heart skipping a beat as I realized they were attempting to escape. "Don't do it. You'll be running for the rest of your lives."

They took another step back, no longer looking at me, but behind me.

"Hey!"

I spun around.

Tank was at the dining car's doorway, standing awkwardly next to Theodore. Jacob was silhouetted behind them, and by him was Katy.

She was waving urgently and shouting something, but I couldn't hear her.

The train's thundering sound was overtaking everything. The whistle screeched again.

That was when I saw it.

A modern electric train, a mile away. It had just come around the bend and was chugging toward us.

The grinding of its wheels on the tracks got louder and louder, echoing across the valley, bouncing off the mountains. I could feel the vibration of the locomotive in every bone in my body.

Another whistle reverberated through the air. The train thundered closer.

"Hey there!" I hollered, running along the tracks, waving my arms in the air. "SOS! Stop! SOS!"

A deafening mechanical screech blasted through the air.

They had seen us.

Steel wheels shrieked against the steel tracks. They were braking hard, but it would take them a while to stop.

I remembered how long our train had taken to come to a complete stop after Robin had spotted the dead body a mile away. This was a much larger, heavy duty, and imposing beast of machinery that would require a lot more energy to halt its momentum.

I could see the driver in the engine cab now, his eyes wide open, as he regarded the scene in front of him in shock.

"Get back!"

I swiveled around, my heart racing.

It was Tetyana, waving her arms, shouting at Katy and the others inside our train. It looked like a scuffle had broken out by the door.

What's going on?

"Katy!" I shouted. "Watch out!"

But it was too late.

The freight train was only yards from us now. The sound of its engine was like thunder, shaking the ground under my feet.

The engineer blew the ear-splitting whistle.

That was a warning.

My gut tightened, like it was preparing for something.

Something bad.

I swiveled my head around, back to the dining car of the steam train.

As I watched in horror, Theodore Henry's grip slackened. His hand slipped, and he fell headfirst onto the tracks, right in front of the oncoming train.

A startled yell came from inside the freight train.

Someone screamed.

Tetyana shouted.

I clapped my hands on my ears.

But I couldn't stop hearing the sickening scrunch of Theodore's bones and flesh as the massive machine rolled over his limp body.

I turned around and vomited on the pristine white snow.

Two Weeks Later

Chapter Sixty

"**B**ut what about the diamonds?"

Win, my young computer expert, was staring at me over the top of her laptop.

She had settled herself at the bakery counter, ignoring protests from her husband, Luc, my head baker.

Everyone had seen snippets of the triple tragedy in Alaska on the news. But no one knew the full story, and all had eagerly gathered in my bakery kitchen to get the scoop.

I didn't realize it then, but I hadn't heard the complete tale either. Not yet.

"Does Tetyana still have the stones on her?" said Sarah, the bakery's sous chef, pushing aside her mixing bowl.

Tetyana was teaching a kickboxing class at the martial arts dojo next door with David. She had returned from our trip with great gusto, pushing her students and working them to the bone, so much so David was worried someone would get injured.

But I knew she was only letting out steam after what had happened during our mission.

"We returned the stones to their rightful owners," said Katy, switching the kettle on.

She turned to Jacob who was sitting at the counter, next to Win. His shoulders were hunched, uncomfortable in this foreign place.

"Tea?" she said.

"Yes, please," he said in his low, soft voice.

"But who are the rightful owners?" said Rosalie, turning off the mixer and wiping her hands on her apron.

Katy and I exchanged a quick glance. That had been a difficult question to figure out.

It had been two weeks since we'd returned home to New York.

Every time I came back from a mission, I appreciated my bakery even more. The sweet warm smells of cinnamon, sugar, and butter swirled in the air as Luc and his team mixed up a batch of cupcakes for a celebrity birthday party at an uptown venue.

I took a deep breath in to savor the atmosphere. This was my heaven on earth. A respite from my investigative ventures.

The Red Heeled Rebels bakery was where I had redesigned my life and found calmness and serenity after a lifetime of daring to stand up to traffickers and their goons who'd vowed to destroy us.

Win, along with Katy, Tetyana, David, Luc, our bakery's self-appointed delivery queen Bibi, and sous chefs Rosalie, and Sarah had all struggled for survival in our youths. Our shared experience had brought us together and kept us together.

We'd watched each other's backs and fought for each other's freedoms. We'd been rejected by our own, but had formed our little multi-national family, where we celebrated what we had in common.

For several nights after our return from Anchorage, I'd woken up at three in the morning, my heart racing, thinking I was still stuck in that burned-out shell of a train in the middle of nowhere, next to Connor's burned corpse.

David always woke up when that happened. He pulled me down and enveloped me in his arms, cradling me until I fell asleep again.

Our Alaska trip had been so out of this world, some days I wondered if it had been a nightmare I'd dreamed up.

That is, until I saw Katy the next morning in her office at the bakery, popping another painkiller for her headaches.

Or when I watched Tetyana punch Bob, the rubber man, at the martial arts studio. One day, she punched him so hard David had to stop her before she broke the equipment.

We each coped in our own ways.

Physical ordeals were easier to get over. The emotional stresses of figuring out the villains and their intentions, then dealing with our part in the aftermath, was far more agonizing.

One question swirled through my mind for days. *Did we do the right thing?*

It was always satisfying when the bad guys got caught and the good guys won. But it was hard when the good guys turned bad, then good again.

Like this time.

"Those diamonds sent us on a goose chase," I said, giving a side glance at Jacob, who was warming his hands around his teacup. "It was a weird red herring."

"But it was part of the puzzle, all along," said Katy, slipping a hot mug in front of me.

"The paintings confused me too," I said.

Jacob gave a grave nod.

Leaning against the wall behind him were three flat objects, four feet by four in diameter, wrapped carefully in brown paper, brought all the way from Alaska.

They stayed quietly in the background, like they were patiently waiting for their creator to acclimatize to the city. They would soon be exchanged for a phenomenal amount of money at the largest art dealership in New York.

Their moment would come.

"Paintings, diamonds, and a dead body on the tracks," said Luc, shaking his head. He waved his icing spatula in the air. "My gosh, what a messy problem to figure out. My biggest problems are self-entitled, bossy clients who want their high tea right now."

"I'm never complaining about my job again," said Sarah.

"Me neither," said Bibi.

She'd just returned from a delivery trip and was standing by the back door, gorging on a pineapple cupcake she'd poached from Luc's cake tray.

"I'll fight downtown Manhattan traffic any day," said Bibi. "That's enough to make me pull my hair out and go insane. I don't know why you keep going on these crazy investigations."

Katy and I exchanged a knowing smile.

"What about the kitten?" said Rosalie, turning to Jacob. "You didn't leave it all by itself at the church, did you?"

"Stella and Matt took her in," said Jacob with a small smile. "That fur ball will outlive me, so it made little sense to keep her."

"Oh, good," said Rosalie. "I was worried about it."

"Stop distracting them, people," said Win, glaring at everyone. "I want to know what happened to those diamonds."

"Stella knew all about the stones," I said, returning to the topic at hand. "She was the one who identified them in her lab when someone brought them up from the mine. Only she, Connor, and Theodore knew what they were."

"How did they end up in Connor McNamara's jacket?" asked Luc, momentarily forgetting his cakes. "Was he trying to steal them?"

"They didn't want anyone else in the company to find out. This was the first time anyone had discovered diamonds in Alaska, so this was a big deal. Theodore wanted to confirm their true value before he made an announcement."

"So, no one else knew about them?" asked Sarah.

I shook my head.

"Stella told Matt, who told Dwayne and Robin. The plan was to pilfer them during the train ride and make them disappear. It was a heist. Just a good old heist. At least, that's what Stella, Dwayne, and Robin thought."

Jacob lifted his head and gave me a quiet look. I knew he was reeling from what had happened, and he'd had much more skin in the game than us.

"Their hearts were in the right place," he said, his somber expression deepening.

"They were planning a robbery," said Win, shooting him a stern look. "Plus, they dug out a dead body. How is that good?"

We waited for Jacob to reply, but he had turned his eyes back to his cup.

Jacob had been a man of few words on the mountain, speaking in riddles and confusing us. Coming to the big city—his first ever foray out of Alaska—had thrown him off balance.

The only reason he had come was because Katy and I had needled him, finally convincing him to bring his paintings to New York.

"What about that dead body? The dead doctor? And the boiler that got blown up?" asked Luc. "Did they do all that to get back at Theodore Henry?"

The day's order was going to be late.

The entire crew had stopped working, their eager eyes staring at Katy and me over their half-done cakes. They looked like a bunch of kids around a campfire, itching to hear how the ghost story ended.

What they didn't realize was this wasn't just another campfire tale.

This one ended with three people dead. Each one of them had probably deserved their ending.

But still.

A death was still a death.

Chapter Sixty-one

"**M**att Ryder complicated everything," said Katy, as she poured herself a cup of tea.

"He spent his entire life looking for the best time to get revenge for his mother's death," I said. "He targeted Connor and Theodore. What he didn't realize was while he was searching for them, they were looking for him."

"Creepy," said Bibi with a shudder.

"Theodore manipulated everything he touched. That's how he became such a powerful man. Matt didn't have a chance."

"Except this time, he was seeking a lost son," said Katy. "He wanted to make amends."

"It's always family, isn't it?" said Rosalie, taking a soda can out of the fridge. "It's always close relationships that mess you up."

"Speaking of," said Rosalie, "what's the deal with Stella and Matt?"

"They're an item. They'd been dating for a while," said Katy.

I nodded. "I didn't see that coming."

"They kept it quiet, but I suspected something," said Katy.

"How did they meet?" said Sarah.

"Matt made friends with as many people in the mining company as he could to get close to Theodore. That's how he met her," said Katy.

"When Stella figured out what Matt's plans were, she had no problem helping him out," I said. "She joined the company years ago for similar reasons. She wanted to bankrupt the man who had destroyed her parents' village. She was patient for years, but you could see the unhappiness on her face."

"Revenge can eat you up from the inside," said Jacob quietly to his teacup. "It can never bring you happiness."

We all nodded.

"What about the train conductor and engineer?" asked Luc.

"They were from the same village that was expropriated for the mine. They thought Matt's plan was to get the diamonds cashed and share the funds among the families who'd lost their homes. That's what Stella had promised, and that's what Matt told them at the beginning."

"But Matt lied," said Katy. "He wanted more. He was nasty."

"If you ask me, that Tank guy sounds the most suspicious," said Rosalie, leaning over her half-done pastries.

"Stella convinced Theodore to hire him," I said. "Tank was family, so Theodore trusted him. All the while, he was really working for her and Matt. She'd promised him a huge payoff from the diamond heist, if he played the game right."

"So, they were the ones who ransacked the train?" said Luc. "I saw a video of the inside on TV. They said it was the explosion that caused it."

"That's not true," said Katy. "Stella and Tank turned the train inside out looking for the stones."

"I don't like those two," said Sarah, shaking her head. "How do you know it wasn't one of them who pushed you in that hole, Asha?"

"No one's confessed, but I'd bet it was Tank who did it under direction from Matt." I shrugged. "It was a small hole. I gathered Tank thought I couldn't die. He was remorseful and helped us out in the end, but I'll never be alone in his company, that's for sure."

"Tank's only nineteen. He was easily manipulated," said Katy. "Matt was the ringleader, and I haven't forgiven him for what he did."

"Tetyana said she'd smash Tank's face if he ever came to town," said a male voice.

I turned around to see David walk in. He came over and looped an arm around my waist.

Class must be over.

"Me too," he said, shaking his head. "I'd make sure he'll never try anything like that again. Why can't you find a safer job to moonlight?"

I gave him a peck on the cheek.

"We came home alive, didn't we, sweetie?"

He made a face.

I knew he hated it when I took these calls, but he knew I could never say no. I wrapped my arm around him and gave him a light squeeze.

Jacob lifted his chin and looked up at me, sadness etched on his face.

"Matt was a good boy once," he said in a slow voice. "I remember when he used to run around, playing hockey on the streets. That all changed after his mother died."

"Murdered, you mean?" said Katy with feeling. "He was left all by himself after that."

Jacob shook his head wearily.

"That he wasn't," he said, speaking so softly we had to lean across the counter to hear. "My wife and I took him in. We gave him a bed and food, and sent him to school."

"*You* adopted Matt?" said Katy in a shocked voice.

I raised an eyebrow. There was more to this story we didn't know yet.

"He worked hard, that boy," continued Jacob. "He was looking for love and validation, and that was really all we could give him." He paused. "We didn't deny him his story. We told him what happened to his mother and to his village. We waited till he was eighteen, but I wonder if we should have waited longer."

"Was that when he plotted his revenge?" said Bibi.

Jacob let out a breath, then hunched over his cup again, like the weight of the world had settled on his back.

"It was a year later he told me what he was going to do," he said. "He was working in Seattle at that time, but he returned to Alaska, that anger festering inside of him. I warned him. I told him he was only hurting himself, that there's always space for forgiveness. But he never listened."

Silence fell inside the bakery.

The only sound was the pleasant hum of Luc's ovens, baking sugary pastries and cupcakes. The sweet and airy smell that enveloped us contrasted heavily with the darkness of our conversation.

"After my wife died," said Jacob, not looking up. "I fell apart. She'd been my strength through it all. It broke my heart to know Matt hadn't given up on his plan. When he told me he found a job as a bush pilot near Black Eagle Town, I decided it was time for me to leave."

"Leave?" said Katy.

Jacob looked at her and nodded.

"I needed to get away from civilization." He coughed. "What is civilization?" he said, shaking his head. "The moose, the bears, and the squirrels on the trees have more humanity than some people I've met in my life, to tell you the truth."

"But not all people are horrible, are they?" said Rosalie, the youngest among us.

Jacob turned to her and gave her a small smile.

"No, my dear. There is much goodness in this world. But when you live as long as I do and have seen the things I have, some days all you want is to live among the wolves and bears who can be much kinder than human folk."

He didn't know our backgrounds.

Some nights when my nightmares plagued me and refused to leave me alone, I wished I could live far away from the rest of the world too.

"Matt found you, didn't he?" I said, pushing my memories to the back of my mind. "He found you in the abandoned mine."

Jacob nodded.

"He asked for your help with the heist, am I right?"

Another sad nod.

"I couldn't stop him."

"Was it Matt who dug up the foreman's grave and put the body on the tracks?" said Luc.

"I told him to never disturb a grave. It's disrespectful. But he was determined. Even telling him that his own mother wouldn't approve didn't stop him from doing what he did."

He looked up.

"I tried to protect him," he said.

I nodded but kept silent.

I knew he wasn't telling us everything.

Because I saw something that last day I hadn't shared with anyone else.

Chapter Sixty-two

"What about the paintings?" said Win. "Why are they so important?"

"Do you know why Stella and Tank didn't find the diamonds in Connor's jacket?" I said.

Win shook her head.

"Because they thought they were someplace else," I said, pausing to look at Jacob. "Like inside the hollow frames of the paintings."

Jacob didn't reply.

"Stella had suggested the idea to Theodore," I said. "That way, she knew where they'd be, but Theodore was smarter than she thought."

Jacob gave a sad nod.

"It was Stella who arranged for Christie's to look at my paintings. Once she negotiated the trade, it was easy to convince Theodore to buy my paintings for cheap and resell them for an exorbitant amount and pocket the cash. Theodore was always the double-dealer, so he couldn't pass on the opportunity."

"He was going to swindle you?" said Rosalie. "That's horrible."

"But Theodore didn't trust anyone," I said. "So he smuggled the stones in Connor's jacket. He and Connor were as thick as thieves.

Though Theodore said he was remorseful for what Connor did to Matt's mother, there was a bond between those two."

"What did Stella plan to do with the uncut stones?" said Bibi.

"She knew the industry players and had connections, so she could sell them on the black market without too many questions asked."

"How did Matt get away with everything?" said Rosalie.

"Matt didn't hang around once the freight train stopped," said Katy. "There were too many of us for anyone to notice someone was missing. He slid into the woods and found his way to the nearest town. He knew the area well, and he took supplies from the church."

"Wait, didn't he inherit everything from his father?" asked Sarah, confused. "It was a big deal. It was even on the news."

"Yes, but do you think he wants it?" said Jacob, turning to her. There was a hard edge to his usual soft voice.

No one replied.

"Last we heard, Matt and Stella were in Costa Rica," said Katy. "Volunteering at some non-profit. I don't think either of them want to see a diamond or a dollar for the rest of their lives."

"What happens to the mining company?" said Luc.

"Stella arranged it with the company lawyers already. The ownership deed was transferred from Matt to the village co-operative," said Jacob.

Everyone stared at him, stunned.

"The town folk own the company now?" said Luc in a shocked voice. "The same people who lost their land, decades ago?"

Jacob nodded.

"Wow," said David. "Just when you think you know what's going on, there's so much more underneath it all."

He was right.

It was easy to sit in this cozy kitchen and talk about diamonds, paintings, and trains, but I couldn't ignore one thing. Three people had died in horrific circumstances.

Tetyana, Katy, the others, and I had agreed on the story we'd tell law enforcement in Anchorage.

The accidental explosion of the old boiler had started it all, we'd told them. The local police had a hard time not believing a remorseful Dwayne and Robin, who took full responsibility for it.

Then, Stella had explained what it had been like to get stuck in the middle of the mountains, with no heat or water. She'd told them how we'd scattered around, desperately looking for shelter in the middle of a hailstorm.

The authorities hadn't suspected her. She was a renowned scientist with a squeaky clean record. Plus, she was a well-respected executive in the state's largest company.

So, they'd believed Doctor Wilson had died of hypothermia after heading off to the woods in a drunken stupor. They'd believed Connor McNamara had perished as he had rushed into the engine compartment when the boiler accidentally exploded.

Dwayne, Robin, and Stella had been adamant neither they nor Matt had planned either death, and we had no choice but to take their word for it.

We had no evidence otherwise.

But it was Theodore Henry's death that had been the easiest to explain.

We didn't have to say anything as Steve, the freight train's engineer, saw Theodore fall onto the tracks.

Steve had requested leave for himself, his wife, Robin and his father-in-law, Dwayne, until they recovered from the incident.

That scene was now indelibly etched in my mind.

The freight train coming to a screeching halt several yards ahead of Theodore's broken body. Steve, the engineer, stumbling down the steps in shock, seeing what his machine had done to the fragile human being. Robin running up and collapsing to the ground with him.

It hadn't been Steve's fault.

We all saw Theodore fall.

But I saw something else.

I'd heard Katy cry out only moments before he fell. When I looked inside the train, someone was silhouetted behind Theodore.

Tank and Katy had pulled back quickly as the freight train came thundering down the tracks, but another person had taken their place and had been standing shoulder to shoulder with Theodore.

That had been Jacob.

The man who'd tried for years to get his adopted son, Matt, to let go of his dangerous revenge plot.

I was sure it wasn't my imagination. I was sure of what I saw that day. Katy had too.

Theodore didn't fall of his own volition.

I turned to Jacob, who was sipping tea on my bakery counter, seeming quietly lost in thought.

"Why did you use the upside-down cross motif as your signature?" I said. "I've seen your other work and none of them have it. You have a proper signature on all of them."

Jacob didn't reply for a minute, merely staring at his cup.

"When Theodore Henry said he wanted to buy all my Aurora Borealis paintings for next to nothing, I decided to send him a subliminal message."

"A subliminal message?"

"To mess with his mind."

I raised an eyebrow.

Just like Doctor Wilson.

Jacob let out a heavy sigh.

"Jim, the foreman, and I used to work together. I was the day shift foreman, he was the night shift supervisor."

"You worked at the mines too?" said Katy.

"Everyone in town did. It was the only place with jobs."

He paused and let out a heavy sigh.

"I saw how Jim treated people. I told him to stop. I complained to the bosses, but no one listened. One day, I saw him kick a kid in the shaft, a kid who'd slowed down after a ten-hour shift. I took the bleeding boy to Doctor Wilson, but he didn't have a chance. Died a few days later. So when I returned, I took matters into my own hands."

I suddenly realized the significance of the cross.

"You carved that cross on his neck, didn't you?" I said.

"I was young and hot blooded. Got into a shouting match with Jim. That quickly turned into a full-on brawl. He had a knife. I had a knife. Next thing I knew, he had me down with his blade at my head, shouting he'd decapitate me and bury me in the mines."

Jacob shook his head.

"But I pushed him off and pinned him under me. I held him down by the throat and carved that devil's cross on his neck, so everybody would know what he was really like."

Everyone in the kitchen had frozen in place, all eyes on him, horror on their faces.

"Theodore Henry knew about the scar?" I said in a low whisper.

Jacob nodded.

"He knew everything that went on down in the mines, but all he cared for was his gold."

No one spoke.

I looked down at my cup.

All that was left were the dredges of leaves gathered at the bottom. I wanted to feel relieved that justice had been served, but I didn't.

I leaned in.

"What's going to happen to the proceeds from these paintings? You're supposed to make a lot of money off them."

Jacob lifted his weary eyes to me.

"Stella set up an account for the village co-operative. Christie's will deposit the royalties straight into it."

Jacob took his last sip and gently pushed his teacup to the side.

So the villagers would get compensated in more ways than one.

Justice for them, finally.

But there was one person who was getting away with murder.

I glanced at the man who sat across from me, looking like the most genial, sweet-mannered grandfather anyone would wish for.

He was uneasy in the big city, more comfortable in the wilderness and the mountains. He looked as ancient as the oldest Douglas fir tree in those coniferous woods.

Old, bent, and wrinkled.

He did what he had to do to save Matt from himself. His adopted son would survive, maybe even thrive in his new life. But Jacob didn't have long to live.

In a strange and twisted way, justice had prevailed.

I smiled.

"Let me get you a cab, Jacob. Don't want you to be late for your Christie's appointment."

He smiled back.

It was a sad and gentle smile, one that seemed to carry all the sorrows of the world.

He knew I knew.

Continue the adventure!

Read the next Merciless Murder Mystery Thriller and find out what Asha and Katy confront next at a friend's winter wedding in a resort on the snowy White Mountains of New Hampshire.

A white Christmas wedding. Red blood on her veil. Till death do us apart...

Flip to the end of this book to read the first chapter.

Or, get Merciless Past right now, right here: www.TikiriHerath.com/Mysteries

Author's Note

D ear reader,

Did you enjoy this book?

My promise is to give you an exciting escape with every novel I write, and I sure hope I have done so.

If you have a minute, I'd much appreciate it if you would leave an honest review of this book on Amazon, Goodreads, or Bookbub. Just one sentence would do.

Honest reader reviews help my books get selected for international book promotions and I get to reach more readers.

Thank you so much.

One more thing.

If you'd like to learn the backstory of Tetyana, Asha, and Katy, flip to the end of this book to learn about the spin-off series that tells their stories.

The Red Heeled Rebels is an international crime series and is the origin story that shows how they all met. It spans four continents and features the back stories of everyone in this found family.

The Tanya Stone FBI K9 Thriller series features Tetyana as Special Agent Tanya Stone and her German Shepherd partner, Max, hunting a devious serial killer in a small seaside town on the West Coast.

Enjoy the reads!
My very best wishes,
Tikiri
Vancouver, Canada

PS: Join the VIP Red Heeled Rebels Club and receive your exclusive gift!

HER DEADLY END is a 250-page twisty thriller about an unusual murder-suicide case that Agent Tanya (Tetyana), Asha, and Katy accidentally stumble upon while vacationing in Paradise Cove. It's a pulse-pounding, nerve-shredding mystery of a devious serial criminal stalking a small seaside town in Washington State.

Click the link below to join the club and get your free gift book.

HER DEADLY END: A gripping thriller with a twisty end
https://books.tikiriherath.com/ts-b0-mmm-herdeadlyend

PPS/ If you didn't enjoy the story or spotted typos, would you drop a line and let me know? Or just write to say hello. I would love to hear from you and personally reply to every email I receive.

My address is: Tikiri@TikiriHerath.com

Merciless Past – Chapter One

The First Kill

Today is the day I die.

This was the only thought racing through her mind as she stumbled through the woods.

There were scrapes on her thighs and bruises on her face. Her shirt was ripped, and her shoulders were bloodied. The ropes had left red marks around her wrists. Still raw.

The wintry morning air was cool and crisp, pinching her skin where it was exposed. Even Mother Nature was being unkind.

But she didn't feel the pain.

She couldn't feel anything other than one simple urge.

I want to live.

The ominous footsteps crashed through the trees behind her. They were getting close. A flash of terror blazed through her spine like a lightning strike, threatening to implode inside her head.

But she didn't dare look back.

Not now.

Her focus was in front as she dodged in between the snow-laden fir trees, trying not to fall into hidden snowbanks.

Oh no.

She grabbed a tree branch and stopped just in time.

The ravine.

She'd forgotten the river that cut through the mountain.

She teetered at the edge of the cliff and stared into the abyss. Everything was white around her, blindingly white, except for the riverbed fifty feet below.

This water never froze. It burst through the narrow galley, crashing over the raggedy black rocks like a furious river god, mad at the world.

Her chest heaved.

She could barely breathe.

What do I do now?

She turned her head.

It was a fleeting sound, but she heard the crack of a twig. A dark shadow loomed from behind the tree.

Then came the hand, reaching to her back.

She opened her mouth to scream, but no sound came out.

One quick thrust was all that was needed.

Her feet gave way.

She hurtled into the gully, clawing at nothing, her mouth wide open in a terrified but silent shriek.

She plunged headfirst through the frigid water. The river gods swirled around her, pushing her forward, pulling her under.

She flailed her arms. Dying to breathe. She came up for a second and tried to yell for help, but fistfuls of icy water pounded into her throat.

She gagged.

Her head bashed against a boulder.

It only took a minute.

Then the world disappeared.

Fifty feet above the gully, at the exact spot where she fell, stood a tall dark shadow, watching her body disappear down the raging river.

This is a beautiful place to die.

A slow smile cracked on their face.

One down. Two more to go.

To be continued...

Continue the Adventure!

MERCILESS PAST the next book in this series, will give you more spine-tingling intrigue, mystery, and lurking killers who Asha will ferret out in the end.

Get the book here: **MERCILESS PAST**

www.TikiriHerath.com/Mysteries

A white wedding. Red blood on her veil. EVIL IS CLOSER THAN SHE THINKS...

Private investigator Asha Kade gets a surprise invitation from an old friend in New Hampshire.

Victoria has found true love. Asha can't wait to see her again and meet the groom she's been gushing about. A man Victoria's known for only six months.

But as a trafficked survivor, Asha knows to trust her instincts. The minute she arrives at the private ski lodge where the wedding will take place, she realizes something is wrong.

Something is wrong with this place.

Something is wrong with Victoria.

When Asha discovers the first body, she knows she has stumbled on a dark family secret worth killing for...

Who is the killer seated among the wedding guests?
Who will they go after next?

Get the book and find out what Asha and Katy confront next. Available around the world, on Amazon stores everywhere. www.TikiriHerath.com/Mysteries

---

Available globally in e-book, paperback, and hardback editions on all Amazon stores. Also available for free in libraries everywhere. Just ask your friendly local librarian to order a copy via Ingram Spark.

Debate this Dozen

Twelve Book Club Questions

1. Who was your favorite character?
2. Which characters did you dislike?
3. Which scene has stuck with you the most? Why?
4. What scenes surprised you?
5. What was your favorite part of the book?
6. What was your least favorite part?
7. Did any part of this book strike a particular emotion in you? Which part and what emotion did the book make you feel?
8. Did you know the author has written an underlying message in this story? What theme or life lesson do you think this story tells?
9. What did you think of the author's writing?
10. How would you adapt this book into a movie? Who would you cast in the leading roles?
11. On a scale of one to ten, how would you rate this story?
12. Would you read another book by this author?

The Reading List

The Red Heeled Rebels universe of mystery thrillers, featuring your favorite kick-ass female characters:

———⟡———

Tanya Stone FBI K9 Mystery Thrillers
www.TikiriHerath.com/Thrillers
NEW FBI thriller series starring Tetyana from the Red Heeled Rebels as Special Agent Tanya Stone, and Max, as her loyal German Shepherd. These are serial killer thrillers set in Black Rock, a small upscale resort town on the coast of Washington state.

Her Deadly End
Her Cold Blood
Her Last Lie
Her Secret Crime
Her Dead Girl
Her Perfect Murder
Her Grisly Grave
Coming soon!

Asha Kade Private Detective Murder Mysteries
  www.TikiriHerath.com/Mysteries
  Each book is a standalone murder mystery thriller, featuring the Red Heeled Rebels, Asha Kade and Katy McCafferty. Asha and Katy receive one million dollars for their favorite children's charity from a secret benefactor's estate every time they solve a cold case.
  Merciless Legacy
  Merciless Games
  Merciless Crimes
  Merciless Lies
  Merciless Past
  Merciless Deaths
  One more to come.

Red Heeled Rebels International Mystery & Crime - The Origin Story
  www.TikiriHerath.com/RedHeeledRebels
  The award-winning origin story of the Red Heeled Rebels characters. Learn how a rag-tag group of trafficked orphans from different places united to fight for their freedom and their lives, and became a found family.
  The Girl Who Crossed the Line
  The Girl Who Ran Away
  The Girl Who Made Them Pay
  The Girl Who Fought to Kill
  The Girl Who Broke Free
  The Girl Who Knew Their Names

The Girl Who Never Forgot
This series is now complete.

The Accidental Traveler
www.TikiriHerath.com
An anthology of personal short stories based on the author's sojourns around the world.

The Rebel Diva Nonfiction Series
www.TikiriHerath.com/Nonfiction
Your Rebel Dreams: 6 simple steps to take back control of your life in uncertain times.

Your Rebel Plans: 4 simple steps to getting unstuck and making progress today.

Your Rebel Life: Easy habit hacks to enhance happiness in the 10 key areas of your life.

Bust Your Fears: 3 simple tools to crush your anxieties and squash your stress.

Collaborations
The Boss Chick's Bodacious Destiny Nonfiction Bundle
Dark Shadows 2: Voodoo and Black Magic of New Orleans

Tikiri's novels are available around the world, on all Amazon stores everywhere. The nonfiction books are available on Apple, Kobo, Barnes & Noble, Indigo Chapters, and all good bookstores around the world.

All these books are also available in libraries everywhere. Just ask your friendly local librarian or your local bookstore to order a copy via Ingram Spark.

Happy reading.

Asha Kade Private Detective Murder Mysteries

How far would you go for a million-dollar payout?

<u>The Merciless Murder Mysteries</u>

Merciless Legacy

Merciless Games

Merciless Crimes

Merciless Lies

Merciless Past

Merciless Deaths

More to come!

Each book is a standalone murder mystery thriller featuring the Red Heeled Rebel, Asha Kade, and her best friend Katy

McCafferty, as private detectives on the hunt for serial killers in small towns USA.

There is no graphic violence, heavy cursing, or explicit sex in these books. What you will find are a series of suspicious deaths, a closed circle of suspects, twists and turns, fast-paced action, and nail-biting suspense.

www.TikiriHerath.com/mysteries

———

A newly minted private investigator, Asha Kade, gets a million dollars from an eccentric client's estate every time she solves a cold case. Asha Kade accepts this bizarre challenge, but what she doesn't bargain for is to be drawn into the dark underworld of her past again.

The only thing that propels her forward now is a burning desire for justice.

———

What readers are saying on Amazon and Goodreads:

"My new favorite series!"

"Thrilling twists, unputdownable!"

"I was hooked right from the start!"

"A twisted whodunnit! Edge of your seat thriller that kept me up late, to finish it, unputdownable!! More, please!"

"Buckle up for a roller coaster of a ride. This one will keep you on the edge of your seat."

"A must read! A macabre start to an excellent book. It had me totally gripped from the start and just got better!"

"A great whodunit with a lot of twists and turns along the way. The story was amazing!"

"I could not stop reading it. It was as if I was there witnessing the murders myself. The characters had depth and personality and backgrounds that were explained nicely. It was awesome!"

"Nothing is more terrifying than the fear of the unknown. Do you have any nails left? Another NAIL-BITING story from a very talented master storyteller!"

———⋈———

A brand-new murder mystery series for a pulse-pounding, bone-chilling adventure from the comfort and warmth of your favorite reading chair at home.

Can you find the killer before Asha Kade does?

———⋈———

To learn more about this exciting series and download the FREE novel—HER DEADLY END—as a gift, go to www.TikiriHerath.com/mysteries.

Sign up to Tikiri's VIP reader club to get the chance to win personalized paperback books, chat with the author and more.

———⋈———

Available globally in e-book, paperback, and hardback editions on all Amazon stores. Print books are available for free in libraries everywhere. Just ask your friendly local librarian or your local bookstore to order a copy via Ingram Spark.

Tanya Stone FBI K9 Mystery Thrillers

How far would you go to avenge your family's brutal murder?

<u>Tanya Stone FBI K9 Serial Killer Thrillers</u>

Her Deadly End

Her Cold Blood

Her Last Lie

Her Secret Crime

Her Dead Girl

Her Perfect Murder

Her Grisly Grave

To come!

—◆—

A brand-new FBI K9 serial killer thriller series for a pulse-pounding, bone-chilling adventure from the comfort and warmth of your favorite reading chair at home.

Can you find the killer before Agent Tanya Stone?

www.TikiriHerath.com/thrillers

Some small-town secrets will haunt your nightmares. Escape if you can...

FBI Special Agent Tanya Stone has a new assignment. Hunt down the serial killers prowling the idyllic West Coast resort towns.

An unspeakable and bone-chilling darkness seethes underneath these picturesque seaside suburbs. A string of violent abductions and gruesome murders wreak hysteria among the perfect lives of the towns' families.

But nothing is what it seems. The monsters wear masks and mingle with the townsfolk, spreading vicious lies.

With her K9 German Shepherd, Agent Stone goes on the warpath. She will fight her own demons as a trafficked survivor to make the perverted psychopaths pay.

But now, they're after her.

Small towns have dark deceptions and sealed lips. If they know you know the truth, they'll never let you leave...

Each book is a standalone murder mystery thriller, featuring Tetyana from the Red Heeled Rebels as Agent Tanya Stone, and Max, her loyal German Shepherd. Red Heeled Rebels Asha Kade and Katy McCafferty and their found family make guest appearances when Tanya needs help.

There is no graphic violence, heavy cursing, or explicit sex in these books.

The dogs featured in this series are never harmed, but the villains are.

To learn more about this exciting new series and download the FREE novel—HER DEADLY END—as a gift, go to www.TikiriHerath.com/thrillers

The Red Heeled Rebels International Mystery & Crime

The Origin Story

Would you like to know the origin story of your favorite characters in the Tanya Stone FBI K9 mystery thrillers and the Asha Kade Merciless murder mysteries?

In the award-winning Red Heeled Rebels international mystery & crime series—the origin story—you'll find out how Asha, Katy, and Tetyana (Tanya) banded together in their troubled youths to fight for freedom against all odds.

The complete Red Heeled Rebels international crime collection:
Prequel Novella: The Girl Who Crossed the Line
Book One: The Girl Who Ran Away

Book Two: The Girl Who Made Them Pay
Book Three: The Girl Who Fought to Kill
Book Four: The Girl Who Broke Free
Book Five: The Girl Who Knew Their Names
Book Six: The Girl Who Never Forgot
The series is now complete!

An epic, pulse-pounding, international crime thriller series that spans four continents featuring a group of spunky, sassy young misfits who have only each other for family.

A multiple-award-winning series which would be best read in order. There is no graphic violence, heavy cursing, or explicit sex in these books. **www.TikiriHerath.com/RedHeeledRebels**

In a world where justice no longer prevails, six iron-willed young women rally to seek vengeance on those who stole their humanity.

If you like gripping thrillers with flawed but strong female leads, vigilante action in exotic locales and twists that leave you at the edge of your seat, you'll love these books by multiple award-winning Canadian novelist, Tikiri Herath.

Go on a heart-pounding international adventure without having to get a passport or even buy an airline ticket!

What readers are saying on Amazon and Goodreads:
"Fast-paced and exciting!"
"An exciting and thought-provoking book."
"A wonderful story! I didn't want to leave the characters."

"I couldn't put down this exciting road trip adventure with a powerful message."

"Another award-worthy adventure novel that keeps you on the edge of your seat."

"A heart-stopping adventure. I just couldn't put the book down till I finished reading it."

"Kept me mesmerized and captivated with the rich descriptions which made me feel like I was actually inside the story."

"This is a fantastic read that will have you traveling the globe. I absolutely loved this book. You won't be able to put it down!"

"A real page-turner and international thriller. Reminds me of why I've always loved to read. Because I can visit worlds and places, I wouldn't ordinarily get to see."

Literary Awards & Praise for The Red Heeled Rebels books:

- Grand Prize Award Finalist - 2019 Eric Hoffer Award, USA

- First Horizon Award Finalist - 2019 Eric Hoffer Award, USA

- Honorable Mention General Fiction - 2019 Eric Hoffer Award, USA

- Winner First-In-Category - 2019 Chanticleer Somerset Award, USA

- Semi-Finalist - 2020 Chanticleer Somerset Award, USA

- Winner in 2019 Readers' Favorite Book Awards, USA

- Winner of 2019 Silver Medal - Excellence E-Lit Award, USA

- Winner in Suspense Category - 2018 New York Big Book Award, USA

- Finalist in Suspense Category - 2018 & 2019 Silver Falchion Awards, USA

- Honorable Mention - 2018-19 Reader Views Literary Classics Award, USA

- Publisher's Weekly Booklife Prize - 2018, USA

To learn more about this addictive series, go to **www.TikiriHerath.com/RedHeeledRebels** and receive the prequel novella - **The Girl Who Crossed The Line** - as a gift.

Sign up to Tikiri's VIP reader club and get short stories, exotic recipes, the chance to win paperbacks, chat with the author and more.

Available globally in e-book, paperback, and hardback editions on all Amazon stores. Print books are available for free in libraries everywhere. Just ask your friendly local librarian or your local bookstore to order a copy via Ingram Spark.

Inspiration

To my childhood superhero author, Agatha Christie. Thank you for whisking me away on magical adventures during those long dark days.

For Train Buffs

Note: These external links are shared for interest and fun and their active status cannot be guaranteed.

The Last Train to Nowhere

www.onlyinyourstate.com/alaska/abandoned-train-ak

Full steam ahead for privately owned passenger railway

www.obj.ca/article/full-steam-ahead-privately-owned-passenger-railway

Train Buffs Are Traveling Cross-Country in Super Luxe Railcars Hitched to Amtrak Trains

www.wsj.com/articles/wealthy-train-buffs-are-traveling-cross-country-in-super-luxe-railcars-hitched-to-amtrak-trains-1521727200

Wilderness Express (Anchorage - Talkeetna - Denali - Fairbanks)

www.alaska.org/detail/wilderness-express
White Pass & Yukon Route Railroad, Alaska
www.youtu.be/zCdG7ZU_DIs
American Rails
www.american-rails.com/akrds.html
....And my absolute personal favorite. The Canadian Pacific Christmas Train! How cool is this?
www.youtube.com/watch?v=cnvii5ojjrM
www.youtube.com/watch?v=fgilGmpr-Qw

Acknowledgments

To my amazing, talented, superstar editor, Stephanie Parent, thank you, as always, for coming on this literary journey with me and for helping make these books the best they can be.

———

To my international team of beta readers who gave me their frank feedback, thank you. In alphabetical order of first name:

Blessmore Chikwakwa, Zimbabwe
Carolyn Pennett-Staresinic, Canada
Kristen Harnish, United States of America
Laura Edwards, United States of America
Michele Kapugi, United States of America
Stephanie Smith, United States of America

———

To all the kind and generous readers who take the time to review my novels and share their frank feedback, thank you so much. Your support is invaluable.

———⁂———

I'm immensely grateful to you all for your kind and generous support, and would love to invite you for a glass of British Columbian wine or a cup of Ceylon tea with chocolates when you come to Vancouver next!

About the Author

T ikiri Herath is the multiple-award-winning author of international thriller and mystery novels and the Rebel Diva books.

----✕----

Tikiri worked in risk management in the intelligence and defense sectors, including in the Canadian Federal Government and at NATO. She has a bachelor's degree from the University of Victoria, British Columbia, and a master's degree from the Solvay Business School in Brussels.

Born in Sri Lanka, Tikiri grew up in East Africa and has studied, worked, and lived in Europe, Southeast Asia, and North America throughout her adult life. An international nomad and fifth-culture kid, she now calls Canada home.

She's an adrenaline junkie who has rock climbed, bungee jumped, rode on the back of a motorcycle across Quebec, flown in an acrobatic airplane upside down, and parachuted solo.

When she's not plotting another thriller scene or planning another adrenaline-filled trip, you'll find her baking in her kitchen with a glass of red Shiraz in hand and vintage jazz playing in the background.

To say hello and get travel stories from around the world, go to **www.TikiriHerath.com**